First published in Great Britain in 2025 by Boldwood Books Ltd.

Copyright © Jane Lovering, 2025

Cover Design by Alexandra Allden

Cover Images: Shutterstock

The moral right of Jane Lovering to be identified as the author of this work has been asserted in accordance with the Copyright, Designs and Patents Act 1988.

All rights reserved. No part of this book may be reproduced in any form or by any electronic or mechanical means, including information storage and retrieval systems, without written permission from the author, except for the use of brief quotations in a book review. This book is a work of fiction and, except in the case of historical fact, any resemblance to actual persons, living or dead, is purely coincidental.

Every effort has been made to obtain the necessary permissions with reference to copyright material, both illustrative and quoted. We apologise for any omissions in this respect and will be pleased to make the appropriate acknowledgements in any future edition.

A CIP catalogue record for this book is available from the British Library.

Paperback ISBN 978-1-83533-241-2

Large Print ISBN 978-1-83533-240-5

Hardback ISBN 978-1-83533-239-9

Ebook ISBN 978-1-83533-242-9

Kindle ISBN 978-1-83533-243-6

Audio CD ISBN 978-1-83533-234-4

MP3 CD ISBN 978-1-83533-235-1

Digital audio download ISBN 978-1-83533-238-2

This book is printed on certified sustainable paper. Boldwood Books is dedicated to putting sustainability at the heart of our business. For more information please visit https://www.boldwoodbooks.com/about-us/sustainability/

Boldwood Books Ltd, 23 Bowerdean Street, London, SW6 3TN

www.boldwoodbooks.com

HAPPILY EVER AFTER

JANE LOVERING

Boldwood

She is too fond of books and it has turned her brain.

— *LITTLE WOMEN*, LOUISA MAY ALCOTT

This book is dedicated to all those who thought life would be like the books we read, then found that it could also be like the books we DIDN'T read. Read more, everyone, not just because then you might read more of my books...

1

MANDERLEY – REBECCA, DAPHNE DU MAURIER

'Are you sure this is right? Only this is Lady Dawe's place, and she's bonkers.'

The taxi driver had an admirable grasp of geography, as the slightly scary drive through the rugged Yorkshire hills from the station had proved, but was clearly not *au fait* with current medical terms and disability discrimination.

'It's where I was told to come. I'm here for an interview,' I said, trying not to sound proud of myself. 'For a job,' I added as the taxi turned between two ancient brick pillars which were sagging beneath the weight of disintegrating urns filled with stone pineapples and now looked more like a bad case of hairy haemorrhoids. 'Cataloguing Lady Dawe's library,' I continued, with a trifle less pride and a touch of uncertainty, the taxi bouncing along an uneven gravelled surface composed equally of potholes and molehills between elegant bushes and curving flowerbeds.

'If you say so,' the driver muttered. 'She's bloody barking though. You take care, lass.'

The bushes parted and gave a glimpse of the house, lying distant below us amid smooth acres of grass and carefully shaped drifts of flower-filled borders. A fountain twinkled falling water into a pond bigger than a swimming pool, beyond which the house lay golden as a slab of butter in the afternoon sun. Behind it, the Yorkshire acres rolled on in swathes of green towards distant woodland and purple-tinted moors etched against the sky. The house looked like Pemberley or Brideshead to my literary-attuned eyes; its stuccoed exterior stretched long and low, mimicking the soft hills on the horizon.

The library would be glorious. Oak shelves, dusty leather, gilt edging and that wonderful smell of thousands of books full of as-yet unknown treasures...

'Aye, totally loony,' the driver went on, clearly on a search for synonyms. 'Proper howling.'

The nerves I'd been keeping well-clamped down made a spirited attempt to kick my adrenal glands. But going back was not an option, so I clasped my shaking hands between my knees, which transferred the sweat from my palms onto my linen skirt, and kept my eyes fixed on the glorious scenery opening in front of me to give a clearer view of the house as we jolted down the drive. Templewood Hall was old, with sixteenth-century origins, the internet had told me. The stucco had fallen off in places to give glimpses of brick beneath; chimneys stuck up without even a nod to symmetry and various crenellations jutted randomly from around the silhouette. With the saggy roof in the middle, the whole place bore an astonishing resemblance to a ribby old piebald horse ambling off into the sunset. Less Pemberley now and more Manderley, after the fire.

I wondered if it were haunted. It *looked* haunted. Or condemned. Two of the windows were askew in their frames, the front door seemed to consist of sheets of metal propped across the gap and a balcony that jutted from beneath an upper floor window had parted company with the stonework on one side. This leant the frontage a slightly threatening air, like half a frown.

It looked as though Downton Abbey had fallen on very hard times and an explosive device.

'Are you *sure*, love?' The taxi crunched to a halt outside the tin door, and the driver turned to look at me. 'The whole family's a bit weird, so they say down in the village, but Lady Dawe's the worst.'

Well, I wanted to say, it's either this or hashtag Vanlife, hashtag Freedom, hashtag BloodyPeeingInABucketAndSleepingOnARolloutMattressOnATabletop. But I didn't. 'I'm sure I'll be fine,' I said instead, pulling my skirt down to try to cover my knees and noticing the big sweaty handprints I'd left on the now creased and crumpled fabric. 'Honestly.'

'All right, if you say so.' The driver muttered his way around the cab and fetched my case from the boot. 'But if you gets chopped into pieces and buried in the woods up there, don't say I didn't warn you.'

'I promise I won't,' I said faintly.

'You won't be able to.' The driver dropped my bag at my feet. 'On account of you being minced an' all.'

The background tinkling of the fountain suddenly sounded sinister, like the piano music in a horror film. No birds sang and there wasn't even the prosaic sound of voices or a dog barking; everything else was silent. As the taxi drove away, the heat of the Yorkshire late summer settled back over the gardens and the building like a huge pillow dropping over the face of the day. *I'm not scared*, I told myself, wiping my hands down my skirt again. *People do this sort of thing every day. It's going to be great. Stately home, big library, welcoming family...*

'You have to knock.' A voice behind my shoulder made me jump, rattling the gravel at my feet and filling my shoes with shingle as I turned around quickly to see a man standing on the immaculate grass near the fountain. He had a huge pair of shears in his hand, which I eyed suspiciously as they came closer, the point waving in my direction. 'They won't know you're here otherwise.'

The man crunched a few steps towards me over the gravel. He was dark haired and scruffy, and wearing a T-shirt which was so baggy that it moved with a life of its own as he advanced, giving me unwanted glimpses of chest hair. He raised the shears above his head and I took a couple of steps back, letting out a tiny squeak of alarm and wondering whether I could hide behind this blue flowering bush thing until he went away, or whether he'd just chase me around the garden with his giant scissors, like a Benny Hill sketch only with more blood.

The man gave a small smile, not directed at me, and brought the handle of the shears down on the metal surface of the door repeatedly, whilst yelling, 'You've got a visitor!' Then he gave me a quick nod, turned, and backed into the nearby bush, sending up a cloud of small insects as he vanished amid the greenery, leaving me with the echoes of his assault on the door fading behind the fountain's now irritating tinkle.

'Oh God,' I muttered. 'I've fallen into a Stephen King novel.'

A movement from an upstairs window made me glance up. At the balcony window, behind the tilted and precarious ironwork that clung to the stone by a few jagged screws, was a face. It was too high for me to ascertain much detail, other than that it was a woman, with long blonde hair, wearing an off-the-shoulder floral dress. For a second she seemed to look down on me, and her face was pale and immobile, yet wearing a look of immeasurable terror, eyes wide and her mouth stretched into a grimace of fear. I gave another little squeak and turned, feet dragged down by the paralysis of sudden dread, took two steps backwards in a feeble attempt at a run – and the metal door creaked, shimmered, and began to open.

2

MANSFIELD PARK – MANSFIELD PARK, JANE AUSTEN

I sat on a horribly skeletal chair, trying to look comfortable and confident whilst feeling that I was perching on Death's lap, watching the woman across the table from me. She was tall, very slim and had the pallid, aristocratic looks of someone for whom a suntan is the mark of the pleb and who only goes outside wearing Factor 150 and a big hat, and then only to interrogate the staff.

Currently, she was interrogating me. She'd introduced herself as Lady Tanith Dawe and I, with the taxi driver's words resounding inside my brain, tried to keep my voice level, my knees together and the absolute hysteria which was trying to manifest, under control.

'You may call me Lady Tanith,' the woman said. She had to be around seventy or so, I thought. Her skin was smooth but her eyes were hooded and her mouth was contained within lines that spoke of a permanently dissatisfied tightness of lips. 'My father was a duke, you know.'

I murmured a polite acknowledgement, trying to keep the eighteenth century out of my vocabulary, so I didn't rush into words such as 'it is truly an honour to make your acquaintance, your ladyship.' Mostly because it felt less of an honour and more of a terror.

'You don't have many qualifications, do you?'

She had a printout of my emailed application on the table in front of her.

She'd printed it in twenty point, so I could see it quite clearly, even upside down, past the piles of books that cluttered the surface of the not-nearly-wide-enough table that separated us. I wriggled.

'No, but your job advert said that you didn't—'

'That I value literacy and a familiarity with books over O Levels or HMRCs or whatever you call them these days, yes. I don't want some hoity-toity university person thumbing through my valuable collection.'

The collection in question was mostly hidden by the sepulchrous darkness of the room, velvet curtains and dust, so I couldn't comment. There was a slight smell of fish too.

Lady Tanith ran her eyes up and down me again. I was beginning to feel like a lame pony and almost offered to let her feel my legs, but her stare was so beady you could have made a necklace from it, so I didn't. Her close contemplation convinced me I was sweaty and rumpled. My dress wasn't the cool, stylish interview-wear I'd envisaged when I'd ordered it; it was shapeless and creased and I had the awful feeling there was a damp patch down my back. 'Hmm,' said Lady Tanith, down her nose.

I wriggled again on the dreadful chair. The smell of fish had intensified. I had nothing against sardines, but I preferred them to stay where they were rather than smell as though they were advancing on me and I wondered whether Lady Tanith, immaculate in her cotton shirt and trousers as she was, had a personal hygiene problem. I wriggled again, and the smell suddenly arrived on my lap, surrounded by the person of a rotund Siamese cat, who pulled a lot of linen threads as it arrived and then stood, perched awkwardly across my knees, its not-inconsiderable weight concentrated into four ridiculously tiny paws.

'Ah!' Lady Tanith's face lost the crease of frown. 'The Master likes you!'

I found myself being stared at. The cat had creamy fur, with espresso-coloured nose, ears and paws and the bluest eyes I'd ever seen. 'He's...' Heavy? Stinky? Fortunately I didn't need to say anything, as she went on, filled with enthusiasm. 'Well, that quite settles it. I may be a little dubious, but The Master is an excellent judge of character.'

A pink mouth, filled with teeth that looked as though they would be more at home being brought back from a jungle expedition as a trophy, yawned in my direction. Sardine-scented air puffed lightly around my face, and then the cat settled down against my chest, kneading the front of my dress into a tangle of loose threads with an air of total self-satisfaction.

'What's... his... name?' I struggled to breathe past the implacable weight. I refused to believe that anyone gave their cat the name The Master. Unless they were a Grade A *Doctor Who* fan, and Lady Tanith had the air of someone who hadn't watched TV since Richard Dimbleby.

'Oh, we never speak his name.' My interviewer was watching the ruination of my clothing complacently. 'He wishes to be known only as The Master.'

The cat finally pulled the last thread and settled down, paws tucked under his rumbling chest, and blinked at me. I'd never had any particular feelings about cats in general, but was working up a real dislike for this one, which seemed not so much cat as an anchovy-scented boulder wrapped in fur. 'Oh,' was all I could say, but inside I was whole-heartedly agreeing with my erstwhile taxi driver.

'I'll have a room made ready for you.' Lady Tanith stood up. 'You may find that The Master wishes to sleep with you. He's a dreadful flirt, I'm afraid.'

With that, she swept out of the room, closing the door behind her and leaving me in the semi-darkness of drawn curtains, with an enormous cat attempting to suffocate me.

I looked at The Master. The Master looked at me, long and unblinking, as though he were assessing his opportunities.

'You are not sleeping with me, sunshine,' I half-whispered, just in case Lady Tanith had her ear to the keyhole. 'So you can get that idea out of your head.'

My bottom was going numb between the bulk of the cat and the knobblyness of the chair, my nose was itching at the dust and the fur and the dim glimmers of sunshine that managed to squeeze past the curtains weren't allowing me much more than a glimpse around the room. I had been told it was the library and would be my workplace for the duration of my job.

Job! I would have laughed if the cat hadn't been suppressing my lungs. Lady Tanith wanted someone to catalogue her books, but the airy library, crammed with first-edition classics, that I'd imagined had been subsumed beneath reality. This library was crammed, but in the same way a hoarder's house is crammed. The vague rays of light which tiptoed between the heavy velvet drapery showed me piles, heaps and tottering mounds of volumes. The books were on shelves, on the floor, on the table, and weighting down the ends of floor-length curtains across the windows. They were stacked on window ledges and propped against the legs of my chair. Spines hung and flopped, half-detached from their volumes, like so many torture victims and some of the book mountains had slumped to form literary foothills of bent pages and collapsed covers. This did not, in short, look like a room where cataloguing was going to be a matter of scanning barcodes and checking dates. I began to suspect that my new job was going to be basic data entry, trapped in this room which felt like somewhere Poe would have deemed slightly too Gothic. Lady Tanith too had a horror vibe about her. She was playing the part of Lady of the House to such extremes that it couldn't be real. Nobody could be *that* posh. But this was, to be honest, all I was fit for with my lack of any qualifications and my desperate desire for a live-in job that meant I wouldn't have to live in a bus with a leaky roof and no toilet.

I sighed, and the cat rose and fell with the movement, adjusting his paws as he went. 'Well you can't stay there,' I told him. 'I ought to... do something.'

No answer. Just a rumbling purr, which came and went as though he had a motor underneath that I could feel through my insides.

The door opened. 'Have you finished, Mother?' a voice said from the oak-lined passageway outside. 'Oh. She's gone.'

The outline of a man stepped into the room, noticed me, and took a half-step back. 'Who the hell are you?'

'My name's Andi Glover. I came to be interviewed for the library job.'

A job that I was now most uncertain whether I wanted to take, as my taxi driver's assessment of the situation here seemed to have been understated to an almost criminal degree.

'Oh! She said – but I thought you were a man.' The shape, outlined by the sun which came in from the window at the end of the hallway, wandered into the room. 'Sorry. It was the name, you see.'

'It's short for Andromeda,' I said wearily. 'My parents are rather alternative.'

'Well then, hello, Andi.' The man approached me, holding out his hand. 'I'm Hugo. My parents were rather traditional. Gosh, it's dark in here.'

A brief handshake and then he moved over to the window and was tugging at one of the twelve-foot lengths of velvet which draped the aperture like the wrapping on an exclusive parcel. Dust billowed extravagantly, there was a ripping noise, and a curtain fell gracefully to the floor like an exhausted ballerina. 'Oh. Whoops.'

But at least now I could see better, although that wasn't much of a recommendation. The library was wood panelled; in addition to the piles of books on the floor, every wall was lined with shelves below the panelling and every one of those shelves was crammed with books to the extent that they lay three deep in some places. A set of library steps curved upwards on one corner, volumes heaped on each step and the blinding sun illuminated dust, some faded furniture, and Hugo who was still standing with one arm raised but now curtainless.

The place didn't need cataloguing. It needed an industrial hoover, a shovel, and a furnace. Or bell, book and candle, because exorcism was also a possibility.

Hugo advanced until I could see him properly. He was wearing a shirt and jeans, had messy pale hair which looked as though he'd just got out of bed, and was incredibly good looking. Sharp bone structure counterpointed huge dark eyes and made him look like a reverse image of Lady Tanith, to whom he bore a very strong resemblance. He had her very slender build with added height, the casual leanness of a greyhound, and I couldn't stop staring at him. Hugo was, in short, absolutely gorgeous.

'Will you take the job?' Hugo asked me casually, as though we'd met at a cocktail party rather than me being stapled to a chair by a cat and him wading through the remains of soft furnishings. 'Do you think?'

I tried to weigh up what to say. 'It's pretty much the only thing I can do' would make me sound desperate. 'Over my dead body', although true, might prejudice him against me, and I really did need the job.

And, whispered that tiny voice inside me, the voice that had kept me going over the years, *you know how this goes, don't you? You fall in love with the son of your employer and marry happily into money and... and... dust, an overweight cat and an absolutely insane mother-in-law*, finished my practical side.

'I'm thinking about it,' I said, truthfully.

I got a radiant smile. 'Good,' he said. 'It would be marvellous to have someone new around the place.'

My eyes rolled wildly, wondering when Igor was going to step out of the shadows. Hugo sounded as though he hadn't met another human for decades, *other than to experiment on,* my mind whispered. But it also practically yelled that he was stupendously attractive, well-mannered and rich. A little bit of family insanity could be overlooked for those advantages, surely?

He left the floor-level curtain and came over, perched on the edge of the table his mother had stared at me over and tipped his head to one side. 'Is The Master bothering you?'

'I would quite like to stand up,' I said, adjusting my buttocks so that the chair didn't cut quite so deeply into my spine. 'But I didn't like to move him, now he's got...' I trailed off as my attention was caught by the portrait at the end of the library, now picked out by a spotlight of sunbeams which were unwisely making their way through the dust. It was *enormous,* bigger than life sized, and the light didn't reach the top so all I could see was a huge overwrought frame and a pair of painted knees. 'What is that?'

'Oh, that's Grandpa,' Hugo said, unconcerned, and he leaned forward to sweep the cat from my lap in a movement which seemed suspiciously practised. 'Bugger *off,* Master.'

The cat, seemingly unperturbed, jumped down as though the movement had been all his own idea and he was fed up with sitting on me anyway. The long, creamy body vanished under the table with a wobble of fur, a twitch of a dark tail and was succeeded by sounds of vigorous fur-licking in the shadowy darkness.

'Your grandfather?' I stood up stiffly and followed Hugo across the book-littered floor to gaze up at the portrait.

'Yes. Wait a moment.' He went to the wall and flicked a switch, whereupon a light suddenly illuminated the entire enormous picture in a spot-lit glare. 'Oswald Matcham Dawe. OBE, Bart, or something. I'm surprised Mother didn't give you chapter and verse on him as soon as you came in.'

The portrait showed a man, somewhere in his mid-fifties at a guess. Grey hair, black suit, rather gaunt but handsome and with an air of supercilious melancholy. He looked, I thought, rather like a Jane Austen hero might, a few decades after the story ended. He was framed in a ridiculously overdone gilt box with curlicues, swoops, swags and elaborate flourishes, like the mind of a German medieval sculptor on hard drugs.

'He was an author. Made his money on the back of some rather dubious business dealings just after the war, retired to take up writing, and established the library. Mother came to Templewood as some kind of companion to his wife, married their son and – well, the rest is history and me and my brother.' Hugo flicked off the light and the enormous man faded back into the darkness, except for his knees, which reflected the sunlight in a disconcerting way. 'Would you like a tour of the house? I'm assuming Mrs Compton will be making you up somewhere to stay – the Blue Room, probably, that's where visitors are usually put.'

The cat under the desk was making horribly squashy noises and the sardine smell kept rising up at me, so I picked up my bag and said, 'Yes, please.'

'Excellent.'

Hugo led the way out of the library and I watched his back view with a degree of complacency. He was attractive, he was attentive and he was interesting. I reckoned we could be announcing our engagement within six months, if I played my cards right.

3

NORTHANGER ABBEY – NORTHANGER ABBEY, JANE AUSTEN

We mounted an enormous staircase, carved in twiddly dark wood, curving like an impressive eyebrow over the hallway and up onto a galleried landing which branched off in various directions. 'This is the *most* haunted part of the house,' Hugo said, leading me off to the right along an upstairs corridor. Occasional glances through the huge windows had told me that this wing of the house looked out over the gardens.

'I'm sorry?' As I spoke, the sun went behind a cloud and the wonderful roseate light died to leave us staring down a wood-panelled box into a murky dimness which was giving off a distinct smell of damp plaster.

'Oh yes. Whole place is riddled with ghosts of course, but this is the worst bit.' Complacently Hugo set out, touching closed doors and naming as he went. 'My room, the Green Room, Scarlet Room...' We rounded the end of the corridor and set out along another, which branched around to the left.

'Hang on, hang on, can we go back to the "ghost" thing, please?' I'd stopped moving now, frozen into immobility on the landing. 'The house is haunted?'

'Oh, yes.' Hugo sounded completely blasé about the walking corpse potential. 'Dreadfully, I'm afraid.' Then he smiled. 'No need for you to worry, though. Stay in your room after dark, don't go wandering around – it's all perfectly all right.' Then he went back to his naming of the rooms. 'The

Panelled Room – Mother uses that one for the Sheraton collection, mostly forgeries of course – the Yellow Room – that one's always kept locked, ah, and this is the Blue Room. We usually put guests up in here, you see.'

He turned the handle and the door swung noiselessly open to show a perfectly ordinary bedroom which had more than a little of the hotel-soullessness about it. There was a big double bed, horrible oak furniture which was too dark for the small amount of light which squeezed in through the inadequate window, and a kettle on a desk. I turned around. 'It's fine.' It was fine. It had a bed. That was really all I asked for. Oh, apart from not being put miles away from the nearest occupants, in a house that was supposedly haunted. 'Where does Lady Tanith sleep?'

'In the other wing. She had a suite of rooms of course, originally, but actually she pretty much has the whole wing to herself now that Father's no longer with us. She doesn't like disturbance, you see.' Hugo said this as though having an entire wing of a house so that you didn't get woken in the night was perfectly normal. Well, of course, it was to him. The idea of just wearing headphones and listening to podcasts so that the drunks arguing outside didn't wake you, wouldn't occur to him because it didn't need to. 'We don't usually go down that way.' He closed the door to the Blue Room and we rounded the end of the corridor. 'This is a storage room, not much used these days.' He touched another door, then another. 'And this is the bathroom.'

This door stood opposite my bedroom, and Hugo flashed me a glimpse of a tiled floor, a high-flush toilet with a cistern the size of a commercial water tank and the end of a roll-top bath. 'This is why we put visitors in the Blue Room, it's close to the facilities. En suite, sadly, rather passed us by.'

Unconcerned at my somewhat stunned reaction to his house, Hugo turned us back and we returned to the 'haunted' corridor, where I stopped again.

'When you say "haunted",' I said cautiously, 'what are we talking, here? Mysterious noises or a sheeted figure that moves inexplicably quickly towards you, or people showing you huge holes in their chests?' M R James had had a hand in my adolescence and took some shaking off, especially in a house like this, straight from *Lost Hearts*.

Under my feet the scarlet carpet had given off little puffs of dust where we'd walked and these were winking and dancing in the sun that had now deigned to shine again through the huge windows.

'Oh, there's all sorts. Up here there's supposed to be a lady who walks,' Hugo said carelessly. 'Fairly modern, that one, and she appears during the day as well as at night. A guest of Grandfather's who fell off the balcony and broke her neck. Or something.'

I thought of the young woman I'd seen through the balcony window. The hair at the back of my neck tingled and the skin of my spine tried to crawl into my underwear and hide. No. Surely not.

'And then there's the noises, footsteps and so on, occasional ghastly scream, that sort of thing, all very standard in a house this old. There's a ghost horse in the old stable block, but that's mostly disused now, and we haven't heard him for *ages*, and sometimes something moans in the Morning Room. I'll show you that in a bit. Are you having your things sent on? Mother wants you to start as soon as possible, I gather.'

For a moment he looked out of the huge window at the acutely angled balcony. I could see from this side that the windows were, in fact, full-length doors that opened, presumably so that the balcony could be accessed, although now it would only be accessible to someone with a desire to see the entire garden at ninety degrees. Below, in one of the borders, the gardener was clipping something with his deadly shears. He still looked scruffy, and the T-shirt clearly only fitted where it touched because it hung around him now like – I tried not to think – an affectionate ghost. The clipping looked to have a degree of ferocity about it too. I shuddered and added him to my list of 'things to be avoided', which was lengthening by the second.

Haunted. Of course Templewood would be haunted. I was overwhelmed with a sudden longing to leave. The bus might be inadequate, but at least it was a known quantity and not full of people who were, in the words of my taxi driver, 'barking'. I could make the best of van life, I'd been doing it my entire life; it was a roof, of sorts, over my head and didn't, as far as I knew, have any ghosts at all.

Ahead of us, where the ornately carved stairway ushered us down into the cavernous reception hallway, the cat appeared, waddling its way up along the carpet towards us, preceded by the smell of elderly fish.

'I don't really have much *to* send on,' I said, trying to decide whether or not to mention that, as my parents were currently *en route* to Montreal and my sister, whose idea this whole awfulness was, lived in Cornwall, there was nobody to send anything anywhere. If I told Hugo that, at least it would establish my credentials as a single woman, available for matrimony. But it would also let him know that nobody would miss me, should the gardener lose what little sanity he had left and stab us all to death in the middle of the night. Or even Hugo himself for that matter. He had, so far, seemed perfectly well-balanced and normal, but you surely couldn't be the offspring of Lady Tanith and live in a place like this without having an awful lot of something restrained under that smooth surface polish.

'Oh. Right-o.'

With one hand on the Gothic balustrading, Hugo began to walk down the gentle half-oval of the polished staircase to the hall below. I followed carefully. The treads were uneven as though something very big and heavy had once walked up alternate steps.

'I live alone,' I said. I wasn't sure now whether I was setting out my credentials for being marriage-worthy or establishing that nobody would come looking for my body for weeks.

'That's nice,' Hugo observed vaguely. He didn't seem inspired to plot my immediate demise, which was encouraging.

Behind us, the cat, disappointed at having reached the top of the stairs just in time for us to start descending, sat like a fat cushion and watched us go.

'In a converted bus,' I tried again for a reaction.

'How very unusual.' He still sounded vague and that annoyed me. This was my one point of interest, my one conversational opening. It normally got some kind of a reaction other than polite acknowledgement.

'My parents are Ed and Iris. Of *Road Life*,' I went on, despite Hugo's obvious lack of follow-up questions, and to let him know that I did have people who would miss me. Eventually. 'You know, the TV programme?'

'I don't watch much television.' Hugo gave me a beaming smile as we reached the bottom of the creaky staircase. 'There's one about somewhere, Mother keeps it for the staff. But this is the Morning Room, come on in and have a look.'

He crossed the hall, with its chequerboard tiling and niches, and opened the door to a small sitting room with yellow walls and a collection of mismatched tables and chairs dotted around, like a furniture orphanage. 'Mother writes her letters in here.'

Suppressing annoyance from his lack of curiosity about me, I continued to follow him around the downstairs. Hugo enumerated the rooms, announcing their name and purpose as though he were an estate agent trying to sell me the place. I stared about me as we went, a little afraid of what I might see. All the rooms were big, with high, chilly ceilings and enormous windows that contained wonderful views like architectural postcards. Curtains that were made from enough fabric to form several circus tents hung, bedraggled and dusty in each, paint peeled in those rooms that were sunny and in those at the back of the house, where the view was of distant moorland safely restrained behind some extensive hedging, there was a smell of ash and burned wood. Either it was chilly enough to need to light fires in there even on summer evenings, or there had been a recent conflagration. From the state of the place, it was hard to tell which of these applied.

Reassuringly, no ghosts manifested, although the chill had begun to seem supernatural.

'And here, obviously, is the library again.' Ignoring the makeshift metal nature of the front door, Hugo swept me around back into the room in which I'd been interviewed and flung open the double doors. 'Ah, Mother.'

Lady Tanith was sitting on one of the overstuffed chairs in a corner, with a book on her lap. She'd turned on the light over Sir Oswald, I noticed, so his slightly resigned features shone above the room, somewhat dimmed by the amount of dust in the air from the fallen curtain which still pooled beneath the window. She looked posed, as though she'd not been sitting reading, but rather waiting for us to come back in.

Behind us, the cat marched determinedly into the room and jumped onto the library steps, causing several books to fall to the floor amid puffs of yet more dust and the cracking of aged covers.

I looked at the little tableau with an increasing feeling of trapped desperation. It wasn't supposed to *be* like this! Templewood Hall was meant to be a shabbily lived-in house, with wonderful possibilities, window seats and comfortable nooks to curl up in. Lady Tanith was supposed to be a delightfully vague and dotty dowager, with amusing habits and a need for rescue.

Narrative causality dictated that I would sweep in, being regularly called a 'breath of fresh air', and redecorate, befriend my employer – possibly causing her to start dating a winsome retired professor from a nearby village, but that was optional – before marrying Hugo and starting a new dynasty who would nurture the Templewood estate into the future.

What narrative causality had failed to mention at any point, was that Lady Tanith would be insanely besotted with a sardine-scented cat, that only demolition would serve to make Templewood more attractive and that I would be staring at a pair of painted knees seen through volcanic levels of dust, trying to impress. Ghosts and the air of incipient horror movie were almost the least disappointing elements.

So far, only Hugo was coming up to expectations.

There was a silence, broken by the sound of the cat beginning to lick itself again and a distant clock ticking.

Eventually, Lady Tanith put her book down on a side table, looked at me and sighed. 'Well, you're here now,' she said. 'You can get started. I need you to catalogue my books onto the computer. It's in here somewhere.' She gazed around as though the computer may be lying in wait under a table. 'Hugo, would you go to the kitchens and tell Mrs Compton that there will be another person for dinner?' She waved a hand of dismissal.

'Of course.' Hugo dipped his head in acknowledgement, but I was mildly encouraged to see him give me a small wink as he did so.

Lady Tanith continued to watch me as I stood completely disorientated. 'Well? Go on then, girl.'

I decided that honesty was best and more likely to endear me to her than a continued failure to act. 'I don't know what you want me to do.'

'Catalogue my books.'

'But *how*? I mean, in what way?' I still couldn't see any sign of a computer. The cat stopped its ablutionary activities and stared at me, twisted into a portly arabesque.

'Just... catalogue. You know. Into... order.'

I began to suspect that she had no idea how one went about cataloguing a library either. 'Shall I just make a list of all the books, maybe author, title and year of publication? On the – computer?'

She waved an irritated hand and the cat bent back to its flank, tongue still protruding. 'Whatever you think,' she snapped, then lowered her voice and leaned slightly forward as though she were about to offer me confidences. 'Cataloguing the library isn't the real reason you're here, you know.'

I felt my shoulders loosen. This was where she confessed that she'd brought me in as a companion to her lonely son. He'd probably had a disappointment – been jilted at the altar or caught his fiancée in bed with another man and sworn to never love again. I was here to bring him out of his shell and teach him about the beauty of life; to fill him with a new positive attitude and, possibly, the desire to build a sanctuary for abused horses, or similar. My arms prickled with her unsaid words. Or maybe it was the dust and cat fur.

'I need you to find something,' Lady Tanith breathed.

Oh, even *better*! A quest. A mysterious artefact. The whole 'save Hugo from himself, fall in love' thing was a *subplot*! I hadn't considered this might be the case. 'Find what?' I bent forward too.

She glanced up at the portrait hanging above us, as though Oswald could be listening in. 'I was his muse, you know.' Her voice had gone a bit dreamy, reliving a past only she could see. 'I came as a companion to his wife Caroline – an invalid, poor woman. Before we knew it, Oswald and I had fallen in love. Of course, nothing could be *said*, and he wouldn't have divorced her; he was utterly, utterly dedicated to Caroline. But we *worked together closely*.' She gave the final three words such a weight and spin that I was imagining them having frantic sex on the tabletop in here before she went on. 'When Caroline died, I thought... but he needed some time. He'd been married to her for most of his adult life, the poor darling, and he didn't want to appear precipitate or cause any form of scandal. So...'

As though a little ashamed of confessing as much as she had, Lady Tanith looked down and began picking cat fur off her trousered leg. I waited. There had to be more.

The Master opened his pink mouth and yowled, a surprisingly human sound. 'I *am* continuing, darling,' Lady Tanith said. I eyeballed the cat with deep suspicion. 'It was decided that he would go abroad for a time. To let the dust settle.' There was absolutely no indication in her tone that this was meant to be anything other than a statement, when any other person would have used the opportunity for a joke, given that the levels of dust in this room were almost tomb-worthy. 'Oswald died. In Switzerland.' There was a lot of emotion behind those words. 'It was very sudden. He never came home to me.'

In the following silence, more dust settled. From outside I could hear the sound of furious snipping, but that was the only noise that penetrated this stuffy, over-furnished room. Lady Tanith was gazing up at the portrait, her eyes shining with affection.

'I'm sorry to hear that,' I said, wondering how the *hell* any of this could be anything to do with cataloguing a library, and hoping that she wasn't going to send me on a quest to bring home Oswald's remains or anything. Cataloguing a library was a suitably romance-heroine task. Grave robbing had *not* featured in my reading material.

'So, I married his son Richard and stayed,' she finished, as though this was the only possible ending. 'Had the boys, and honoured Oswald's memory every day.' Another glance at the painted face. I forbore to point out that she seemed to have honoured his memory by allowing his house to slide gradually into dereliction, but then remembered Miss Havisham, and didn't. A momentary twinge of pity for Lady Tanith and her disappointing love life plucked at my heart. She'd clearly loved Oswald very much and loving a married man only to lose him at the point when she thought he'd be hers must have hit her hard.

'However, somewhere in here, are his diaries.' Lady Tanith seemed to dismiss all extraneous details, like emotion or getting to the point. 'Oswald used to work in here all the time, on his novels, the dear man. It's my favourite room, you know.' She gazed fondly around at the shelving.

I made another encouraging noise, hoping she would actually tell me what I needed to know soon. I could feel a sneeze coming, and sneezing hugely would break the mood of anticipation that Lady Tanith was clearly building, with rather too much foreshadowing for my liking. It felt a little like waiting for a terrible curse to be revealed.

'I want you to find the diaries.' *Ah, here we go*, I thought. Hardly lost treasure, but good enough. 'I'd like to publish them,' Lady Tanith went on. 'It's been fifty years this year, since he passed away, I think Caroline's memory has been sufficiently honoured. Now is the time to let the world see what lay behind his creative genius.'

I was mentally trying to draw a timeline, work out how old she was; how old she'd been when Hugo was born, because he looked to be in his early to mid-thirties; whether Oswald had strayed into 'dirty old man seducing young companion' territory; and basically, what the hell had gone on here. 'Just that?' I asked. 'Find the diaries?'

'And catalogue the books, of course,' Lady Tanith continued, as though this would be the work of moments. 'But the diaries are the important thing, obviously.'

'Obviously,' I echoed faintly. There had to be *thousands* of books in here. 'I presume you've already had a look.'

Lady Tanith pursed her lips at me and crossed her legs. She was still slim and elegant, like her son. Her face was mostly unlined and she had wonderful bone structure, if somewhat sharp-edged – yes, I could see what Oswald had seen in her. Older man with invalid wife, pretty young thing coming into the household. I bet he'd mused the hell out of her in every room. I had another momentary pang of pity for this woman, ageing away in this crumbling house and pining for her lost love. 'Of course I have,' she said, as though this should be obvious. 'But I couldn't have a very thorough look because I don't want the boys to know. They understand that I had a very *special* relationship with their grandfather' – another, beatific gaze at the portrait – 'and that he took much of his inspiration from me, but I don't want our love for one another to become...' She stopped, as though groping for the right word. 'Salacious,' she finished. 'I want to prepare the diaries for publication and I don't want the boys reading them first. Oswald was always *most* discreet, but there may be – comments. I'm sure you understand.'

She didn't enlarge on the nature of the comments, for which I was overwhelmingly relieved. My imagination was already on double overtime.

'And the diaries are definitely in here?' I looked around again. There could be an entire NASA space probe in here, plus astronauts, there was so much stuff.

'Definitely.' Lady Tanith also looked around. She clearly wasn't seeing what I was seeing, because there was a wistful smile tugging at her cheeks. 'Oswald did his best work in here.'

I tried very hard not to imagine her and Oswald 'doing their best work' in here.

'He would have left the diaries with me, of course, but the trip to Switzerland was very impromptu; Oswald had friends in Geneva who'd invited him out, to help him get over Caroline's death, you know.' She stared mistily at the portrait again. 'He always said that one day posterity would own him. He'd say it just like that, Andromeda – "One day Posterity will own me."'

I blew out a silent breath. Posterity, clearly, had not known what it was letting itself in for.

'But I have to edit them sensitively. They cannot be left for the boys to find. And you're not to tell Hugo, obviously.'

'Obviously,' I echoed faintly.

'So, you can start now.' Lady Tanith stood up. 'The Master will leave with me.'

'Good,' I muttered.

The cat gave me a stare that could have stripped paint, and Lady Tanith frowned. 'I firmly believe,' she said, with extreme hauteur, 'that Oswald has come back to me, in the form of The Master.'

With that, the pair of them stalked, heads high and with regal bearing, from the room. I stuck my tongue out at their retreating backs, and began the hunt for the computer.

* * *

Dinner was... interesting. We sat in the dining room, although Lady Tanith's demeanour rather indicated that she thought 'The Help' should eat alone in her room, and spooned up obviously tinned soup from a tureen in the centre of the table. After that, a doughty lady wearing a brightly coloured pinafore overall, marched in, slammed down a plate of cold meat and salad and said, 'You'll have to serve yourselves, I'm off home, my legs is playing up something cruel.'

'Thank you, Mrs Compton,' Hugo said as calmly as though she'd curtsied and served us personally.

'I'll be in to do her ladyship's breakfast,' Mrs Compton said, giving me a wicked, narrow-eyed glare, 'but the rest of you can fend for yourselves.'

'I am sure we shall rise to the occasion, Mrs Compton. Goodnight.'

Mrs Compton 'harrumphed', which I'd never heard done in real life before. And, whilst I was trying to decide whether she was more Mrs Danvers from *Rebecca*, or Mrs Reynolds from *Pride and Prejudice*, she marched out of the room and closed the door behind her with a firmness that told of a wish to slam it, but too much class to do so.

Nobody remarked on this behaviour, so I presumed it was Mrs Compton's normal way of communicating. Hugo passed me the plate of cold meat. 'So, you said that you lived in a converted bus, Andi?'

'Er,' I said, wishing that I hadn't mentioned it. Did Hugo have to choose *now* to find me interesting? 'Yes.'

'And your parents are television personalities?'

Now Lady Tanith raised her head. 'You have famous parents, Andromeda?'

I gulped. 'They have a television programme. They started out making programmes for YouTube on living in a converted bus and travelling around Britain and Europe and the show got picked up by the BBC. It's apparently cult viewing.' I cut my meat into tiny pieces and tried not to notice that there seemed to be a caterpillar on my salad.

'Hm. Are they well off?'

'Mother!' Hugo remonstrated, but gently. 'We don't talk about things like that, remember? It's déclassé.'

I poked at the caterpillar and it wandered off over the edge of my plate. Once it had gone, I ate the salad. One thing you learned from growing up with my parents, was to eat what you were given, when you were given it. They could be a little lackadaisical about meals and mealtimes when they were busy.

'Oh, Andromeda doesn't mind,' Lady Tanith said, blithely. 'The working class are always keen to discuss how much money they make.' She folded a lettuce leaf, speared it with her fork and tucked it into her mouth in one movement, without looking at it first. I hoped my caterpillar hadn't had friends in that salad bowl.

'My father' – I didn't know quite how to go about phrasing things – 'made a lot of money in the city. When he was younger. Then he married Mum, took very early retirement and they bought the bus. They had me and my sister, and then they started a blog about life on the road – that turned into the YouTube channel and then they got taken on by mainstream TV.

They've gone to Montreal, to tour Canada in a Winnebago, for the new series.'

Hashtag OnTheRoad, I thought, bitterly. Hashtag LeaveYourDaughterToManage. Hashtag WhatTheBloodyHellAmIDoingHere.

'Their loss is our gain,' Hugo said, with an admirable attempt at levity. With a flash of horror I wondered if they were going to kidnap me and ransom me back to my parents. Should I have revealed as much as I had? Had I put myself in danger?

Then I thought of my parents being presented with a ransom demand for me, and reality cut back in again. They had probably forgotten that I'd moved out by now and any attempts to extort money for my return would be met with puzzled stares and a feature-length episode. While my parents were lovely people and undoubtedly fond of me and my sister, the alternative lifestyle they led meant that they could be somewhat vague about details, such as where I was currently living and why.

'I didn't go to school much.' I thought I might as well just come out with all of it now and save the embarrassing Q&A session. 'We moved about all the time when I was young and I never really had the chance, so I read a lot instead.'

And everything I know about life comes from books. I had to teach myself how life worked, the conventions, how to behave, from sitting for hours in local libraries. I didn't have friends, I didn't go to parties, because we never put down roots. I just sat, and I read.

It was beginning to dawn on me that perhaps Jane Austen, the Brontës and Daphne du Maurier hadn't been the best preparation for life in general.

'So, you have siblings?' Hugo asked. He'd put his elbows on the table and was looking at me as though he was fascinated.

'Yes, I've got a sister. Judith. She lives in Cornwall now with her husband and two children.' Whom I narrowly escaped having to move in with, I didn't add, and it was only because Jude had found the advert for this job, and you didn't seem fussy, that saved me from that fate. Although now, I thought, looking at Lady Tanith eating a tomato with a knife and fork, and Hugo watching me as though I were some kind of scientific experiment, maybe I would have been better off moving into Jude's granny annexe and taking a cleaning job, as my parents had suggested.

'Andromeda and... Judith?' Lady Tanith speared another tomato. 'Not exactly a duo that rolls off the tongue.'

'Mother!'

'She was actually called Nebula,' I said, happy to drop my sister in it. 'But she decided when she was five that she was going to be called Judith. She got my parents to send her away to school too.' That was how she'd got a normal life, I thought sadly, remembering my sister, aged about seven, hands on her hips and a copy of *Malory Towers* on her lap, insisting that our parents should send her to boarding school. My sister's life had been affected by reading as much as mine had, but her books had given her courage rather than the knowledge of how to tie a cravat and how to conduct oneself at balls.

Maybe, if *I* had discovered school stories before *Northanger Abbey* and Dickens, I would have turned out like Judith. Then I caught Hugo's eye across the table. He gave me a broad, angular-cheekboned smile, and I stamped down the feeling that I'd been ill-used. Jude was married to a marketing director, whose rugby playing physique had long since turned to podge. Hugo was definitely better looking than Ollie. And he was heir to all this...

The handle fell off my fork and I hastened to try to attach the two bits back together. Hugo's smile increased, and he passed me another fork from the stack on the sideboard behind him. I thanked him silently, and the smile got even wider.

'Judith is a nice name,' Lady Tanith said. 'You might have been a Judith, Hugo.'

There was a sudden noise as Hugo knocked the pile of forks off the sideboard and they clattered to the floor. 'Sorry,' he said, 'caught them with my sleeve.'

'Your brother, of course, was always going to be Jasper.' Lady Tanith turned to me again. 'Jasper is my elder son, you see.'

Oh. That meant that Hugo wasn't the heir to the estate. Oh, bugger. I'd been brought in to marry the *second* son. I had to remind myself that, these days, this no longer meant that he'd have to go into the army, and I could find myself as a soldier's wife, a calling that I was fairly certain I would not be suited to. Although, right now I was beginning to waver in my certainty that marrying Hugo was my happy ending in waiting. The atmosphere was definitely leaning towards the 'acid bath' finale.

'Jazz renounced the estate in my favour,' Hugo said. 'The bastard.'

'Hugo! Language!'

'Sorry, Mother.' Then, turning back to me. 'He lives in a cottage on the estate now. But he didn't want to take on the management and all that entails, so I will take it all on, after Mother... um... Father left the estate to her, you see.'

'Richard was very forward thinking.' Lady Tanith pushed her plate away with a sigh. 'And, of course, you were both so very young when he died. Oh, there you are, my darling.'

I looked up. I didn't know who I expected to see coming in, possibly the elusive Jasper, but it was just the cat. It forced the door open sufficiently to allow its creamy-furred bulk through, wandered across the floor, and jumped up onto the table, presenting me with an unwanted view of a backside, tail held high in the air.

Neither Hugo nor Lady Tanith reacted as though this was anything other than a perfectly reasonable occurrence.

'May I... may I go to my room?' I asked faintly. The cat's tail was sweeping generally around the salad plate and I was horribly afraid that the front was licking the remaining ham. 'I'm a little tired after the journey.'

'Of course.' Hugo half stood. 'Would you like me to help you with your bags?'

'There's only the one and it's out in the hall,' I said. 'The Blue Room is mine?'

'I thought you were going to continue work tonight,' Lady Tanith sniffed.

'I'll carry on first thing tomorrow.' I was already through the door. Hugo gave me a small bow as I passed. 'I promise.'

4

GODSEND CASTLE – I CAPTURE THE CASTLE, DODIE SMITH

Contrary to my first impressions, the bed in the Blue Room was comfortable. The room had overtones of a Regency Premier Inn, with its functional furniture in the ubiquitous oak and I'd imagined that I'd spend my first night lying wakeful and restless, hearing strange occult noises and mysterious footsteps. But, in fact, I fell asleep almost as soon as my head hit the pillow and, apart from a few minutes in the middle of the night, when I woke suddenly and heard some heavy creaking from the 'always kept locked' Yellow Room next door, which was probably just the wind, I slept all night.

I woke early to silence. I made a dash for the bathroom and managed to persuade some lukewarm water out of the antiquated shower fittings, then went downstairs.

Nobody was about and the whole house had a deserted feel. The air smelled of dust, with a slight undertone of damp plaster and neglect, and I stood in the huge hallway, wondering what to do. Running away was heading the list at the moment. Between Lady Tanith's air of repression and Hugo's lack of immediate attraction to me I was doubting the whole situation fairly hard. Only the lack of transport and anywhere to run to, plus my desire to show Jude and my parents that I really could make something of my life, stopped me from repacking my bag and heading off into the dawn.

A small beam of sunlight inched its way in through a side window and cast itself at my feet. The light made me feel better and I squared my shoulders. There was no such thing as ghosts. Lady Tanith was simply a besotted old woman and Hugo was a somewhat foppish heir to an estate. Nobody had murdered me in the night, the mysteriously mentioned Jasper hadn't burst into my room begging to be rescued. Now, I was hungry. Did I dare try to find the kitchen and make myself some breakfast? I took a few steps along the dank corridor that led to where I remembered Hugo showing me the kitchens, scullery and various empty little caves which had once been grand and busy. Then I remembered the bad-tempered Mrs Compton and her legs, and decided to wait until I was cushioned by the presence of Hugo before encountering her again. My stomach still had the clench of nervousness and the fear of doing something wrong and being sent packing to live at Jude's or, even worse, to take possession of the bus. That was currently languishing in a farmer's field and my lack of a licence to drive large vehicles meant I'd have to live in it there, where bullocks peered in through the windows and there was no running water.

At least here, I thought, walking aimlessly around peering in the empty niches in case Oswald's diaries had carelessly been pushed into one, I had a proper bed, running water and a lack of small children bouncing me awake at 4.30. And I was Doing a Job! My parents' casual assurance that nobody needed qualifications these days, all you really had to have was a willingness to work and/or an eye for interiors had, so far, failed to be true. Apart from shifts behind the bar at the local pub, where I was unpopular because I didn't know how to banter, I had singularly failed in the job-hunting world.

I pressed a few of the plaster mouldings that surrounded the walls, just in case a previously unsuspected secret panel slid out or a priest hole became visible. Nothing happened, apart from one plaster rose breaking beneath my fingers into dust and paint fragments. *This wasn't supposed to happen.* None of it. Even this bit, the Templewood Hall and Hugo being the heir, was way down the list of how I'd expected life to go. I had thought, encouraged by the small local library near where we'd ended up before the Montreal offer, that I'd go to work for a local businessman who, despite my adorably ditzy ways with his appointments and some misunderstandings with another woman, would fall for me and give me promotion and an engagement ring. Either that, or a billionaire would need an emergency date for a society wedding and we would, via some humorous mix up, end up sharing a hotel room with the inevitable consequences.

What the novels I had devoured had neglected to mention was that, as I wasn't gorgeous with long legs and an ability to quip, I was not heroine material. I didn't have the curvy figure and incorrigible hair, the innate way with winsomely adorable orphans or the sparkly brilliant conversation that caused riotous laughter. Instead of inspiring lust or adoration, I mostly just made people annoyed.

So this, here, was my best hope for now. The sun, which had been beaming its cheering early light in through the upper windows of the double height hall and showing up the chips, cracks and scratches in the tiled flooring, went in. It illustrated my state of mind nicely – the dying of hope for any real future, a lack of inspiration and the dawning knowledge that my life was probably going to be lived in my sister's shadow or a mouldering forty-nine-seater, forever.

I shook myself. I was here now. This was a real job, and maybe I could persuade good enough references from Lady Tanith, whom I had already begun to call Tanith in my head, because I had read enough mythology to know where the name originated and to suspect that Thanatos might be hanging around in this house, to find myself something similar somewhere else. Or, I thought, with hope beginning to peep at me from behind the cloud of realism it had hidden behind, I *could* marry Hugo? I could see beyond the neglect and damp that this house had wonderful bones. Sixteenth-century history could be a draw too; perhaps it would convert into a luxurious, if somewhat cavernous B&B? The gardens, what I'd seen of them, were spectacular; maybe cream teas on the lawns in the season? There would be a great deal of work to do, of course, to get it up to standard, but I could see myself cheerily beavering away, hair tied casually and cutely with a cloth, buffing woodwork and scouring floors to the accompaniment of an indie-rock backing track.

Then, once more, reality bounced back. I thought of Lady Tanith's acerbic personality being faced with visitors and shuddered. Then I squared my shoulders and looked for something to do.

I could go back to the library, switch on the ageing computer which had turned out to be stuck in a corner forming a useful shelf for more books, and clear another tiny section. Or hunt about amid the volumes for anything that looked as though they might be diaries. I had my hand on the library door handle before the thought of the silence which lay in that room, overseen by the enormous figure of Oswald himself, gave me second thoughts. No, before work, before breakfast, I'd allow myself a few minutes of illusion and wander the acres, looking pensive. The fresh air, after all this dust and brooding, would be good for me and I could pretend to be an Austen heroine again, despite the lack of muslin, reticule and willing clergymen.

The front door was immovable. However the metal sheets were jammed in, I couldn't budge them, and I had no idea where there was another door to the outside, so I improvised. I hauled at one of the long sash windows in the moan-free Morning Room until I wiggled it high enough for me to be able to squeeze myself through and managed, with a great loss of dignity, to clamber out and drop the considerable height down onto the narrow area of lawn which lay outside.

It was further down than I'd thought, and I landed awkwardly, pitching forward to lie on the grass, which was damp. But it felt wonderful to be out of the house and to feel the sunshine first hand, so I just lay for a moment, face down, enjoying the smell of the gardens, the soft prickle of the grass against my skin and the warmth on the back of my neck. Maybe it wasn't *so* bad here, after all.

Then I rolled over and screamed.

The gardener was standing over me, armed, this time not with shears but with a huge metal rake with enormous tines. Backlit by the bright early sun, this gave him an Edward Scissorhands silhouette.

'Are you all right?' He looked down on me, shifting the rake so its metal teeth now lay level with my head.

'Yes,' was all I could say, still prone and now aware of dew seeping through my shirt.

'Need a hand?' He moved the rake again. I couldn't take my eyes off its threatening shininess.

'No, no thanks, I'm fine,' I gasped.

He was wearing a slightly better-fitting T-shirt this morning, I noticed. His hair was longish and dark and his legs, which were very visible between his cut-off jeans and huge boots, were tanned. I was thwarted in my momentary recall of *Lady Chatterley's Lover*, read furtively under the covers over a couple of very overheated summer nights, when he grunted, nodded to me briefly, and headed off away across the smooth acres of mown lawn, with the teeth of the rake bobbing and springing beside him like an enthusiastic metal terrier.

I waited until he was well out of sight before I stood up. Then, forgetting to be an Austen heroine, I went and sat by the edge of the pond for a while, until someone turned the fountain on, when I decided it was probably time to go back in and see if anyone was awake.

I wandered around to the back of the house, where I found an open door which led into the kitchen, where Hugo was sitting on a stool eating Rice Krispies dry out of the packet with his hand.

'Oh, good morning!' He sounded bright and breezy and not at all surprised to see me trailing in, slightly damp from the fountain's unexpected resurgence, and dusted with more than a few grass cuttings from my close encounter with the lawn. 'We'll have to forage for ourselves this morning. Mrs Compton sometimes does breakfast, but she's having one of her "moments" lately and only doing it for Mother. She's devoted to Mother, for some reason. Perhaps she's quietly putting rat poison in all her food, or something.' He fisted another batch of Krispies into his mouth thoughtfully. 'Wasting her time, of course, Mother's immune to most of the major causes of death.'

He gave me another beaming smile which took the sting out of his words a little but did make me wonder about the familial relationships.

Marry Hugo, I thought. *Turn house into hotel. Exorcise ghosts. Rescue imprisoned older brother. Never, ever have to throw myself on Jude's mercy for somewhere to live...* 'How long have the family owned Templewood?' I asked, trying for pertness, and sitting down on the stool next to Hugo.

'It's not ancestral or anything.' Hugo pushed the Krispies box towards me and shook it, but I averted my eyes. There was a loaf of bread sitting on the long oak table and I'd spotted a toaster. 'Well, it is, sort of. It was Grandma's family home, although Mother tries to spin it so that it was Oswald who bought it. But really it came when he married her, although I think *her* father bought it from an impoverished aristocrat in eighteen hundred and something. Hardly Norman conquest stuff.'

I got off the stool and began to make toast. I had been hoping that the bread would be a handmade artisan loaf, although I had to work hard to imagine the irritable Mrs Compton handmaking anything that you couldn't use a steamroller to manufacture, but it turned out to be a supermarket loaf deprived of its wrapper.

'And it's just you and your brother? No other siblings?' Hugo was easy to talk to anyway, which was encouraging. And he wasn't married, unless his wife was chained up in the attic. Which absolutely wouldn't surprise me.

'Yes, and there's nine years between us. But, as I said, Jazz doesn't want the bother of managing the estate or the house; he has a cottage out there, in the estate village.' A vague thumb indicated the window. 'And Mother won't change anything that was here in Oswald's time. So we live with crumbling tiles and peeling walls, in case the Great Man gets upset, even though he's been dead for fifty years.' Hugo sighed.

'What would you like to do with the place? When...' I stopped myself in time from saying 'when your mother dies', because I was half-convinced that Lady Tanith kept herself going with the blood of virgins already. '...When you inherit.'

The kitchen was beginning to smell of toasting bread now, a little bit more homely and less like a post-apocalyptic *Pride and Prejudice*.

Hugo sighed again. 'Honestly?'

I nodded.

'Sell it. I want to go and live in Paris. Or America. Anywhere but here. Or, maybe, travel around, see places. I envy you your upbringing so much, always somewhere new, new things to see and experience. I never go anywhere.'

He was looking at me now as though I were some shining example of ambition. As though being born in a bus and never staying anywhere long enough to make friends, or form any social connection of any kind, was something laudable. But then, if he sold this place he'd be able to afford to travel first class and stay in hotels where, presumably, he wouldn't have to fill the water bowser every morning and chip the ice off the blankets in winter.

I was enjoying feeling as though, in Hugo's eyes at least, I was an achiever. I had something of value – I'd travelled. 'Yes,' I said, determined to

Kerouac my childhood as much as necessary, 'it was full of wonderful experiences.' *Also some pretty shit ones, but we won't go into those right now.*

The toast popped, and Hugo and I sat side by side on wooden stools at a table which could have seated twenty, eating. I kept looking around, agog at so much space just to prepare food; at the massive range oven along one wall, the racks of pans suspended from the ceiling and the dusty shelves of plates and serving ware filling the walls. I tried to ignore the ominous crack which ran the width of the ceiling and the fact that the fridge humming to itself in a corner, like an unattended child, was tiny.

'Right.' Hugo jumped up at last, folding the now-empty packet into a small square of cardboard and dropping it neatly into a plastic tub. 'I'll be upstairs, if anyone wants me, not that they will, but Mother may ask.'

'I'll go and start work in the library, again.' I'd only done about an hour so far, and was already dreading that echoing silence.

'Cheerio, then. I'll see you at lunch.' Hugo waved a hand and sauntered out of the kitchen, leaving me wondering what he did around here all day. Did he work? Was he managing the estate? Although I found it impossible to imagine him giving orders to staff. There was a kind of floppy reticence to Hugo that made me think he wouldn't be that effective at management.

But that didn't matter. We got on. The possibility of our falling deeply in love and doing lots of staring into the depths of one another's eyes to see our souls reflected still existed. I wouldn't object to Templewood being sold either, I thought, looking at the fractured ceiling and the row upon row of unused crockery. Hell, I'd hold the flamethrower myself, if it came to it.

I thought, mistily, of all those books where the heroine had set sail for foreign parts and imagined myself on the deck of a yacht, clamping a large-brimmed hat tightly to my head whilst my skirts blew in the breeze of transit. I couldn't somehow imagine Hugo traipsing up a mountain wearing a sweaty rucksack in search of a view; he had far more of the organised helicopter tour about him. And with that thought satisfyingly in place, I tipped my toast crumbs into the sink, rinsed off my plate, and went off to the library and more data entry.

5

BLY – THE TURN OF THE SCREW, HENRY JAMES

Two weeks passed. Or rather, they inched slowly along, eased only by the fibre of occasional meetings with Hugo, usually in the kitchen. I learned my way around the house, mostly by trial and error which meant a lot of openings of doors, surprising Lady Tanith or The Master, apologising and closing the door again. Mrs Compton stomped her way to and from the kitchen doing I knew not what, and serving us meals every evening that seemed to have come straight from the School Dinner Cookbook. Lady Tanith would sometimes loom over me as I tapped yet another 'Author, Title, Date' into the spreadsheet on the computer and enquire whether I'd made any progress in looking for Oswald's diaries. As I considered that finding them would be my end goal, I didn't see how I could 'make progress' in the task – perhaps they were spread throughout the library as separate sheets? – I supposed that she was really checking up on me to make sure I hadn't legged it down the drive and headed for civilisation as fast as I could go.

As the only places I had to go *to* were a rusting static bus in a field or my sister's complacency, I had decided, on balance, to stay put.

Templewood seemed to be built on mystery and I slotted in as well as any heroine could be expected to, under the circumstances.

The whole place was sinister. Locked rooms and who only knew what was going on inside them? Noises so soft as to be almost inaudible but with no visible cause. Footsteps in the dark. I half expected to come down one morning to find a body in the library, which would actually be a relief. There was a breath-holding quality to Templewood as though a crime were about to be perpetrated but was awaiting the right time.

I came across other workers every now and then – a sad-eyed joiner patiently nailing something to a gate, a man shouting at bullocks in the fields beyond the garden. After a quick glance that seemed to have something of *The Gulag Archipelago* about it, they dismissed me as clearly unworthy of notice. Hugo's brother did not appear. He was occasionally referenced by Lady Tanith in a casual, throwaway way, to which Hugo reacted like a sullen teenager. I gathered that there was no love lost between the brothers although I didn't know why. Surely becoming the heir to the estate wasn't something to resent? Jasper's renouncing the title meant that Hugo would never have to find a job or move away – his life was here, amid these glorious gardens and this house full of potential. So why did Hugo grunt and look down at his plate whenever Lady Tanith asked if he wanted to come with her to visit Jasper? Did Jasper even *exist*, hinted my brain, trying to veer me into dark thoughts of bodies behind doors again. Was he real or Hugo's alter-ego, hived off to become a separate identity because of some hideous crime committed in childhood?

I didn't ask. I *couldn't* ask. I was too afraid of the answers.

And so, here I was, on what was probably a Tuesday but it didn't really matter as every day at Templewood was the same as the one before, although I had nominally negotiated for Sundays off. I finished inputting the books from the pile I'd scraped from a shelf, shared a dinner of frozen-in-the-middle cottage pie with Hugo, Lady Tanith being nowhere to be seen, and headed for bed, my steps dogged, or rather catted, by The Master. Every night he tried to get into my room and every night I managed, by some careful bodily arrangement, to prevent him. He continued to try, like an unsuccessful Tinder date, to force his way past me, but his beefy attributes always jammed him between my leg and the door edge in a wobbly mass of fur and embarrassment.

Tonight, I'd fallen asleep to the sound of discontented fur-cleaning from outside the door, and with *Great Expectations* lying crumple-paged across my chest. When the half million cups of tea that I'd drunk – I filled a vacuum flask every morning; there was no chance that anyone in this house was going to bring me continual top-ups during the day – percolated down to my bladder earlier than usual, I found myself awake with a book spine uncomfortably pressed into my ribcage.

It was still dark. Usually I woke after dawn, to the sound of birds in the attic above my head. At least, I was going to choose to believe it was birds that scuffled and clattered about. Some of the sounds were distressingly close to footsteps, coming and going with the sort of shuffling creak that made me imagine Dread Things. However, I'd seen starlings swoop above the window, so if there *was* a ghost up there I could carry on in ignorance of its existence.

But now, everything was silent and still. I slept with my window and curtains open, mostly to let out the smell of general neglect and Mrs Compton's attempts to make the place seem cleaned by spraying furniture polish into the air. I'd come upon her doing it once or twice, whilst I'd been finding my way around the house. She'd open a door, stand just inside the room, spray Mr Sheen randomly and then close the door quickly to trap the scent. When she'd turned around to see me watching I got a look so vitriolic that it almost ignited the aerosol fumes.

I had half wondered if she was trying to cover up the smell of death and kept a wary eye open for unnatural numbers of flies swarming outside a door. Despite frequent mentions, Jasper had still not made an appearance at Templewood and I had now started imagining him lying bloodstained and lifeless in one of the many rooms that nobody appeared ever to enter.

Templewood had got into my soul, and not in a good way.

I went and stood at the window. Outside there was nothing but blackness, punctuated by darker blackness where trees and shrubs deepened the night. Above, the stars shone, white-hot diamonds in the cold sky, filling the air with a grey almost-light. I took a deep breath, enjoying the feeling of freshness. The air smelled of water, a vague perfume from some of the flowers, and newly-mown grass and it almost made me want to climb out of the window and run barefoot far and fast away from this place.

Instead I sighed and opened my bedroom door to head to the bathroom. I turned the knob quietly, partly because I didn't want to wake anyone, even if they were sleeping four acres away, and partly because I didn't want the cat to know I was up. I wouldn't have put it past the feline interloper to slide into my room and be in my bed with a come-hither expression and a spritz of mackerel cologne when I got back.

As I stepped out onto the landing, the ghost was there. Frozen static with her back to me, her blonde hair piled high on her head and her ball gown swirling around her legs, she was standing by the window where I'd seen her on my first arrival. My brain took in her image in one solid gulp of terror. Tall and willowy, blonde and slender, wearing a pink satin dress that fell from a draped bodice to just above the floor, with a pair of kitten heels peeking out from underneath, she continued to stand, gazing out into the night. Or possibly seeing daylight in another time; waiting her turn to step out onto the balcony and die again.

My mouth instantly dried, open in a half shriek that I killed as the ghost began to turn towards me. I shot back into my room, my bladder no longer of any concern, terrified beyond understanding at the thought that she might see me, looking out of eyes ruined by her last fall. I closed the door, then locked it, which took some considerable effort, as the huge metal key didn't seem to have been turned since the queen before last.

I fled to my bed and dragged myself deep under the covers, but that was worse, because then I couldn't see whether the ghost had followed me in – as it slowly dawned on me that a locked door probably wasn't much of a deterrent to the Other Side – so I inched one eye and half my nose out until I was hunched on the mattress with the duvet and coverlet draped around me and gathered under my chin.

There was no sign of ghostly following. Nor was there any sound at all. I half expected a ghastly scream, a re-enactment of the accident that had caused her to hang around in these draughty corridors, maybe a slam of the balcony doors. But there was nothing. Not even a sigh of wind rattling the window in its sash. It was as though the entire night was holding its breath along with me, so as not to antagonise the supernatural.

As I continued not to be visited by a spectre, the terror began to lift, assisted by the first tweeting and muttering from the birds in the garden beyond, and a gradual thinning of the darkness into early dawn. The dim light gave me courage, which, added to my insatiable curiosity and bulging bladder, drove me out from beneath my swaddling and sent me trepidatiously to my door. I pressed my ear to the wood, after a momentary recoil in case a ghostly arm was about to stretch through the panels and grab me, but couldn't hear anything. Did ghosts even make a noise? Unless reliving the trauma of their death, weren't they *meant* to be silent, anyway?

I opened the door slowly and peered around its leading edge. The landing, balcony, and double windows were empty. There was absolutely nothing, no bloody handprints on the walls, no mysteriously tattered garments, no skeletal forms clattering along the boards. Nothing.

Gaining a little more courage at the lack of uncanny occurrences, I walked along to where I'd seen the figure. Was that a trace of perfume I could smell? Or was my imagination racing ahead of me and attributing a female scent to the ever-lingering furniture polish smell? I didn't know, and only the gradual greying at the window revealing that the morning was cantering in with full birdsong and a rising sun, made me brave enough to walk along to the head of the stairs, where there was still no sign of anything at all.

I trailed a hand along the wall as I walked back down the deep carpet, visited the bathroom in a world-record breaking time, and then went back to my room. This plaster, this paper, it must have seen so much drama over the years it had, evidently, been here. Perhaps it occasionally replayed scenes from that drama, like a DVD stuck on a favourite clip. I shuddered. This house was hundreds of years old, it must have entertained such a lot of anger, fear and pain. Now was absolutely *not* the time that I needed to find out that I was psychic or had any kind of affiliation for Things Unseen.

Some of the scarier passages from my recent reading lurched up from my subconscious to make me aware that there could be horrors lurking in any of the unsightly cupboards or behind any of these doors. It almost made me glad to hurtle back into my room and leap into bed, although unless the duvet was soaked in holy water and embroidered with religious symbols it probably wouldn't be much of a deterrent to some of the things I'd read about. I clutched my knees up under my chin and wrapped my arms around them, making myself as small a target for the Otherworld as I could, thankful that the sheets were still warm to my chilled body and I could dig my feet in to whatever the mattress was made of for extra heat.

Templewood really *was* a haunted house. Great. That would just put the proverbial cherry on top of the metaphorical icing. Searching for lost diaries for a woman who didn't seem to realise that slavery was illegal and her diffident-to-the-point-of-invisibility son, in a room where the books didn't so much need recovering as a full-on archaeological expedition, in a house that might suddenly reveal terrors beyond my wildest imaginings was *not* in the life plan.

And I was stuck here by my lack of anywhere else to go and the need to earn money.

I gathered more of the duvet around me and squared my shoulders. *Plenty* of women, my life gleaned from reading had told me, had to earn a living. Many of them found themselves in less-than-savoury positions, driven there by impecuniousness and lack of family 'background'. I was hardly a governess to an unruly child, with a master of the house who kept vanishing for weeks at a time. I was getting paid, board and lodging – even if the board was still half frozen and served with intense disinterest by Mrs Compton and the lodging was haunted. I tried to square my shoulders again but this was as good as it got, huddled under a bedcover, waiting for full daylight so that I could get up and start work again.

My imagination was in overdrive. If I breathed quietly I could almost convince myself that there were sounds coming from the Yellow Room next door; quiet, furtive sounds like half stifled sobs, so muted as to only come through as ethereal whispers. My skin tightened into goose pimples again and, to distract myself from spectral thoughts, I tried to imagine Jude, snuggled up with her sturdy husband in her comfortable house, with the sound of the sea in the background, while her adorable children slept on in their beautifully decorated bedrooms with the circus wallpaper, hand-painted toy boxes and racks of alphabetically ordered reading books.

As I was trying not to compare our circumstances, and counting my blessings ferociously that I didn't need to be woken by being bounced on and *Peppa Pig*, I felt a touch on my leg. A warm sensation, as though silk were being dragged down my bare skin. I froze, only to unfreeze seconds later when the telltale smell of old and unwashed fishing boat billowed around me and a Siamese head popped out of the side of the bedding to stare at me with fathomless blue eyes.

'No, no, no, no, no!' I jumped out of the other side of the bed and stood, cold footed, on the rug. 'You cannot be in here!'

The Master sat with a sheet draped lightly over his creamy body and his head and tail protruding. His ears twitched and he began, lazily, to lick a paw and swipe it across his dark whiskers, keeping his eyes on mine. The stare was so direct and challenging that I forgot my dismissal of any idea of reincarnation and began to worry whether Oswald really *might* have come back as a cat.

This idea, coupled with the possibility of a ghost on the landing, the low-level hatred from Lady Tanith, the mundanity of my job and its relentlessness, plus the seemingly hopeless task of finding *anything* in a library so cluttered that I would only be half surprised to find mammoths lurking behind some of the cabinets, was too much.

I hurtled myself out of the door. Dawn had broken like an egg over the building, laying a smooth golden yolk of light over everything and I wasn't sure whether it was the reassurance of daylight or sheer indignation that drove me back along the landing and down the stairs, desperate for escape.

Now I knew where all the doors were, it was an easy matter to let myself out of the door to the kitchens, through a boot room full of antiquated fishing rods, piles of snooker cues, collapsed wellingtons and cast-off garden shoes, and out into the lemon-fresh air beyond.

I ran a few trailing steps, aware that a heavy dew had settled on the grass and showed my passage in glimmering facets, as though a path of diamond had been built behind me. But there were no following phantoms, the cat was now presumably taking possession of my bed in its self-satisfied way, and Lady Tanith wouldn't be up for a good few hours. This was going to be as good as it got.

Then I spotted the gardener. He had his back to me, doing something with twine and a particularly vigorous-looking bush. I wondered what he was doing out here so early, but as I didn't know anything about gardening and there might well be jobs that could only be done in the first light of dawn, I didn't want to question him and look stupid.

'Good morning!' I called, trying to sound bright and sprightly, and not as though I'd been terrified out of the house wearing pyjamas that had not just seen better days but witnessed some truly spectacular past decades.

He didn't even acknowledge me to the extent of a raised hand of greeting. Well, sod him then. I'd add him to my list of grievances although, to be honest, that list was so long that it was beginning to feel a little indulgent.

Round about now, I told myself, as I perched on the edge of the pond and peered between lily pads to try to see the fish I knew were in there, I should be making a friend. Finding a confidante. This was how the stories went, just enough misery to lay the conditions as intolerable, and then someone comes along with sympathy and understanding to listen to my troubles. A best friend for me to explain my mental musings to and to help the reader more closely identify with my inner turmoil.

I raised my eyes from the lack of pond action. Nobody. Nobody for miles, just acres of dew-dotted grass, the long shadows of trees, carefully sculpted beds planted up with long-stemmed flowers that lolled out across the edging like artists after a night on the absinthe. I supposed I could tell my problems to a peony, although that was moving dangerously close to Lady Tanith's territory and I didn't think the fish would give a finny fuck about my trials and tribulations.

Hell, I knew life away from everything I'd known would be difficult. But I never thought it would be this *lonely*. My parents had been omnipresent around the bus, scripting out new episodes for the YouTube channel and then, latterly, there had been the constant comings and goings of a film crew, directors, sound and cameramen, all of whom had ignored me completely. All right, I know I'd said I wanted no part in the whole TV series about travelling around in a bus. And they'd had to sign waivers to ensure that I was never on screen. But that didn't mean they had to never talk to me or interact with me in any way – and some of those camera guys had been quite good looking. Even so... none of it had been as lonely as life around Templewood Hall was proving to be.

'Hey!'

It was the gardener. So, he'd decided to notice me now, had he? Although he didn't approach, he just stood, half-encompassed by a shoulder-level stand of bushes, so that his head stuck out like a particularly convincing statue. I gave him the briefest of glances and then looked away, hoping that my coolness gave a hint at how put out I was about his rudeness at ignoring me earlier.

'Hey!' he shouted again and waved an arm. I sighed. Nothing to be gained by being rude back, I supposed. Two wrongs not making a right, and all that. I waved back, a languorous movement of my arm that mimicked the way the long-stemmed plants were beginning to waft in the early breeze. Then I dropped my gaze back to the fish. The ball was in his court now, he could come over and talk to me properly – as long as he wasn't carrying those scary shears again – or go back to his little enclave of rudeness amongst the bushes.

He did neither. He stopped waving but didn't approach. He just stood and kept watching me, which meant that he had a front row seat when the fountain spurted into life right beside me and soaked me to the skin.

6

PEMBERLEY – PRIDE AND PREJUDICE, JANE AUSTEN

I had to have a bath to get rid of the smell of pond water, which meant that I was late down for breakfast. Normally this wouldn't have mattered; it would have been Hugo eating something like a five-year-old who's been left unsupervised and chatting lightly to me about whatever came into his head.

Today, however, it seemed that Lady Tanith had decreed we would be having a Formal Breakfast. When I came down the stairs with my hair in a towel, because I'd had to wash it – there had been weed in the fountain water – Mrs Compton was waiting for me at the bottom of the stairs.

'Lady Tanith and Master Hugo are in the Breakfast Room,' she said with disdain leaking from every syllable. 'You're late.'

'I didn't know there was anything to be late *for*,' I pointed out.

'Well, it's the twenty-first, isn't it?'

'Is it?' I replied, as though this made things any clearer.

Mrs Compton gave me a look such as might have been given by a stern father to a daughter who has forgotten her stepmother's birthday. 'Yes, it is, so you'd better get your gold-digging self into the Breakfast Room before her ladyship disturbs herself coming to look for you!'

My mouth fell open. *Gold digger?* Was Mrs Compton really calling me a gold digger?

She further compounded her statement by muttering 'hussy', and shoulder charging me towards the door to the little Breakfast Room which lay between the Morning Room and the Study, and which served only to play host to orphaned furniture and unwanted paintings as far as I could remember.

'She's here,' Mrs Compton announced me in her own, unique style. 'At last.'

I shuffled over the threshold to see that the table was laid immaculately. There were covered tureens on a sideboard, silverware on a cloth so white it made my eyes ache, some wonderful china which looked old, and a smell of sausages and bacon that made me start to dribble.

Hugo half rose in his seat. 'Ah. Andi, good morning,' he said pleasantly.

'Eventually.' Lady Tanith was drinking coffee. 'We eat *together* on the twenty-first of every month, Andromeda.'

'Oh.' I refused to be abashed. I'd learned this much in my few weeks here; Lady Tanith would be scathing whether I was apologetic or unabashed, and it was less painful to me if I just shrugged and let her sarcasm bounce off. 'Nobody told me. Why?'

I heard Hugo give a little gasp, and when I looked towards him he was making little 'cut throat' mimes.

Lady Tanith stood up. For a moment I thought she might pour her coffee over my head. 'Because,' she enunciated, as though I were a very stupid child, 'the twenty-first is the date on which darling Oswald died.'

I'd stopped being afraid of her, that was it. She needed me to find Oswald's diaries; I couldn't see anyone else being desperate enough for a job to stick around this haunted, wobbly place for more than a couple of days listening to her being rude, even if they did intend to marry her son. Besides, I did feel a bit sorry for her and her devotion to the deceased Oswald. She had clearly loved him very much and every time I thought of her solitary loyalty to the memory of a man who'd been dead half a century, I had a tiny heart-twang of pity.

I raised my eyebrows at Hugo. He pulled his mouth down sideways, stopped the mime and looked firmly down at his plate, where half a rasher of bacon and some egg stains showed that I had missed the start of breakfast by some margin.

'I'm very sorry, Lady Tanith. I didn't know,' I said, but without the obsequiousness that I'd had when I first started here. 'It would have been helpful if someone had informed me last night,' I continued, still speaking like someone in a 1920's drama.

Both she and Hugo had sat in the library yesterday evening. Hugo had been reading the paper, and Lady Tanith had kept her hawk-like stare trained on me the entire time. I think she wanted to make sure that, had I actually suddenly found Oswald's diaries, I wasn't going to announce the fact in front of her son. Either one of them could have mentioned this 'eating together' tradition, and I hoped I'd managed to inject the tiniest amount of sarcasm into my words to get this point over.

'Well.' Lady Tanith subsided in the face of incontrovertible fact. 'We'll say no more about it, but please bear it in mind for next month, Andromeda. If you are still with us, of course.'

I knew I was meant to take this as a rebuke, as a threat that she could fire me at any time. As I'd not only come to the conclusion that she *wouldn't*, I'd also decided that I'd be only too delighted to be sacked, and I'd regard living in the draughty and rusty old bus again as an improvement, because at least it wasn't haunted, I just smiled and sat down.

Hugo visibly relaxed and ate the rest of his bacon.

Nobody made any attempt to tell me where the food was or what I was meant to do, so I got up again and went to investigate the tureens. Lady Tanith began a conversation with Hugo which seemed so pointedly obscure that I knew I was meant to feel left out, but I was so enthused by the sight of more bacon, and eggs done three ways, plus a pile of toast that had been covered by a napkin to keep warm, a dish of butter and some crumpets, that I didn't even bother to try listening in. It was something to do with the estate, I got that much.

The food was delicious. I'd endured two weeks of Mrs Compton's random dinners, whatever cereal Hugo didn't want and a vacuum flask of tea, so I dug in. Once I'd heaped my plate with bacon, sausage and toast and poured myself a cup of coffee, I sat down again, to find that Lady Tanith had stopped talking and was staring at me.

'Are you going to eat all that?'

'Yep,' I said, with my mouth already full.

Hugo grinned at me. His hair looked as though it needed cutting; it was beginning to flop, but the unstructured look suited him and his incredible bone structure. I grinned back, around a sausage, and renewed my intention to marry him and put ground glass in Lady Tanith's food.

'A *lady*,' Lady Tanith continued, 'should watch her weight. Elegance in all things, Andromeda.'

'Uh-huh.' Butter dripped down my chin. I wiped it on my hair towel.

'I trust you will be joining us for the service of thanksgiving in the chapel this afternoon?' she tried again, and this time I looked at her.

Lady Tanith was sipping her coffee delicately. She looked a little tired and I had that little twist of empathy for her again. Poor woman, still mourning her lost love after all this time and living in his house with all his things around her to try to feel close to him. Grief, I knew, could do strange things to people and it had obviously stuck Tanith in time, pinned to Templewood as it had been when Oswald had been alive. It really was dreadfully sad.

I knew there was no point in saying any of this to her. Lady Tanith was far too upper class to admit to any emotions, and I didn't want to antagonise her, not when she might be my future mother-in-law. It was bad enough having Mrs Compton calling me names, I didn't have that many people who cared whether I lived or died that I could rile one of the few who actually needed me. So I nodded.

'Good.' Lady Tanith stood up now. 'I'm visiting Jasper this morning, Hugo. Any message?'

Hugo shook his head and Lady Tanith left the room, closing the door firmly behind her. I put more sausages on my plate and listened for sounds of her opening a door somewhere in the house to rising screams. They didn't come and I had to assume that Jasper wasn't chained up anywhere within earshot. Why didn't he come to the family breakfast, if the twenty-first was so important?

'Do you do this *every* twenty-first?' I asked.

'It keeps her happy,' he replied.

I wanted to say 'that's *happy*?' but didn't. She was his mother, over the top insane though she may be. 'Your brother doesn't come and join you?'

'No.' This was definitely tight-lipped and I saw Hugo narrow his eyes at the bacon still remaining on his place. Questions about the invisible Jasper obviously made Hugo uncomfortable.

'Where's the chapel?' I asked, to change the subject.

'Over there.' He pointed with a corner of toast towards the window.

'How far away?'

'Oh, it's still on the estate. We just don't use it very often, because it's inconvenient and none of us has had even the slightest interest in religion since we left pre-prep.'

'But you go along with Oswald's remembrance services.'

'It doesn't cost anything and it keeps Mother happy,' Hugo repeated, putting his cup into the saucer. 'Anyway. How are you, Andi? Did you sleep well?'

I remembered the disturbed night. The ghostly vision on the landing. 'Actually, no,' I said. 'I got up to use the bathroom and saw – well, I'm not sure what I saw. A ghost?'

Hugo didn't seem surprised. 'What did it look like?'

I tried to remember. Actual horror was what I could mostly recall. 'Tall, blonde. Wearing a dress of some kind. I didn't really look, to be honest, I was too scared.'

He nodded slowly and took a sip from his cup. 'Her name was Marie. Oswald apparently used to host huge parties for the literati up from London. Everyone got really drunk and there was scandalous behaviour.'

I wondered if Oswald had held these parties simply to cover up his affair with Lady Tanith – what's a little more 'scandalous behaviour' when everyone is up to it?

'Marie was the "friend" of someone at one of the parties. Apparently she wandered off upstairs, went out onto the balcony very drunk, and it came away from the wall. She fell onto the path and died of a broken neck.'

So the ghost was real. I had no idea how to process that thought. I had seen a real, genuine ghost. Ghosts walked Templewood. Any fear I'd felt on that dark landing had gone now, replaced by a tremulous sympathy, and the prosaic way in which Hugo spoke about her death made me even less fearful. Whatever ghosts were, it was just a 'thing'. Another weirdness in Templewood, where the oddnesses were stacked up so far that they almost reached the ceiling.

No wonder the slim, elegant Marie still walked the landing. I tried to imagine what she must have felt as she fell, and hoped she'd been too drunk to know what was happening. 'That all sounds straight out of a standard ghost story,' I said.

Hugo gave me a look I found impossible to interpret. I wondered if my levity had upset him; after all, this was his family home. Then he drank more tea and stood up. 'Ah well,' he said. 'Like I said before, probably best if you don't go out of your room after dark, if you're worried about meeting ghosts. This place is riddled. Right. I have to go and do some work. I'm guessing you'll be in the library? I'll come and fetch you when it's time to head over to the chapel. Oh, don't worry, the service is very informal, a couple of hymns and a quick homily and we're back in time for high tea. Mrs Compton always puts on a good spread on the twenty-first.'

'*Every* twenty-first?' I buttered another crumpet. If it was going to be a whole month before we got food like this again, then I was going to stock up while I could. 'You have a memorial service every month?'

Hugo came back into the room and closed the door again. 'My mother,' he began, and gazed at the ceiling for inspiration. 'My mother was *devoted* to Oswald.'

I remembered Lady Tanith's shining face when she spoke about him, and the twinge of sympathy I felt for her plight. 'But wasn't he her father-in-law or something?'

'Yes. And forty years older than her, which was why she and my father had quite an age-gap relationship. But she admired Oswald's writing and he – well, he drew inspiration from her, according to Mother.'

I'm not sure that's all he got from her, I was too full of crumpet to say. The thought of Lady Tanith loosening her stays sufficiently to have wild, abandoned sex, and the grim Oswald letting go enough to be any good at it, really upset my world view.

'She was so devastated when he died, Mrs Compton told me in strictest confidence that they thought they might have to have her put away.'

'Well, it's never too late,' I said cheerily.

'I'm sorry?'

She could be your mother-in-law... 'I meant, it's never too late to celebrate someone's life,' I said quickly. 'So I suppose having memorial services for fifty years after someone has died is…' I tailed off. There wasn't a single spin I could put on it that didn't make Lady Tanith sound unhinged.

'It's all we've ever known,' Hugo said simply. 'The twenty-first is Oswald Day. Not so bad for me, but tough on Jasper. His birthday is the twenty-first of November; I don't think he ever had a birthday celebrated on the actual day as it's been taken up by family meals and then the service in the chapel.'

I felt a momentary sympathy for the as-yet-unseen Jasper. 'What does your brother do now? If he's renounced the estate?'

'He's a designer,' Hugo said vaguely. 'Anyway. Better pop.'

I waved him off and filled my pockets with toast-and-bacon sandwiches to take to the library. I had really begun to wonder about the absent Jasper. Surely the son of the house, even one who had renounced his birthright, might be expected to be around sometimes? If the twenty-first was important to Tanith, why did her eldest son not pop over, for old times' sake?

The memory of those footsteps in the attic plucked gently at the back of my brain and I shivered. No. It was birds, that was all. Birds. Definitely.

With the reassurance of a proper lunch warm and bacon-scented in my hand, I headed back to work.

7

SATIS HOUSE – GREAT EXPECTATIONS, CHARLES DICKENS

It was another day of dust and data. I'd cleared one complete shelving unit now and several floor piles and felt quietly proud of myself for the empty space, the organised stacking and the text-filled computer screen.

'No sign of your diaries yet though, Ozzie, my man,' I said to the portrait. I had to talk to him as there was nobody else present, apart from Old Fishbreath, who had taken up residence under the desk and enlivened moments by occasionally seeping forth to stare at me. 'Where on earth did you put them? And why hide them?'

Oswald continued with his fixed grimness. I did have to admit that there were traces of handsomeness there, in his cheekbones and the firm set of his chin. I bet he'd turned a few heads when he was younger, alive and not made of paint and canvas. Like his grandson, his eyes were dark brown under stern eyebrows, and there was a sensuousness to the twist of his mouth that made me wonder just what he and Lady Tanith had got up to. I just hoped they hadn't got up to it on this table.

I was bored with inputting books, so I got up for a stroll around the walls again. These were panelled in a dark wood which increased the air of foreboding, as though any panel may conceal a passage leading to a dead body. Where they weren't wainscot they were either tattered silk paper, cupboard or shelf. I'd opened every cupboard and moved all the random piles of books, just in case a stack of diaries was behind something else but hadn't found so much as an old calendar. The room smelled like a second-hand bookshop which had had a flood in the last ten years and looked as though a mobile library had crashed into Thornfield Hall and nobody had bothered to pull the survivors from the wreckage.

Why did I keep thinking about death and corpses? I had another momentary vision of that figure on the landing this morning amid the memory of the sounds from the attic and some of the other stories Hugo had told me about the house. Death and corpses. Maybe even Oswald was still hanging around, drawn in by longing and loss to tap at windows in the middle of the night?

'Maybe they aren't even in here,' I carried on monologuing to Oswald's portrait to distract myself from my imaginings. After all, if he *were* to be still here in some form, being friendly towards him could only help. 'Maybe you gave them to a friend to keep. Or you destroyed them. Were they full of lots of Forbidden Love stuff, I wonder? Or were you more of a "today it was hot and we had sponge pudding for dinner" man? No, you were a professional, I bet your diaries were full of long, luscious descriptions of the way your beloved's hair moved in the breeze from the window and the way she looked lying naked on your…'

I stopped. The cat had poked its head out from under the table and was watching me again. It had a disconcerting way of behaving as though it understood everything I said.

'What?' I asked it irritably.

The cat gave me two solemn blinks of those blue eyes and withdrew back beneath the table again.

I wondered where Hugo was and why he hadn't accompanied his mother on her visit to his brother. There definitely seemed to be some animosity there, I thought, opening another spreadsheet page on the computer. Hugo clearly felt forced to take on the estate because Jasper had renounced his right to inherit – I wondered what Jasper was like and how he had managed to get his own way with Lady Tanith, who looked as though she'd rather bulldoze the place to the ground than let it go out of the Dawe family. Then I thought about what Hugo had said about selling it when she died, and travelling around the world, and whether Lady Tanith had the faintest idea of what he had planned. If she had, I wouldn't put it past her to just not die, but keep going, getting more and more withered, until Hugo gave up and died first. She already had the lean and dehydrated look of a kiln dried log, a very 'preserved' look, not enough body fat and a touch too much make-up. She could probably keep that up for another fifty years if she had to. Plus I was still taking private bets that she drank human blood, and that somewhere in a back room there were the desiccated corpses of lesser estate workers.

Hugo and I at least had something in common, something we could bond over – our generalised resentment of our siblings. I stopped, my hands resting on the computer keys, seeing my face reflected in the screen. I looked a lot like Jude, I knew, despite being two and a half years older. A round face, which gave us a touch of the 'naughty choirboy' look, fair hair, although mine was wavy whilst hers was straight. We both tended to a little too much bust and not quite enough hip to balance it out, so we were less hourglass and more balloon that's been squeezed at one end. She was four inches taller, so on her, it looked good. On me... on me, it made me not heroine material. Not thin enough, not enough of the ingenue and the waif. I didn't look like someone who needed taking care of, I looked like someone who is at home with the business end of a screwdriver and who knows her way around the internal combustion engine without having to watch a YouTube tutorial. Which, I supposed, was true enough, as Dad had often had me help when the bus wouldn't start, or when it started making graunching noises halfway up a hill in Dorset.

Jude, of course, hadn't been there *to* help. She'd been away at school, learning maths and geography and how to behave around other people; being taught things without having to find them out for herself in whichever library we were currently parked near.

I was tapping at the keyboard, restlessly. Tap tap, random letters expressing my jealousy, my unhappiness that my sister had been assertive enough to get our parents to send her to school. That *I* had been left behind, teaching myself life from Jane Austen, Charles Dickens and the Brontës. A string of meaningless consonants showing how unfair I thought it that here I was, inputting data for an obsessive woman, with a ghost on the landing and the son of the house resolutely refusing to become besotted with me, whilst Jude lived a life filled with the normality and domestication that I craved.

Maybe Hugo felt that way about Jasper? That he got to live a normal life, while Hugo festered away here, trying to keep their mother happy? The thought was cheering. So far, Hugo had been pleasant but distant. He was an attractive slender shadow around the house, chatty in an impersonal way and always managing to look busy without actually being seen to do anything in a terribly well-bred way. I wondered what he thought, what he felt, about his life and if he wanted to talk about the resentment he felt towards his sibling.

Maybe I could ask him. After all, I was here to become attached to the heir to an estate. My life so far had been sufficiently unusual for me to know that this wouldn't be a smooth transition, and sufficiently blighted by having a very attractive sister to know that men didn't instantly desire me. I sighed and looked at all the little cells that I'd filled in with my restless tapping. Half a page of 'zzzzzz' and 'bdbdbdbdb'. At least it made it look as though I'd done something though.

The library door opened and made me jump. Beneath the table the cat made a little 'brrp' noise of startled alarm too and shuffled around my ankles in a disconcerting sweep of blubbery fur.

'Andi! It's time to leave for the service!' Hugo came in, looking around in the dimness for me, which was encouraging. He was wearing a very smart suit, immaculately tailored, and very shiny shoes, which was also encouraging. Maybe he'd dressed up to show himself off to me? It was working. His sharp bone structure looked wonderful above the clean lines of shirt and tie, and his blond hair was neatly brushed. 'Oh.'

'What's the matter?'

'Oh, nothing. You look as lovely as ever.' He smiled at me. 'It's just that Mother pulls out all the bells and whistles for the service and you may feel a little bit – out of place? Have you got a nice dress you could pop on?'

Half of me gritted my teeth in annoyance. Lady Tanith was not the boss of me! Except she was, although not really the kind of boss who had any say in what her employees ought to wear. And it might be nice to have a chance to wear a dress and show Hugo that I actually had rather good legs (although I said so myself because I had to, nobody else noticed), and maybe get to talk to him properly.

The other half of me was clenched with worry. *Did* I have a dress? There wasn't a lot of call for dressing up when you lived in a bus. All I'd got was the linen one that I'd bought specially for the interview that had brought me here, but that was all in the way of 'smart clothes'. If I wore that then Lady Tanith would know that was all I had and no doubt look at me scornfully, because, didn't I know that all employees would be required to dress like *Vogue* cover models once every month? I sighed. Lady Tanith looked at me scornfully all the time, anyway.

'I'll go and change,' I said, and then, 'I'll be quick,' to his worried frown.

'Two minutes then.' Hugo settled himself on the big velvet seat behind the table, where his mother usually sat. 'Spit spot!'

I dashed out of the room, up the stairs two at a time – which nearly killed me; the staircase had the broad oak treads which made going up at speed feel like a workout – and into my room, where I found the linen dress discarded on the floor with a telltale ring of cat hair on it.

A quick look around told me there was nothing more suitable. Jeans, leggings and T-shirts made up almost the entirety of my wardrobe. Practicality had always been more important than being well turned out and you couldn't clear a blocked fuel pipe in chiffon so I had never had the need for 'nice dresses'. The floral printed linen was all I had so I pulled the dress on, buckled on the sandals which had looked so cutely winsome in the shop but which had rubbed my ankles even though I'd hardly had to walk in them, and flew back down again, clip-clopping on the tiles in the hall like a small pony.

At least my hair was clean and brushed, I thought, silently thanking the fountain incident of the morning as I tried to stretch the wrinkles and pleats out of the dress and knock off the cat fur. 'Ready, Hugo!' I trilled, as though we were already married and off for a night out. Although where anyone would go for a night out from Templewood was anyone's guess – the village was a good eight miles away and didn't seem over endowed with five-star restaurants and nightclubs. Perhaps the Hellfire Club had a mobile branch?

'So you are.' Hugo came out to meet me, accompanied by The Master, who sneered. 'You look…' He trailed off. The words had had a 'prepared' feel; perhaps he'd been working on what to say when he saw me while he sat in the darkness of the library? The fact he felt he needed to say anything at all made me feel slightly warm. 'Er. It's linen, yes? I'm sure the wrinkles will come out on the walk. Did you buy it online? There really is some wonderful stuff about that hardly looks chain-store at all,' he finished.

I looked down at myself. The dress being left on the floor had not done the fabric any favours. The pink roses of the pattern were pleated and creased into patches and swirls of colour as though a sudden frost had passed, and the pale stretches bore distinct paw prints. It looked like a dress that had been worn to commit a bloody murder and then inadequately cleaned.

'It's all I've got,' I said. 'And we'll be sitting down, won't we?'

Hugo looked cheerful again. 'Perfectly true,' he said jauntily. 'Now, let's get a trot on.'

He led me out of the front door of the house, and around to a narrow path that wound through the grounds. If we hadn't been hurrying, I hadn't been desperately trying to iron my dress smooth by pulling bits of it taut, and my sandals hadn't instantly started to rub, it would have been pleasant. Hugo had taken my arm in a gentlemanly fashion and was pointing out sites of interest as we went.

'That's the old icehouse there, under that mound. Over there is the biggest specimen of Douglas Fir outside the Highlands; that's a ceanothus, we're quite proud of that one, very regular flowerer. That looks like a flowerbed there, but in the middle of the planting is where the controls for the fountain are. My maternal great grandfather liked to keep the workings out of sight – being able to see switches and so forth was a little too plebeian for him.'

I wondered if it was too soon to stumble and pretend to sprain my ankle. Suspecting that Hugo would not have carried me back to the house and tended to me, but would have sat me carefully on the side of the path for collection on his way back from the memorial service, I made sure I looked carefully at where I was putting my feet.

'And through this gate is the chapel, and the estate village.' Hugo opened a small metal gate in a huge yew hedge, which, he had informed me, dated back over three hundred years. The bushes had half-collapsed onto one another, so the entire hedge line sagged and dipped like elderly buttocks. We passed through the gate and on the other side lay a graveyard, a tiny church and, beyond, a tumble of old thatched cottages. The village was incredibly pretty, if slightly overshadowed by the encircling hedge, and made me think of Hobbits. 'We came the private way, from the house. Oh good, we're not late.' Hugo stood back to allow me through first.

Lady Tanith, wearing a black hat and veil so large that she looked like a helicopter landing pad in mourning, was leading the way into the church. Behind her followed a straggle of people; Mrs Compton was among them so I supposed they were estate workers. Hugo and I tagged along at the back, but, once inside the church, he led us down the aisle to sit next to Lady Tanith in the front pew.

The chapel smelled like the library, I thought, as the service, conducted by a man so wizened that he looked as though he was being eaten by his vestments, got underway. A bit damp, a bit bookish. Furniture polish. Flowers, from the huge floral arrangements that stood either side of the chancel. Insufficient light filtered through the hedge which loomed in at the window, watching proceedings from its encirclement of the churchyard. My parents had no notable interest in religion, so churches hadn't been a regular feature of my childhood, although I'd taken to visiting historic-looking ones when I was old enough, envisaging Jane Eyre, and then myself, standing small and plain at the altar. I wondered whether Lady Tanith had married Richard in this church, and tried to imagine a Dawe family wedding, but could only come up with Count Dracula marrying the mistletoe bride amid a corpse-filled congregation. Probably a little unfair, but it was impossible to imagine Lady Tanith as a blushing young bride.

Lady Tanith kept her eyes focused on the vicar during the entire service. She didn't acknowledge Hugo or me, or any of the twenty or so people who sat scattered through the pews behind us, all obviously wearing their best clothes in the dark dampness, like beads from a dropped necklace. She dabbed at her eyes occasionally through the veil, particularly when the vicar mentioned Oswald's name, and sang her way in a faint fashion, through a hymn I didn't know the words to. There were no hymnbooks or orders of service to help me, I just had to make a sort of throaty burbling attempt to follow the tune.

Side glances at anyone else I could catch sight of made me think that this was such a regular occurrence for them that they were making their way through the service by rote. Mrs Compton sat, stood and prayed in a determined and rigid way in the pew opposite, and just behind her I could see the figure of the gardener, going through the motions. I wondered who all the others were. I'd seen occasional distant figures about the place; the mystery joiner and bullock-shouting-man. I knew there was a man who sorted the plumbing too because I'd seen him unblocking a drain once, and Hugo had spoken about carpenters and farmers who worked on the estate, but I'd never met any of them. Here they, and their wives and husbands, evidently felt it necessary to put in an appearance. Perhaps it was a condition of working at Templewood. The gardener was certainly giving every sign of being here under duress, barely kneeling during prayers and apparently not even attempting to sing.

I gritted my teeth and ironed the dress between my fingers again. It had been *his* fault that I'd got sprayed with filthy green water this morning. He could have told me he was turning on the fountain, rather than just shouting.

I half turned my head to give him a haughty look and caught him looking at me with a smile that I didn't really like. When our eyes met, he winked, which only served to remind me again that he'd seen me soaked to the skin in my pyjamas, with pondweed hanging from my head. I hadn't been at all sure that he hadn't been laughing as I'd fled my way back into the house, trying to cover up the transparent nature of my cotton night things with my hands.

I did not smile back. Instead I huddled a little closer to Hugo and knelt ostentatiously for the final prayer, on a kneeler that gave off an 'oof' when I made contact with it. After that we clattered our way back down the aisle behind Lady Tanith, into the welcome fresh air and green, filtered sunlight, which called to mind the pond water again.

The little crowd of estate workers dispersed instantly, leaving the three of us in the graveyard. Even the vicar dissipated – the touch of daylight probably turned him to dust – and Hugo pointed to an enormous granite obelisk which protruded from the centre of the churchyard in such a way that the two surrounding tombs with their semi-circular headstones gave it the look of a giant penis, accompanied by a pair of sandstone bollocks.

'That's Oswald's memorial,' Hugo half whispered.

A posy of flowers lay at its base, in a pubic frill. Laid, I supposed, by Lady

Tanith before we'd arrived. There was something touching about the smallness of the bunch, almost as though Lady Tanith hadn't wanted the flowers to be noticed by anyone other than Oswald, a little nod to the ages that had passed since his death.

'I thought he died in Switzerland or somewhere?' I whispered back.

'He did. He's not buried here. Mother had the stone put up to... ah. Lovely service as ever, Mother!' Hugo's tone changed as Lady Tanith stalked up to us.

'Hm. The vicar's cutting it. We were two verses short, and that sermon sounded rushed to me. Did it sound rushed to you?' Lady Tanith adjusted her hat. Behind the veil her features were smudged into beady inquisition.

'It sounded perfectly fine. Oswald will have loved it,' Hugo said placatingly. He took his mother's arm now, and I was left standing in the churchyard on my own, with my abrasive sandals and crumpled dress, as they made their way together through the iron gate and back towards the house.

I felt the old, familiar sensation of being unwanted descend over me. It was so familiar as to be almost welcome, a known quantity among the strangeness of my surroundings. My parents had always been busy, doing, planning, filming. When I was a baby, before the YouTube years, they'd written articles for resolutely left-wing magazines on the 'freedom of the road', carefully not mentioning that said freedom had been sponsored by a previous capitalist career and inherited wealth. My sister had been away or had a trail of admirers or friends from school who'd come to stay and exclaimed excitedly about the novelty of living in a bus and travelling. And there I had been, in the corner with *Madame Bovary*, *Great Expectations* or, during one particularly bleak period, *Anna Karenina*.

Here I was again, on my own, overlooked in favour of someone who shouted their wants more loudly. I nodded to myself in acceptance. Yep. Of course. And naturally Hugo should help his mother, she was upset...

'Upset over a death that had happened fifty years ago.' My gritted teeth juddered over the words as I heard the gate clang shut. Hugo hadn't checked to see if I was following.

'You dried out, then.' A voice beside me made me jump and I twisted around, sustaining a minor ankle injury from a sandal strap, to see the gardener leaning nonchalantly on a nearby headstone. In common with the other men attending the service, he was wearing a suit, although his jacket was unbuttoned, his tie was under one ear and he was wearing wellington boots on his feet, with the trouser legs pulled down over them so that only rubber-coated toes gave him away.

'Obviously.' I pulled at my skirt again.

'I did try to warn you.' His hair was messy too, long and untidy, and looked like it needed a good brush.

'Well, just a word of advice, shouting "hey" is not really a sufficient warning. Next time, try "I'm going to turn the fountain on." It might be of more use to your victims.' I snapped the words, turned so sharply that the straps of my sandals did my ankles another injury, and stalked off towards the gate in the hedge. 'And saying "good morning" when someone greets you might be a nice touch too!' I called back over my shoulder but didn't give him the satisfaction of actually checking on his reaction. I was trying to concentrate on stalking, which was harder than I'd thought over the loose gravel of the path and in sandals that were slowly cutting off the circulation to both feet.

The gardener did not reply. When I had my first chance to look back – stopping to open the gate and peering back under my arm – he'd gone.

I sat down on the grass edging to the path and took the sandals off. Restraining myself from the urge to hurl them one at a time towards the place where his head had been, I set off back towards the house.

8

BLANDINGS CASTLE – JEEVES AND WOOSTER, P G WODEHOUSE

As soon as I got back, I changed out of the dress, back into my usual workwear of jeans and a T-shirt, and had my hand on the door to the library, when Lady Tanith opened it from the inside and stood framed by blackness in the doorway, like a movie vampire.

'Andromeda,' she said. 'Can you explain... *this*?'

She was still wearing her memorial clothes, a smart dark navy dress with jacket, although she'd taken the hat off. I instantly felt like a downstairs maid who'd been caught not polishing the brass.

'What?' I asked faintly.

Lady Tanith led the way over to the computer. Having been interrupted by Hugo and having had to change, I'd left it switched on and displaying the book catalogue spreadsheet. My randomly filled cells, with their collection of meaningless letters, occupied the screen.

'This.' Lady Tanith pointed at the computer, as though I'd left a small turd on the keyboard. 'This... nonsense.'

I opened my mouth and closed it again. I didn't think that 'I was revenge-typing' would cut it with Lady Tanith, who seemed to have *retribution* close-printed on her soul.

'I hope you haven't been occupying your time by typing this complete rubbish every day,' Lady Tanith went on, still with her arm held out to indicate the screen. 'I feel I have been lax, allowing you to continue in your own time. In future, I shall be supervising your work more closely.'

I thought about Lady Tanith sitting opposite me while I worked every day, her eyes fixed on my every movement unless she was staring mistily up at Oswald's portrait glaring down on us, and opened my mouth again. Still no excuses were springing to mind.

Suddenly there was a movement. From underneath the table The Master stalked, his eyes fixed on me in a way that was not totally unlike the baleful stare his mistress was giving me. Elegant, despite his bulk, he jumped onto the chair I had been sitting at to work, up onto the table, and then, in an attempt to attract Lady Tanith's attention, he walked onto the keyboard and strode up and down it, making little chirruping noises.

The keys clattered. More cells filled with random letters.

The cat sat solidly on the space bar and enormous gaps began to appear on the screen as he let out an almost human-sounding yowl, blinked twice at Lady Tanith, and then got up again to butt his head against her still-pointing hand.

I said nothing.

Lady Tanith looked down at the cat, looked at the screen, lowered her arm with a quick stroke over the chocolate-coloured ears and turned on her heel. As she reached the library door, she muttered over her shoulder at me, 'Don't leave the machine switched on if you aren't in the room. He could injure himself.'

I kept my eyes on the cat.

The door closed firmly and I let out a huge breath. 'Thanks, puss,' I said, and gave the top of his head a sweep of my palm. 'Although I'm not sure how you're meant to injure yourself on flat plastic keys. Maybe she thinks you can Qwert yourself to death.'

Blue eyes blinked at me, and The Master stood up, pushing the full weight of his head into my hand as he stropped up and down a few times against me. The keyboard made a high-pitched note of complaint and I gave the furry bottom a gentle push to clear him from the machine. 'I owe you.'

With a hefty plop that dipped the floorboards, the cat jumped down off the table, mewed at me in a puff of anchovies, then stalked in a fashion very similar to Lady Tanith, to the door, where I got a ferocious stare until I opened the door to let him out. As soon as the dark tail had swept clear, I closed the door and leaned back against the nearest shelf, hands on my knees and laughing to myself. Great. Now I was indebted to Old Fishbreath, not that he was in a position to hold it over me, of course, but I did feel a little more warmly towards him. He'd certainly saved me from a future of being watched over by Lady Tanith during every working moment, like being observed by a deity with a short temper and a ready hand with the thunderbolts.

I straightened up again and looked towards the window. The curtain that Hugo had pulled down on my first day still lay on the floor, its mate hanging anxiously from tattering fitments alongside, as though attending the difficult birth of more dust. What this room needed, I thought, was a lot more light. How was I supposed to look for anything when the gloom was so thick you had to force your way through it, like wading through chest-deep gravy? I gave the remaining curtain a tug, and it dropped wearily in a sigh of cobwebs and rending velvet over my head, at which point the library door opened again and Hugo appeared. I could see his outline through the worn material, hovering uncertainly in the doorway, then coming in cautiously.

Not knowing what to do, bearing in mind that I'd just broken something that belonged, technically, to him, I stood still for a moment. Saw, filtered through velvet, Hugo suddenly notice this person-sized lump of fabric, and with vague ideas of asking him to help me get it off my head I took a few steps forward, hands held out to keep me from tripping over the pool of material at my feet. Hugo screamed, fell backwards until he was half-crumpled against the door and put his hands over his face.

'It's all right.' I fought my way clear of the curtain. 'It's only me.'

Hugo was blanched white with a greenish tinge, still cowering. 'Andi?' he asked faintly.

'Yes. Just pulling down this last curtain so I can actually see. Sorry, did I frighten you?'

He stood up, lowering his hands to put them over his heart. 'You... you startled me,' he said, sounding like a small child who'd had a nightmare. 'I came... Mother said...' He went even paler. 'I'm sorry, I think I'm going to be sick,' he said, wrenching the door open behind him and fleeing through the gap. I heard his footsteps out across the hall and then decreasing in volume as he dashed down the corridor towards the kitchens.

'Well, that was odd,' I said to Oswald now as he was the only thing left to talk to, again. 'Hugo's always seemed very blasé about the ghosts here. He makes Marie on the landing sound like the most normal thing in the world, but he got scared of what was obviously a person with a curtain over their head?'

Oswald continued his censorious stare, only slightly better illuminated now that the light could come further into the library. He seemed a little disappointed in his grandson, but then I realised that it was *my* disappointment I was seeing reflected in that painted face. Dashing off to vomit from fear had hardly been Hugo's finest hour and, whilst I was not looking for heroics or any of that ghastly alpha-male behaviour that so many romantic heroes seemed to indulge in, I'd hoped for a little more than screaming and running off in my intended. I hadn't even looked particularly ghostly. Plus, he knew I was in here, he knew what the curtains looked like. I was hardly a phantom shade in a winding sheet stalking the floor of the library. And, besides, he *knew* the house was haunted! What was one more ghost among the hordes that seemed to throng Templewood, like an M R James basket of discarded ideas?

Outside, where the afternoon sun was now far more visible as it was no longer screened by several metres of velvet, I could see my nemesis, the gardener, driving a ride-on lawn mower with what looked like gleeful abandon, along one of the grassy sweeps that led down towards the road. He might be an arse, he might be rude and dismissive, and he might have seen me in transparent nightwear, but he was the only other human within conversational distance. Maybe I could go out there and be contemptuous at him? It would beat wondering about Hugo's overreaction and why his mother had sent him in here, although the memory of the expression on her face when she thought her cat had been the one to fill in the spreadsheet was giving me warm feelings. Perhaps she'd sent him to apologise?

I tried to imagine Lady Tanith apologising to anyone, and just couldn't do it. She'd probably sent Hugo to keep an eye on me, to make sure I was dedicating myself to her library rather than disporting myself wantonly, although chance would be a fine thing around here, where there was only

Hugo to disport myself wantonly *at*. I drew the line at any of the other contenders, a portrait, a cat and a housekeeper of such intense malevolence that Mrs Danvers would have conceded precedence.

No. I needed a real person. Even if they were on the horizon and carving random shapes in the grass with a mower, exposure to anyone who wasn't part of this insane household would make me feel better. I could just watch him garden for a bit, at least until I forgot about Hugo's screaming attack and his mother's accusations. Fresh air was what I needed. Fresh air, smell some flowers, get some exercise and clear the extra dust from my lungs. Normality.

I opened the library window and climbed out.

I'd learned the art of climbing out of the windows. Although I now more usually used the kitchen door in a conventional fashion, it sometimes felt too long a way from the front of the house when I needed a quick breath of fresh air or to stretch my legs. As far as I could tell, the front door was hardly ever used and I couldn't work out how to actually open it, so I had no option but to go out of the library window. The secret of the window exit was to try to land on both feet, and to crouch as you hit the ground, so I did this and managed not to fall forwards onto the grass.

When I straightened up, everything smelled of cucumber from the freshly mown lawn. A slight undertone of earth hung in the air with a bitterness from where the shrubs which overhung the path at the far end had been clipped with the mower. Lots of beheaded daisies scattered the green, the fairy equivalent of finding a horse's head in your bed, I thought, poking my bare toes through the detritus of the lawns, listening for the sound of the machine approaching, although it seemed to now be performing mower dressage somewhere off behind the birch grove. I wandered off in that direction.

The gardener was mowing swathes in patterns, swinging the wheel about seemingly randomly so that the cutting pattern swept from left to right and then around, blades rising and dropping in a choreographic fashion. Not wanting to be seen, or for him to think I was watching, I climbed to the top of the rise that was the icehouse, sunken into the garden but forming a small hillock, and looked down.

Unless I was very much mistaken, the gardener was cutting 'FUCK OFF' into the grass, only visible from above, and I found I was smiling. From ground level it was just swirls and loops but from up here the letters were unmistakeable. Well, well, it seemed that our dedicated gardener was not quite the loyal and devoted member of staff he had seemed to be when he'd been dressed up at the memorial service.

The machine puttered into silence and I decided to go down and tell him I'd noticed, just in case he was going to try to go on about my wet pyjamas. If he could hold seeing my nipples over me, then I could hold carving swear words into his employer's lawn over him. I clambered down off the icehouse and went towards where he'd parked the little tractor.

He was standing with his back to me, half in the yew hedge which curved back to form the boundary of the garden out here. The roof of the chapel was visible way off to our left and the hedge ran down to the ha-ha which divided the garden from the field beyond and stopped the cattle from trampling the ceanothus, whatever that was. Hugo had explained it all to me the other day, when I'd been staring out of the library window, pretending to be interested in the estate but really wondering what he'd do if I asked him out for a drink.

I'd gone off the drink idea now. If I wanted to woo Hugo, I was going to have to go hardcore. I might have to try the see-through night things on him.

'I can see what you've done,' I said, approaching the gardener's back view. '"Fuck off"? I do hope that isn't directed at her ladyship.'

He didn't react, just stayed where he was, facing the shrubbery.

'Are you always this rude?' I touched him on the shoulder. He gave a strangled sort of gasp and whipped around, whereupon it became obvious that he'd been having a quiet pee in the bushes, and I had interrupted him.

'What the hell...?' He was trying simultaneously to tuck himself back into his shorts, work out who had tapped him on the shoulder and try to pretend that he hadn't, in fact, been spraying pee up the venerable example of *Taxus* that had been on the family estate for generations.

'I did announce my presence,' I said, not sure whether to be amused, appalled or, my very quick glance had informed me, impressed.

'I'm sorry?'

He was staring hard at me, head slightly to one side, as though he was trying to work something out. He was frowning ferociously, and there were grass clippings in his hair.

'I said, I...'

'Hold on a minute.' He dug around in the pocket of his shorts for a second, pulled out two tiny plastic objects, and hooked them over each ear. 'That's better. Say again, now I've got my hearing aids in.'

Oh. *Oh*. He was *deaf*. No wonder he hadn't heard me. 'I'm sorry,' I said, chastened. 'I didn't know.'

'No reason you should.' Another 'tucking' manoeuvre and he zipped up the shorts. 'Well, I guess that's us quits then. I've seen you looking like you were entering a Miss Wet T-Shirt competition, and you've caught me with my dick in my hand.'

'There's no need to make it sound so seedy,' I muttered, to the ground.

'You'll have to speak up. And look at me if you're talking to me.' Unabashed, he grinned. 'These are hearing aids, not psychic receptors.'

'You're horrible,' I said, more loudly now.

'And proud of it.' I got another grin. 'Things not going well with Our Lady of the Veils and the son and heir?'

'No,' I admitted, although grudgingly. 'I'm supposed to be looking for Oswald's diaries and I'm having no luck, and everyone's bonkers.'

'The cat's all right.'

'No it isn't. It keeps trying to get into bed with me. And it smells.'

A hand was cautiously extended towards me. It was ingrained with grass juice and the fingernails were filthy, and I wasn't sure that I wanted to shake it.

'They call me Jay,' the gardener said. 'Who are you?'

'Andi. And I'm not sure I want to shake a hand you've just been holding your willy in.'

'That was this one.' His other hand waved at me. 'I'm left-handed, it's quite safe.'

Gingerly I took the hand. There were callouses all over his palm, hidden under the dirt, but his grip was warm and firm and I felt a wash of reassurance for a second as we shook. He felt normal and seemed uncomplicated, and it was nice to be talking to someone from outside the Dawe family, with all it implied.

'Why were you mowing "fuck off" into the grass?' I asked.

He leaned against one of the birch trees, one foot up so he looked relaxed and at home. 'Ah. You saw that.'

'From up there.' I pointed to the top of the icehouse mound.

Jay shrugged. 'It's all right, I mow it all out again. It's just a way of letting some frustration out.'

'On innocent grass?'

He sighed and rested his head back against the bark of the tree. His hair was long and swept against the neck of his T-shirt, and when he folded his arms I noticed that he had a tiny tattoo on his wrist.

'Grass isn't innocent,' he said wearily. 'It's evil. Everything round here is evil.'

'Even the ghosts?'

His head rolled along the trunk of the tree so that he could look at me. 'Did you say "ghosts"?'

'Mmmm. Marie of the landing, that sort of thing.'

'Marie of the what, now? Who the hell is that?'

I found myself explaining about the ghostly figure at the balcony, her origin story and that I'd seen her myself, twice. Jay just stood and listened, frowning, then rubbed his hand through his hair. 'Never heard of her,' he said. 'All sounds dodgy as hell to me.'

'Well, unless Hugo is keeping a secret woman in the house…'

'Who'd blame him? Lady Tanith probably won't let him go out with anyone until he's over forty, and she's pre-approved them. If he wanted a girlfriend he'd *have* to keep her hidden.'

I thought about the scuffling noises in the attic above my head. About the soft, sorrowful sounds from the Yellow Room, which I'd managed to convince myself had been rats. 'Do you think so?' Then I thought of Hugo's diffidence and deference to his mother. 'No. He wouldn't dare.'

'So he's not tried to seduce you yet then?' Jay had his hands on his hips. 'A red-blooded male denied female companionship – he'll have a secret lover away in a priest hole somewhere.'

For some reason I felt as though I ought to defend Hugo. 'I don't think he's like that.'

Jay raised his eyebrows.

'What about you then? Where's your "female companionship"?'

'I don't need a woman.' Jay turned away and began to walk back across the grass. 'I just take my pleasure with the ride-on mower if I feel the urge.'

'You really are horrible,' I said, but he'd got his back to me and was already taking out his hearing aids and climbing back up into the seat of the little tractor. He waved a hand at me and started the engine, executing a neat spin around the grove and back to the incriminating letters carved into the lawn, where he dropped the blades and began mowing them out.

9

WUTHERING HEIGHTS – WUTHERING HEIGHTS, EMILY BRONTË

Between having frightened Hugo, Lady Tanith's 'misunderstanding', and my minor falling-out with the gardener, I kept my head down for a few days. I worked diligently enough to keep everyone at bay, and cleared acres of floor space in the library, getting all the books entered on the system as the newly liberated light streamed in through the big window and made my working conditions far more pleasurable. I even tolerated The Master coming to sit under the table, with occasional breaks for rubbing against my ankles while I worked.

But I was tired. Every night now, thanks to Jay, I would lie awake listening out for sounds of Hugo tiptoeing downstairs to let in his 'secret woman', or creeping up to the attics to 'entertain'. The house was given to sporadic noises, wispy sounds from the Yellow Room next door, those footstep-like creaks from overhead, none of which did anything for the state of my nerves. I sometimes sat with my ear against the door, alert just in case a ghostly arm should reach through, to hear nothing more alarming than the raspberry blowing of The Master, puffing air through his fur as he cleaned himself, ineffectually, on my threshold.

The house continued mostly as silent as – well, I tried not to think 'the grave'. I had to admit that Hugo having a secret lover was more likely than Marie haunting the landing, but from what I knew of Hugo it wasn't an enormous probability gap. He had failed, totally, to try to seduce me in proper *droit de seigneur* fashion and instead kept up a light-hearted and chatty relationship, which was at least an improvement on what I got from his mother, who would sit in dark silence in the library at times, like a black hole that's got lost on its way to a universe.

Jay gave me the occasional wave if he saw me, but now I knew that he didn't wear his hearing aids when he was working, I didn't bother to shout a greeting. I'd return his wave, with an inner comment on his dreadful shorts or the brown hairy legs that protruded beneath them, ending in work boots or wellingtons depending on the wetness of that day's task.

I'd spent one day off walking down towards the village and hoping to meet someone, *anyone*, from outside the household to talk to. I had failed on both counts. The tiny collection of thatched-roof cottages was deserted, so I had only gone as far as the church.

Without the pressure of the memorial service and the presence of Lady Tanith, the building had seemed more welcoming. I'd always liked churches. There was something comfortingly enduring about the way they sat in towns and villages, overlooked and quite often overgrown, but sensibly *there*. This one was little more than a squat tower and four grey walls etched with the marks of now-absent windows and the scars of recently removed ivy. From the pathway I could see the silent houses beyond, uniform in their thatch and fencing. There was something of the *Midwich Cuckoos* about them, a slight tinge of the sinister and I'd turned away, poked once or twice around the graveyard which hadn't helped matters at all because it had only reminded me further of the presence of the dead, and gone back to the house.

The weather turned hot, not that we really noticed inside the dampness of Templewood, which sucked all the heat from the air and turned it into a vaguely plaster-scented chill permeating the entire building. The Master went outside and spent his days lounging under the edging shade of the bushes, airing his surprisingly pale stomach and blinking in the unaccustomed daylight. I hated to admit it, but the library was lonelier without him, and as another day trailed miserably to another end, I made myself a sandwich in the kitchen and went to bed early to lie in my pyjamas in the moist heat of my room.

I had almost stopped noticing the noises now, but with the oppressive humidity preventing me from sleeping, everything seemed so much more sinister tonight. The slow, furtive tread overhead, audible as each board creaked beneath an anomalous weight and then settled back into position, was unignorable. The soft and sinister brush-against-the-wall from the Yellow Room, with the hint of assignation and whisper of stifled laughter that I could no longer ascribe to rats, unless they were rodents of inordinate good humour and long fur, made my flesh prickle.

I'd borrowed a Bible from the library and it sat fat and complacent beside the bed, unopened. While I had no religion whatsoever, other than occasionally offering up prayers to any deity which might control recalcitrant bus engines, I had the hope that the ghosts would have been devout believers when alive. The Bible, therefore, was my first line of defence, should anything non-corporeal come floating through my bedroom door. It would also have come in handy should anyone corporeal but unwanted feel like having a go at me – Mrs Compton sprang to mind – and it came in useful as a very small bedside table too. I had had great intentions of taking the Bible and starting a ghost hunt one evening, but ghost hunting was only fun if there was someone else to back up assertions that the noises couldn't possibly be a haunting. Alone in the dark, listening to the relentless tread, the occasional sound from downstairs which might have been rodents knocking furniture or might have been a phantom dinner party and my own breathing, had taken away any desire I'd had for brave and affirmative action.

Now, here I was, wondering yet again what I was doing. My lack of action on the exorcising of ghosts was matched by my failure to locate Oswald's diaries. I flapped around on the mattress, thinking. I'd tapped all the panels, opened all the cupboards and found nothing, all the while having Oswald stare down at me from his painted chair, as though dissatisfied with everything he saw.

Maybe he'd had the diaries bound to look like ordinary books? I half sat against the pillows, facing the panelled walls of my room, not seeing those but instead the shelves and stacks of books in the library. How would I know? Except... except, those books wouldn't have a title page, would they? They might look, on the outside, like ordinary books, but I'd be able to see as soon as I opened them if they were really handwritten memoirs, or whatever Oswald had chosen to note down. As I'd currently logged a few hundred tomes and didn't relish the thought of having to go back and look at them again, I flopped back with relief. No. I couldn't have missed them. Maybe they weren't really in there at all.

I fell asleep, window wide to allow the muggy air to circulate. It also allowed the flash of lightning to wake me a few hours later, followed by a crescendo of thunder that boomed and rolled like celestial dustbin day.

From outside the door I heard The Master cry. It wasn't his usual 'I want to come in/out' yowl, this was more protracted and held what I thought was a hint of distress. Perhaps the cat didn't like storms?

I shrugged my way around in the bed, trying to get comfortable. The mattress felt hot and sticky against me, the sheets damp and yet still too warm and the air was heavy with dark. Another flicker as lightning danced somewhere in the skies beyond, and the tympanic growl of the thunder, followed by another yowl.

Annoyed, I shouldered myself up to sitting. Well, I wasn't going to be able to sleep anyway, unless I shut the window and drew the curtains, and I would rather face the storm than worry about what might be hanging from the Virginia creeper trying to peer in when I couldn't see it, so I got up.

The Master had been sitting pressed up against my door, his fur ruffled with agitation. As soon as I opened the door a crack, he shot through, squeezing his body like a tube of toothpaste in order to fit, fled across the room and launched himself at my bed, where he burrowed under the covers and became nothing but the end of a twitching tail. I was about to go over and scoop him out, but three things stopped me. Firstly, he was obviously disturbed by the storm, and if being under cover made him feel better, then who was I to throw him back into the corridor of despair. Secondly, I owed the cat a favour after his computer-walk the other day. It had saved me from possible daily observation from Lady Tanith, and the thought of having to sit in that stuffy room inputting book details under the weight of her death-stare made me shudder. Thirdly... thirdly, the lightning flash that had accompanied my door opening had shown me a glimpse of what had looked like a female figure, making its way towards the staircase.

The momentary nature of the timing meant that I couldn't be absolutely certain what I'd seen. After all, I was half-expecting to catch a glimpse of Marie anyway, frozen pre-balcony disaster. Perhaps my mind had simply thrown me an image woven out of deep shadow and sudden light. I saw what I was afraid I *might* see.

But, the blonde, elegant figure of the woman that I had thought I'd caught sight of, had been heading *down* the landing. Marie, as Hugo had told me, was haunting the landing and balcony window, the last places on earth that she had seen. I could just about buy into that – especially since these walls seemed to hang on to every mote of dust or fingerprint from the last century, why would they not hold on to memories in the same way? So, if I accepted that Marie was a ghost, that she was held in some kind of loop and doomed to repeat her last, drunken walk up to the balcony – why the hell would she be walking back down the stairs?

Jay's words about Hugo having a secret lover began to echo around in my head as I stood, undecided. In a place the size of Templewood, with his mother occupying a separate wing and mysterious locked rooms, I had to admit it was a possibility that took on a firmer and more certain shape here in the darkness of the silent hallway.

Footsteps in attics. Strange movements in the room next door that nobody went into. And a tiny part of my vanity that had absorbed more than words from all those books I'd grown up with whispered, the mystery of Hugo not falling for me as the main love interest in his life. Here we were, on this huge estate, no parties, no pubs, no – well, anything? Just Hugo and me. I was choosing to believe that life would follow the traditional route of the classics. Boy meets girl and, in the absence of any real competition other than maybe a scheming rich girl whose father wants the land, he was *supposed* to fall for me! And, while Hugo was friendly and chatty, it was a superficial kind of friendliness. There had been no long, late night discussions about hopes and dreams, he hadn't sought to reassure me that my quiet plainness was the perfect antidote to the artificial women he knew already.

He had to marry me, damn it! Otherwise it was a future of a granny annexe over a garage or a quietly rotting makeshift caravan. Love and affection would follow and could take care of themselves. It had worked for all those heroines in the yellow-paged books I'd pored over; arranged marriages had been the norm until relatively recently. A love match would be a bonus, but I would settle for convenience and proximity bringing us together. Love was not for the poor and the undereducated, the basically unquirky girls took what was offered. I just needed Hugo to offer.

I took a deep breath. At least I could clear up this mystery, right now, if I followed Marie down that dark, imposing staircase.

I looked behind me at the inviting comfort of my bed. Clicked once or twice at the wall light, but nothing happened; the electricity was unreliable at best here and the storm had clearly thrown it out again. Under my duvet, The Master was a flattened lump down the middle of the bed, reducing my chances of any kind of sleep to a narrow balance-bar down either side.

Another breath. Right.

I picked up the Bible, although I wasn't quite certain whether I wanted it as spiritual comfort or a weapon, and leaving the door slightly ajar, I tiptoed along the landing. Past the Yellow Room, around the corner and past Hugo's room, where the door was closed and all was silent, with no flicker of romantic candlelight showing in the small gap underneath, no music playing and no sign that he had recently been 'entertaining'. Was Hugo leaving his mysterious lover to find her own way out of the house on what was building up to be a traditionally dark and stormy night? Not very gentlemanly of him, surely. Not good manners. And Hugo's manners had, so far, appeared to be polished to a high gloss.

I'd waited sufficiently long for Marie to have cleared the staircase, which had half been my intention. I didn't want to meet an apparition at all, and most *definitely* not on a rickety-banistered staircase with a five-metre drop to the tiled-floored hallway. So, with my sticky footsteps hushed by the dusty carpet, I tiptoed on down the stairs and into the inky black of the hall.

Another flash of lightning zig-zagged in through the hall windows either side of the tin door, illuminating the entire space in a white flare that burned my retinas. But it had shown me what I feared to see, the back of Marie, a slowly swaying shape in heels along the corridor that led to the kitchen, the darkest part of the house.

My heroines were brave. All those hours in library corners, reading, while Mum and Dad filmed the town; having patient people teach me how the community computer worked so that I could look up some of the more obscure points of literary reference; all these things had shown me that fictional people were brave. They didn't hesitate to follow ghosts, or track smugglers, or creep into rooms at night in time to extinguish fires in the bed hangings. They had been better than me, stronger, fiercer. They had fought for what they wanted, and got it. But they weren't me. Their worlds weren't real, their happiness hung on the turn of a pen, not a moment. Their strength came from authorly imagination, not a life of struggle and endurance, and without it there was no story. This was me. This was real life, and I was terrified.

I heard the rain start, hammering on the roof, a double height above me as the hallway soared up past the landing and onto a small glass dome, inspired, as Hugo had told me, by Castle Howard, and installed by Oswald's predecessor. It proved to be not quite watertight, and small drops splashed down past me to pool on the tiles at my feet. I gritted my teeth, hugged the Bible to my chest and took a few steps in the wake of the phantom Marie.

Deeper into the house now, and I lost the sound of the rain and the thunder. The odd flash of lightning licked its way ahead of me, scouring the walls with vicious brightness, making me afraid of what I might see. Was Marie making her way to the place of her death? Reliving that last alcohol-soaked party? Or was she more corporeal, finding her way out of the house having given Hugo what he wanted? Maybe her car was parked around the back? Or was she going to walk back to the estate village through the storm, in properly picturesque romance-heroine fashion?

I crept along the passageway, knowing where I was, despite the Stygian gloom, from walking this corridor every morning to get to breakfast. Apart from the regular twenty-first of the month Oswald Day, breakfast was always taken, rather grimly, in the main kitchen, toast and cereal with milk of dubious vintage. I trailed my hand down the wall, feeling that final lump in the plaster that indicated where modern electrics had been inadequately covered over on installation, and then I was standing in the kitchen doorway.

Marie was there. She'd put a saucepan of water on the gas hob and was leaning against the wall, smoking a cigarette.

My heart had gone from adrenaline-inspired hefty thumping to full jazz-hands, all-out-cardiac-incident, but when I saw the blue flame under the pan and the glowing end of the cigarette, it steadied back down. No ghost would need to light the gas. Marie was as real as I was, and that gave rise to a whole other lot of questions.

A well-timed lightning bolt jagged the air, illuminating me in the doorway at the same moment as Marie looked up. The cigarette tip curved a light in the resulting darkness, flying up out of her hand and away to glimmer faintly under the table.

'Fuck me!'

A moment of scampering, and then Marie seemed to realise that I was blocking the only doorway, and she slumped onto one of the stools at the table. The gas burner threw her shadow down onto the scrubbed wood as she leaned forward and gasped, but by then I'd got a handle on the situation.

'Hugo, what the hell are you doing creeping around in a dress?'

I was quite proud of that. Given that I felt as though I could faint, my blood was so full of adrenaline that I could taste it, and the sound of the storm beyond the narrow windows of the kitchen was adding a shovel full of pathetic fallacy to the scene, I thought I'd been nicely succinct in my summation of the circumstance.

'Oh, shit,' said Hugo, crumpling further over the table, his wig sliding around his head to a comedy angle. 'Oh, shit.'

The wig had gone sideways, so he was peering out from half a curtain of hair, looking pale and frightened. The off-the-shoulder ballgown he was wearing had come down and rested in his armpit, exposing a line of chest hair and a lot of pale, bony sternum.

'What the hell?' I said, although, to be honest, it was pretty obvious.

Hugo shot to his feet. 'I can't talk about this!' Suddenly he pushed past me in a haze of French perfume and ran, surprisingly nimble in what looked like designer high-heeled evening shoes, down the corridor and out through the back door into the night.

10

THE CASTLE OF OTRANTO – THE CASTLE OF OTRANTO, HORACE WALPOLE

I followed, but he'd vanished into the dark and the rain. Thunder growled overhead again and another stab of lightning speared the air. 'Hugo!' I called, but there was no answer.

'Bloody idiot.' I hovered in the doorway for a moment, looking out at the savage night. He'd looked so desperate, so horrified, I ought to try to tell him that it was all right, that I understood. Well, maybe I didn't understand, as such – this was a whole psychology that Jane Austen and the Brontës had somewhat skated over – but I didn't want Hugo to do something reckless under the belief that I was going to go straight to his mother with my tale. So, with one last hopeless look at the weather, I plunged out after him.

I was barefoot, but Hugo was wearing heels. Nobody could run in heels, I thought, picking my wincing way over the gravel to the grass. He couldn't get far, particularly as the weight of water the sky was throwing down would saturate his full-length dress and slow him down.

'Hugo!' I shouted again into another thunderclap.

No reply. No sign. I hoped he wasn't sheltering under a tree. Getting up in the morning to find her son and heir fried to a crisp in a ballgown and stilettos would probably rid Lady Tanith of what little sanity she had left.

I had to find him. Had to tell him that his secret was safe with me, and that, actually, discovering it had made me feel a good deal better. I knew enough to know that wearing women's clothes didn't necessarily mean that Hugo's sexuality put him completely out of my reach, but the fear of discovery would have put a crimp in any desire he may have felt for me. It wasn't that I was a hideously unlovable monster, even given my rather top-heavy figure. The problem had all been on Hugo's side. It was, I had to admit, a rather different 'hero flaw' than I'd been led to expect – those had leaned far more toward the 'questionable morals re smuggling' or 'seeming attachment to lady of good fortune' than a predilection for frocks – but it did make Hugo more relatable and more approachable now.

I was soaked and the 'refreshing, after a muggy night' coolness of the rain had given way to 'bloody freezing'. These poor pyjamas, that had suffered the indignities of the fountain incident, now were being subjected to a midnight dousing and I was going to have to invest in some new ones if this sort of thing carried on.

I stood near the pond with the wind thrashing my pyjama legs around my thighs and looked. Nothing moved out there in the blackness, apart from the undergrowth which was flailing as the wind passed, carrying yet more rain. I turned a small circle, my feet freezing in the sopping grass, which was beginning to squelch quietly; the rain falling on its hard-packed surface wasn't draining away but was sitting and puddling. There was no Hugo to be seen.

My gaze fell on the rise of land that was the icehouse. Maybe I could go up onto the top and get a better view? Without being struck by lightning hopefully. I ran, muddy water splashing up my legs as I went, meeting the overflow from my hair coming down the other way. Wet cotton flapped against me and gave inadequate coverage against the weather, my shoulder straps had stretched until my once-cute camisole top was now more of a bust-bandage and the pyjama legs encircled my calves in clinging desperation as I reached the top of the hillock and looked out across the carefully mown acres.

It was too dark to make out much. I had hoped that a bloke in a ballgown and heels might stand out against the night, but I hadn't really counted on the sheer darkness out here. No streetlights, no stars, no illumination at all.

Just sheets of rain and the occasional blinding flash, and now my hair was in my eyes. I could hardly even see my own hands, let alone a figure in the distance.

'What the hell are you doing?' A voice came from somewhere around my ankles. 'You're going to get fifty thousand volts through the head if you keep standing there.'

Tonight had already been so far outside my experience that, for the tiniest second, I entertained the idea that some particularly earthy branch of the fae was speaking to me, but then I looked down.

'What are you doing in there?'

'Restoring a 1975 Ford Escort, what do you *think* I'm doing in here?'

It was Jay. It was one in the morning in the middle of a thunderstorm, and here he was, standing in the entrance to the icehouse fully dressed, as though this were the most normal thing in the world.

'More to the point, what the hell are *you* doing out *there*?' He held out a hand to arrest my slide down the small waterfall that the icehouse mound had become, and pulled me into the cubby of an entranceway. 'There's a thunderstorm going on.'

'Well I thought I'd take an evening stroll,' I said, sarcasm dripping almost more than the rest of me. 'I was...' No. Hugo's clothing-confusion was nothing to do with Jay. 'I thought I saw someone out here.'

'You did. Me.'

'And, again, what are you doing out here?' He'd got both his hearing aids in, I noticed, although they were largely concealed by his hair, and I wondered who he'd been talking to in this brick-lined tunnel.

'I am a dark, tortured soul who walks the grounds by moonlight to ease my... err... dark torturedness.' Jay shuffled back further into the little porchway until his back was against the locked metal gate of the icehouse proper, which gave me room to get further in. He was dry and warm and I began to shiver.

'Cobblers,' I said, trying to stop my jaw wobbling.

'Probably. Are you all right?'

It was an unexpected question and, in my soaked, frozen and worried-about-Hugo state it reduced me to tears. 'No! I want to go home, but I haven't really got one, and I thought...' I stopped. Again, this wasn't Jay's business. 'And I'm tired and there's a cat in my bed,' I finished, sniffing heftily.

'I just meant, you're cold and wet. You should get in and dried off before – well, before your clothing disintegrates.' Jay nodded towards my chest, where the midriff of my top had rolled up when I'd sat down and my boobs were now only covered by a strip of wet fabric.

I sniffed again. 'I'll just wait for the rain to ease off.'

We sat in silence for a while. After a few minutes, Jay took off the jumper he was wearing and draped it over my shoulders, without saying a word. We sat a bit more. Trickles of water began to slide from the entrance down to where we were crouched, like little muddy tongues trying to lick us.

'It's not easing off,' Jay observed at last. 'Are you going to stay here all night?'

'Are you?'

'You just asking me the same question doesn't count as an answer, you know.' He sounded amused. 'I only live over there, in the estate village. You've got to get all the way back to the house. Look, the storm seems to have passed over, it's just the rain now. If you run really quickly you can get back inside and into a shower or something.'

'Are you trying to get rid of me?' I had no idea why, but the presence of Jay in this little stone building was reassuring. As though he represented a normality that everything else about tonight was severely lacking.

'Not really, but I'm going to head home to bed and I don't really want to leave you here. You might die of hypothermia and I'm running out of garden to bury the bodies in.'

'Shut up,' I said mildly.

'Come on then.' A hand closed around my wrist and pulled me to my feet, which slithered slightly on the muddy channel of a floor. 'Get on inside and out of those wet... whatever they are.'

'All right, Dad.'

Now he grinned. 'And put my jumper on. No daughter of mine is going to be wandering around with, well, it's noticeable that you're cold, put it that way.'

I smiled back, pulled his jumper over my head and, with the extra layer of reinforcement against the elements, I made a dash for the kitchen door, which stood slightly open in the courtyard wall.

I turned to look back, just once. Jay was still standing in the shelter of the icehouse, watching me go and I wondered again what he had been doing out in the storm. But then I thought of Lady Tanith's twenty-four-hour work ethic and maybe there were jobs that could only be done at night?

I pattered soggily back up to my room, stripped off my soaking pyjamas and, snuggled up to the furry warmth of the cat, I fell asleep.

11

BORLEY – THE HAUNTING OF BORLEY RECTORY, SEAN O'CONNOR

Hugo was not at breakfast that morning. This wasn't totally unheard of, but I was still a little worried as I settled myself into the library for another dynamic day of staccato typing. The storm had died into a misty dampness that veiled the view, so I had nothing else to look at, just Oswald and the computer screen. Even The Master had chosen to stay where he was, tucked under my covers, so I was alone in the grey, dusty light, moving piles of books from place to place. I set up camp with my flask and some biscuits that I'd found in the back of the pantry, where Mrs Compton waged a low-grade war on the household by hiding any tasty comestibles, and started work.

Three piles of books later and the door opened cautiously.

'Can... err... can I come in?' It was Hugo.

'Of course you can, it's your house.' I swivelled away from the screen to watch him slither through the door gap. He looked as though he hadn't slept all night. His chin was stubbled, his eyes were red and there were dark shadows underneath them, and he kept swinging his arms and flexing his fingers as though he were a boxer about to go into the ring.

'I think... look. We need to talk. About last night,' he added, as though there was an entire string of past indiscretions for us to discuss. 'But not in here.'

'Oswald won't tell,' I said, pulling another pile of books over. I'd really only just warmed up properly after my soaking, and I wasn't filled with the desire to go back outside again.

'No, I know. It's just... Mother might come in. And I'd rather she didn't... I mean, it's delicate and...' Hugo swung his arms again, as though his whole body didn't fit him properly this morning. 'And I want to talk to you, properly.'

I stood up. 'All right. But, please, not the icehouse.'

Hugo stared, wide-eyed. 'Why on *earth* should I want to go to the icehouse?'

'No reason. Long story. So, where?'

I followed him out of the library and up the stairs. 'In here,' he said, pulling a key out of his pocket and stopping at the door to the Yellow Room. 'We can lock the door and Mother can't... I mean, she won't come down here anyway but... just in case.'

He unlocked the door and threw it open. I went in to see a small bedroom, charmingly wallpapered in a yellow floral pattern, and holding no furniture except three full-length wardrobes. Hugo, after an ostentatiously careful check of the landing, locked the door after us, and then hovered in the middle of the room, practically vibrating with nerves.

'So,' I said, when it became obvious that he didn't know where to start. 'Marie doesn't exist? You made it all up?'

He shrugged. 'I thought you'd seen me, on the day you arrived. I had to come up with *something*. Then, when you caught me that night, well, I thought a good ghost story might keep you from wandering around.'

'So Templewood isn't haunted *at all*?' I asked, thinking of the footsteps in the attic.

'Not as far as I am aware, why?'

'No reason.' I couldn't bring myself to tell him about those eldritch sounds that made me unwilling to lie awake for long, those rhythmic creaking boards that spoke of *something that moved*. 'Just wondered.'

Idly, he walked up to the first wardrobe. It was huge, oak, and looked like something that might play host to snowy lands and gas lamps, but when he opened the door it was crammed full of evening dresses.

'I know that Mother has been half-hoping that you and I might... she'd like to see another generation, know that the place is in safe hands, all that.' Hugo gave me a shame-faced grin. 'I'm really sorry.'

'Oh, Hugo,' I said helplessly.

'And, I mean, I'm not gay and I don't want to transition. Not at all. Quite the reverse. But I know this' – he waved a hand at the frocks – 'isn't for everyone.' He opened the next wardrobe. It was similarly filled to the brim with expensive-looking dresses. 'Mother must never know.'

'So, all those noises I've heard in here at night? That I thought was rats or ghosts?'

He dropped his eyes to the toes of his shoes. 'I only dress at night,' he said. 'Can't run the risk of Mother catching me. She goes to bed at nine with an Ativan and she's out for the count until seven.' Now he looked up at me. 'It's truly not a sexual thing, it might be better if it were. Can you forgive me, Andi?'

'Forgive you for what? Liking dresses? That's not really something that needs forgiving, is it?'

He gave a huge sigh. 'Thank you. And no, not just for that. For being here, for letting Mother keep up her fantasies that you and I... that I'm just here to provide another generation. As I said, once Mother has... gone, I'll be selling the estate. She wants to keep it, for Oswald's memory, but I don't *have* any memory of Oswald. He died sixteen years before I was even born.'

I inwardly cursed all my reading. Whilst the Brontës, Dickens, Hardy et al had given me a grounding in life of sorts, they really hadn't covered crossdressing in anything like the detail that I could have done with.

Hugo looked so... so abject. As though his life was sitting around his knees in ruins and his every hope had died. I knew how that felt. I'd gone from a hope of marrying the heir to this estate, or at least a man with the money to travel in the kind of style you didn't see very often when you lived in a bus, to knowing that I didn't want my future to be a husband who looked better in clothes than I did. But the alternatives – the bus or my sister – could I compromise? I had no problem with anyone who decided they wanted to be someone else in whatever form that took; hadn't I reinvented myself to a certain extent just to be here? And Hugo said it wasn't sexual; he liked to wear women's clothes, that was all. *Could* I be with someone who liked dresses? It was only clothes.

'Show me,' I said, and his entire face brightened.

'*Really*? You're interested?'

Not really, I wanted to say. But if talking to someone about his preferences made him feel better, then why not?

'Just show me.'

I'd never seen Hugo so animated before. This was obviously the first time he'd ever had chance to share his interest with someone, and it was rather sweet to watch him pull each dress down from its hanger, take off the wrapping and talk about its history, the fabric, the hang and fit. The clothes were all expensive, designer and had history.

'And *this* one' – he unzipped a dress bag to release a blue silk dress – 'I got from an auction. It used to belong to Elizabeth Taylor.' He stroked the flowing folds of the skirt. 'It wears so beautifully, although I don't often put it on; it's not really my size.'

'Oh, Hugo,' I said again, softly.

'When I saw you in the library with that curtain on your head, for one second I thought it was some kind of judgement on me.' He gabbled the words out really quickly. 'I'd told you all those ghost stories to try to keep you hiding in your room at night, and then I thought that maybe there really *was* a ghost and it was coming to get me for making up that rubbish.' He passed another hand over the beautiful silk. 'But really it was just my conscience. Keeping secrets isn't easy. And my brother...' He stopped, his face twisting.

'I hate my sister,' I blurted out. 'That's my secret. No, that's not fair, I don't *hate* her. I wish I was more like her. She put her foot down with our parents.' I remembered Jude again, aged about seven, stamping and hands on hips, telling our mother that it was ridiculous that she didn't go to school, brandishing that copy of the Enid Blyton boarding school book that she'd been reading. She'd stuck to her guns and got Dad to invest some of his large savings in her education at a very good boarding school in the Cotswolds. 'She's pretty and she's assertive and she gets what she wants. And what she wanted was a normal life.'

'Well, you're… not unattractive.' Hugo put the dress back into the wardrobe again. 'And I'm sure there's a life out there somewhere for you.'

'That's not enough.'

His baffled frown told me that he didn't get it. But why would he? Good looking, even as the second son of the estate, his future would be assured, by his batty mother.

'My parents always told me that I could have the life I wanted. Whatever I wanted to do, to be, I could do it, it didn't matter that I had no experience, no qualifications, no "special talents".'

'And that's an admirable sentiment.' Hugo tidied up some shoe boxes, piling them back onto the floor of the third wardrobe.

'It is. But it's a lie. Look, I was raised in a bus. We moved all the time, never settled anywhere. I got all my education from reading, books were my only constant. And the books lied to me too. They said that all I had to do was to know what I wanted, and go for it.' I stopped. The words were falling out of me in painful lumps, backed by all the emotion that I'd recently come to understand. But this was a man who liked to wear dresses. If anyone could come close to knowing how I felt at finding out that life wasn't as easy as everyone made out, it would be him.

'In what way isn't it true?'

'It might be true that you can grow up in a bus and go and – I dunno, set up your own company or be seduced by a billionaire or travel the world and all that. But only if you've got more. Only if you're more than me. People expect someone who grows up like I did to be a kooky, ditzy pretty girl with a brain like razor wire. If you're just ordinary, then nobody cares. You've got no education, no particular talent and you're not even decorative. Life lied to me. *Books* lied to me. And my sister got a great life because she didn't fall for the lie.'

'Oh, Andi.'

Hugo came over and hugged me. It was a warm hug but totally fraternal.

'Not to mention that I got a stupid name!' I said, muffled against his shoulder. 'I mean, Andromeda! I ask you. I don't even look like an Andromeda – I ought to be all willowy and a bit wafty and "at one with the universe". I should have been beautiful and wear a size six and have lovely hair.'

'There is nothing wrong with you.' Hugo gave me a little shake. 'Don't talk yourself down. You might not have masses of qualifications, but here you are, you've got a job. You're doing good things.'

I stepped away. 'Am I, though? Am I not really just doing some pointless data entry?' I nearly slipped and mentioned my search for the diaries but managed to keep my lip buttoned on that.

'You are giving my mother someone else to focus on, apart from me and Jasper, and that is an action worthy of beatification,' Hugo said firmly. 'When she's complaining about you, or supervising you, then she's leaving us alone, and my mother has taken an unhealthy interest in my brother and me since we were born. Oh, not like that.' He must have seen my expression. 'Nothing worthy of the tabloid press. It's more that she has very firm ideas of how she wants our lives to go. I'm jealous of my brother, too,' he added.

'Because he got away with renouncing his birthright? How did he manage it, by the way?'

Hugo looked conflicted for a moment. 'It's not my story to tell, sorry,' he said. 'But it means that Mother has concentrated her efforts on me, and making me take on estate responsibilities. I *can't* tell her I don't want it either, the shock might kill her.'

There was a momentary silence; presumably we were both weighing up the pros of this happening. There didn't appear to be any cons.

'So, you see,' he went on. 'I could never tell her about this.' A waved hand indicated the racks of frocks. 'She so wants me to conform utterly. Saying that I can only marry a woman who can deal with a man who likes to wear dresses in his downtime – it wouldn't go down well, let's put it that way. Telling her that I'm going to sell the entire estate as soon as I inherit, pack up my collection and go somewhere where I can live the way I want to...' He shook his head. 'Not going to happen.'

I looked at him standing there, slender and attractive and yet with a dark loneliness about him. 'Can't you get away? You must have friends, people you could go and stay with to find a life away from the estate?'

Hugo shook his head again. 'I'm not really the sociable sort,' he said. 'All the boys from school meet up now and again and I've been along once or twice to the reunions, but it's all so – loud. It's a bit like none of them have grown up at all, they're all in their father's firms or in banking or some such, but they all seem to be playing at life.' He sighed. 'Too much money and too much privilege. All I have is a crumbling old house and an estate full of people who pretend to be faithful retainers whilst plotting to move to the city and earn proper money doing proper jobs.'

'Oh, Hugo.' He looked sadly forlorn, standing in front of the wardrobe but staring out of the window into the darkness. My heart pleated with pity.

'I'm not really cut out for this Lord of the Manor lark,' he said. 'But Mother is determined that I'll run the place with a rod of iron, so she keeps trying to instil a ferocity into me that's just not there.' Now his handsome face was pulled tight around the eyes with hopelessness. 'I haven't got it in me to bark orders and demand obedience. Even the cat doesn't listen to me; what hope have I got of getting a workforce to? It ought to have been Jasper. He's good at all the officious stuff, but the bugger managed to worm his way out of it and left Mother to me.'

'Life can be a bit of a shit really, can't it?' I patted his arm.

'Indeed it can.' Hugo gave me a wan smile. 'All we can do is make the best of what we've got. Play the hand we were dealt, and all that.'

I went to the door. 'Anyway, I had better go back to cataloguing that bloody library, because right now it's all that's providing me with a sense of self-worth.'

Hugo smiled. 'Can I recommend a pair of Manolos for that?'

I had to laugh. 'Not really going to work for me. But you have at it.'

He unlocked the door and we both went out onto the landing, meeting The Master coming from the direction of my room with a determined expression. The cat and I descended back to the grim dark of the dust-haunted room, while Hugo went off to do his own thing, hopefully feeling a lot lighter and a lot happier now that his secret was out in the open.

I felt, mostly, cheated.

After a morning's work, I went for a walk in the grounds again. I needed to avoid Hugo for a while, I decided. Not because of anything he'd done – I didn't feel the disgust or horror that he had clearly feared I would, but I needed time to think. If marrying Hugo wasn't totally out of the question, and it did seem to be something Lady Tanith was working towards and even Hugo didn't seem revolted at the prospect, plus now I had his misplaced sense of guilt on my side – was it something I felt I could do?

I stuck my hands in the pockets of my jeans and strolled along one of the winding paths through the shrubbery. I could marry Hugo. I already knew his secret, so he would feel he could be open with me, and that was healthy. I could live here until Lady Tanith died – all right, it wouldn't be my first choice, but the house could be lovely if someone who wasn't obsessed with the previous owner took over and actually *changed things*. And then – then we could travel. Tour the world. Probably with heavy emphasis on couture clothing shops and places that sold designer shoes in size ten, but still. We could.

But then I thought of the trade-off. My husband would wear women's clothes whenever he could. We'd go designer shopping, not for me, but for him, and Hugo had the tall, slender build that looked great in sample size clothing. We'd be at all the fashion shows, London Fashion Week, Paris, and all the while he would be handling fabrics, thinking of how they would drape, the fit, the cut. Everyone would look at me and think how lucky I was that my husband bought me couture, or vintage dresses with history, possibly with a side order of what a waste it was, buying such lovely things for such an ordinary looking girl. Then there was the enormous factor of my not fancying a man who wore dresses. Hugo in male garb, yes, absolutely. But I couldn't look at him in azure silk and tassels and feel the same way.

Not even to save me from the bus. Not even to stop me having to go cap in hand to my sister. The parents would probably go down a storm in their new series, touring North America in the Winnebago and come home full of plans and contracts and the possibility of an extended stay in the States or Australia. They wouldn't even notice that I was still there, still hiding out in libraries and trying to pretend that hashtag Vanlife was working for me.

I shook my head and stopped by a small tree with branches weighed down by the formation of berries. I banged my head slowly against the trunk. Stay here, with Hugo, or go home? Either option seemed equally dreadful right now.

'What has that tree done to you?' It was Jay, emerging from cover like a scruffier version of the god Pan. 'And have you got my jumper? I'm going to need that, it's bloody cold first thing in the morning.'

'Sorry, no,' I said vaguely. 'I didn't know I was going to see you.'

Jay looked at me, his head tilted to one side. 'Did you sort out your person?' he asked.

'Person?'

'The one you saw outside last night. Did you find them?'

I was instantly thrown back to Hugo, running off into the night and my stomach gave a jolt. *A bus or a man who wears dresses.* 'Oh, yes. Yes, thank you, I did.'

'Hmmm.' He came closer, fiddling with the hearing aids, tucking them more firmly behind his ears. 'You don't look happy about it.'

'It has thrown up something of a dilemma.'

'Want to talk about it?' Jay threw an arm out. 'Come and have a coffee.'

'Where?'

'I've got a flask.' The tattoo on his wrist flickered in and out of vision under the sleeve of his donkey jacket as he waved his arm again at a canvas knapsack on the grass the other side of the tree. 'You look like you could do with a chat.'

'I can't really say anything; it's not my secret to tell,' I said, suddenly awkward.

'Ah well, maybe you could give me the précised highlights then. Leave out any incriminating details?'

'I think that would leave me with the words "the", "and" and "wardrobe", actually.'

Jay laughed and pulled a flask out of the bag, then sat down on the grass, his bare legs stretched out in front of him, and poured two cups from the old-fashioned tartan covered vacuum flask. 'Narnia stopped being a secret about sixty years ago. Sit down. Tell me as much as you can, as much as you feel comfortable with. You'll feel better, I promise.'

He looked at me over the rim of his plastic mug, sipping. The coffee smelled good, breakfast had been a long time ago and I really didn't feel up to trying to force lunch out of Mrs Compton who had a propensity for asking why I needed another meal when I could do with losing a few pounds, and I was being paid to work, not eat.

I sat down next to him and took the other coffee cup, then found myself telling Jay about Hugo. That deep well of loneliness that he seemed to be perching over, trying to keep his mother happy by taking on the management of an estate that he resented. I managed to steer clear of mentioning the dresses, none of that seemed to matter as much once I'd heard him talk about the future that was being thrust upon him. His life revolved around being the second son, unprepared for the lifetime commitment that Templewood had become, and his bitterness towards his brother for breaking out. This led to me blurting out all the stuff about my sister and our relationship; about having to find myself a life without any real preparation apart from books. I went on for quite some time.

Jay drank his coffee and listened. He was very good at it, keeping his head tilted, presumably to hear better, his eyes flickering between my face and his booted feet, and not interrupting. He didn't seem to have suffered as much as I or Hugo had from the late night and the soaking. There were no shadows under his eyes, although he clearly hadn't shaved for a couple of days.

At last I stopped. The coffee was almost cold, but he'd been right, I did feel better.

'So, you can't tell me what it is that you found out?' He took the coffee cup from me, tipped the cool dregs onto the grass and refilled it. 'But you don't want to be with Hugo now?'

'I'm not entirely sure that I ever *wanted* to be with him,' I said thoughtfully. 'It's more that – fiction gave me expectations, I suppose. And now I feel stupid.'

'Real life doesn't have a narrative.' Jay poured himself another cup of coffee. The cuff of his jacket rolled back and revealed his tattoo fully to the half-hearted sunlight. The design was small but looked like a posy of flowers tied into a bunch with a rainbow-coloured ribbon. 'That's the thing. It's messy and confusing and heartbreaking, and things don't always happen in the right order. Heartbreak doesn't always mean that you get the guy in the end; sometimes you just get more heartbreak.'

'But that's not fair,' I said.

'No, but it *is* life. Books have to have lots of stuff going on and well-reasoned endings, otherwise nobody would read them. But life isn't tidy like that. Bad stuff happens for no reason, then there's five hundred pages of getting up, going to work, and going to bed. No happy ending, no narrative causality. Just shit and boredom and unhappiness.'

He sounded sad and slightly bitter. I drank the last of the coffee.

'It's not fair,' I said again, putting the cup down.

'No. It's not unlike books that *have* to be fair, usually. The detective always solves the crime, the spaceship always discovers the lost planet.' He gave me a rueful smile. 'The hero always gets the girl. Or boy.' He fiddled with the hearing aid again. 'If the book doesn't end the way the reader expects, then the reader feels cheated. It makes them feel stupid, that they invested all that time in a story that didn't give them what they wanted.'

I sighed. 'Life cheats all the time. It doesn't have to give us what we want.'

He flashed me a smile. 'No. I was born with a hearing defect. I thought that would be as bad as it got, but – well...' Now his eyes went to the tattoo on his wrist and he rubbed it with a finger. 'There were other complications. Like I said, no fairy stories here. At least, only of the evil, dark fairy kind.' For a second he looked as haunted as I'd believed Templewood to have been, then he glanced back up at my face, and smiled. 'We make our own stories, I guess,' he said.

'And my sister made her story so different from mine that it itches.' I felt slightly embarrassed by seeing Jay's pain. Almost as though I had to remind myself that I was also entitled to unhappiness. Mine may not be tragedy on tragedy, more *Northanger Abbey* than *Hamlet,* but it was all relative. My unhappiness was all relatives. 'If I could have been more like her...'

'Then you wouldn't be you,' Jay interrupted briskly. 'And you'd have none of this.' A wide arm indicated the lush grassland, with its backdrop of gently flowering shrubs and elegantly draped trees. 'So you can't compare non-existent lives. If you had been someone else, you may have been heartbroken by now and vowing to hide out in that bus and never meet another man.'

'"Hurt and must never love again"?' Some of those stories where the heroine or hero had promised themselves that they would never fall in love because they'd been dumped once had been, I had thought, unnecessarily overwrought.

'That sort of thing. Or – or worse things could have happened.' Jay looked back down at the grass again. He stroked it gently with one finger, revealing the tattoo again, so that the colours changed and flexed with the movement of the muscles of his arm. 'Trust me.' He looked up and into my eyes. 'You're doing all right.'

Brisk then, as though he felt he'd said more than he should have done, he tapped his cup against the ground to empty the remains of the coffee and began screwing the flask back together.

His sudden movement made me feel dismissed. 'I suppose I ought to go back,' I said.

'To the dust and the spreadsheets?' Jay stayed sitting while I clambered to my feet and handed him back the mug.

'Yes. And because I don't want Hugo to think I'm hiding from him. I don't want him to feel that I... that I think less of him because of... what I found out today,' I edited carefully.

'You're very kind.' The words didn't have the expected undertone of amused sarcasm; they sounded as though he meant them.

'Maybe. Thank you for the coffee.' I lingered for a moment. Walking away felt – not right, somehow. As though Jay and I had shared something more than coffee, something that had bound us together, although I had no idea why I should feel like this. He'd hardly spoken, while I'd gabbled enough for two.

'I'll see you again soon.' He began to pack the flask back into the rucksack that had held it. 'I have to; you've got my jumper.'

'Yes.' I was backing away slowly, leaving without leaving.

'Go on, go!' He was laughing now. He'd lost that strange, bitter tone that he'd had when he'd talked about life. 'Spreadsheets wait for no man.'

'They do, actually. They wait for me, anyway.'

'Well, Lady Tanith won't.' He nodded behind me. 'I think she's coming for you.'

I turned around. Lady Tanith was, indeed, crossing the lawn at a vigorous pace. The Master trotted in her wake with his tail in the air, like a very small pageboy.

'Andromeda. Why are you not in the library?'

I turned around to say something to Jay, but he'd gone. Evaporated into the bushes, knapsack, coffee dregs and all, leaving nothing but a small patch of crushed grass and some waving branches marking his passing.

'I'm on my lunchbreak,' I said.

'A lunchbreak which has extended for' – Lady Tanith ostentatiously looked at the slim gold watch on her wrist – 'an hour and twelve minutes. I should like you to get back to work now. Thank you.'

She turned again and set off back towards the house. The Master hesitated. He looked up at me and twitched his tail.

'Traitor,' I said quietly. He blinked at me. 'Come on, then.'

Together we set out across the grass, following Lady Tanith's earth-scorching passage, back to the library.

12

ILLYRIA – TWELFTH NIGHT, WILLIAM SHAKESPEARE

Lady Tanith was looking up at Oswald's portrait when we came in. Without the curtains, the sun shone fully on his countenance and I could see that he must have been painted at about the age of forty or so. He looked like a thoughtful older man with a face only now starting to feel the effects of gravity, his hair had traces of grey at the swept-back temples but was still mostly the same dark shade as his grandson, and his back was erect.

Lady Tanith was murmuring sweet nothings to the painted visage and gently stroking the edge of his frame.

'How old was Oswald? When he died, I mean,' I asked casually, flipping the computer back on again carefully where she could see, so that she'd know I now turned it off when I wasn't in the room. Hopefully talking about Oswald would distract her from my twelve-minute lunch hour overrun and I could learn something more about him. Any information which might lead me to the diaries would be welcome.

Lady Tanith pointed to a small brass plaque set into the bottom of the frame. 'Oswald Matcham Dawe,' it said. '19 January 1912 – 21 February 1975.'

'Sixty-three? No age at all.' I sat down.

'Taken too soon,' Lady Tanith sniffed. 'In his prime.'

'How old was he when this portrait was painted?'

She gave me a narrow-eyed look as though she suspected me of some kind of wicked calculation. 'Forty-seven. He was very well preserved. Very active, for his age. Of course, he didn't meet me until later. I came to the house in 1969, as companion to Caroline, his wife.'

'That must have been—'

'We fell for one another instantly,' Lady Tanith went on, talking over the top of me. 'It was a true meeting of minds. We understood one another without saying a word.'

'Lucky old him,' I muttered into my collar. I was now deeply regretting getting her on the subject of Ozzie. It wasn't going to lead me to the whereabouts of the diaries, it was going to lead to more borderline salacious details about their relationship. Which I *so* did not want to hear.

'But, of course, Caroline was so frail, so dependent, and Oswald was such a gentleman. She needed him so utterly.' Lady Tanith gazed up at Oswald's face again, her tone softened. 'I used to sit with him in this library, while he wrote his poetry and his novels, and suggest ideas to him.' She stroked the frame again. 'He was always so grateful.'

I had a horrible mental flash of a very young Tanith 'suggesting ideas' to an older man with a frail wife and, again, hoped that none of those ideas had come to fruition on this table. I found I was wiping it with my sleeve, just in case. The thought that Lady Tanith might have hastened Caroline's departure from this veil of tears to get Oswald all to herself struck me suddenly and horrifically.

'How did Caroline die?' I asked tentatively, a little worried that a fall down the stairs or other nasty 'accident' might be the next thing I had to worry about.

'She'd been ill for a long time,' Lady Tanith said, still wearing the expression of misty fondness that she always adopted when staring at Oswald's picture. 'It was a release at the end.'

That did *not* answer my question.

'I had the plaque with the dates put onto the portrait, after he... passed.' Lady Tanith started stroking the plaque now. 'So that nobody could forget. Oh,' she sighed. 'He was a genius, Andromeda. A genius. The world will never see his like again.'

A silence fell. I didn't feel that I could go and get another pile of books, not whilst she was having misty remembrances.

'So, you married his son?' I tried to bring her back a little more into the here and now.

'Mmm? Oh, Richard, yes. Of course, he was a *lot* older than me, but, with Oswald gone – it kept me close to the family.'

I felt a pang of sympathy for poor Richard, who seemed to have been an also-ran to his own father. I wondered if Lady Tanith had ever loved him, or even liked him, or whether she'd only married him because of his father.

'Then, of course, the boys came along and Richard died.' She turned away from the portrait now. 'But now I feel the time is right to find and publish Oswald's diaries, to let the world know what lay behind his genius and what we meant to one another. He idolised me, you know. Idolised. Far more so than Richard ever did, but the boys are old enough now to learn the truth. Edited, of course. I'd prefer them to think of their grandfather as the creative talent he was, without stressing the importance of my own contributions.'

I held my breath for a minute, in case any great revelations were about to appear about the parentage of her sons, but then I realised that Oswald had been dead for some while before they were born and I was trying to force a book narrative onto real life. Of course her father-in-law wouldn't be the father of her children, that wasn't how real life worked. That sort of relationship belonged to the concupiscent world of daytime television and the tabloid press, not Lady Tanith's world. Jay was right. Life was messy and didn't have proper endings.

'Caroline had the portrait commissioned as a birthday present,' Lady Tanith carried on. Even spreadsheets were starting to look appealing now. 'Oswald asked to have it hung in here; the library was very much his space, you see.'

And of course he'd have wanted a gigantic version of his own face staring at him every time he sat down for a read or to write, I thought, and wondered if Caroline had been as off the wall as Lady Tanith was, and whether that had been Oswald's 'type'.

'It's very...' I tried to think of a word. Big wouldn't do. Neither would ominous, oppressive, egocentric or off-putting. 'Powerful,' I settled on.

Lady Tanith nodded. 'It was painted by someone quite famous. Spencer, possibly. Caroline did tell me but I really don't remember.' The dismissive way she said this told me an awful lot about how she'd felt about Oswald's wife. Maybe Lady Tanith really *had* hastened Caroline's end. Then I remembered what Hugo had told me, about this being Caroline's family home and Oswald 'marrying in' and wondered whether Lady Tanith had a big chip on her shoulder about it. 'But I don't know why we're talking about dear Oswald. You are supposed to be sorting my books.'

I couldn't say 'well, bugger off and let me get on with it, then,' so I just raised my eyebrows, which she couldn't see, and opened a new sheet on the screen.

> *'The stringing of the fencing wire*
> *Hangs tighter than the player's lyre.*
> *Whilst all around the pigeons flock,*
> *And with their calls, the humans mock.'*

'That was one of Oswald's verses. It's from a poem he called "Party on the Estate Lawn". I know all his work by heart, obviously.'

I stopped, my fingers hovering over the keyboard. That had to be the worst piece of poetry I thought I'd ever heard, but I couldn't say so. 'Are his published books in here?' I asked. 'I haven't come across one yet.'

'Oh.' Lady Tanith looked around vaguely at the shelves. 'They're all in the house somewhere. He wrote fifteen novels and three collections of poetry, all privately printed, of course. He was far too much of a gentleman to deal with editors and all that nastiness.'

I was beginning to utterly loathe Oswald Bloody Dawe now. 'Interesting,' I said, half-heartedly. 'I'm sure I'll come across his books at some point.' And then burn them, if that poem was a typical example of his work, for the good of mankind.

'But the *diaries*.' Lady Tanith lowered her voice. 'The diaries are what you're really here for, Andromeda. Please, do try to find them. I feel they could be such an important contribution to the world of literature, a true historic voyage into the working mind of a creative genius.'

But they *weren't* here, were they? For the look of it, and because Lady Tanith was watching me expectantly, I fetched another armful of books from the nearby shelf and plonked them down on the table with a resulting puff of dust. I also peered into the gap the books had left, in case the pile of diaries was in there, double stacked and waiting. They weren't.

I wanted to tell Lady Tanith what Jay had told me. Life isn't like the books. Being brought into the house to find the diaries didn't mean that I *was* going to find the diaries. Find the diaries, marry her son, wait for her to die and then open the house as a hotel or sell up and move to somewhere where Hugo could wear his beautiful dresses all day. Wasn't that how the story was shaping up?

The library door opened and Hugo put his head through the gap. 'Ah, you're back,' he said, seeing me sitting. 'I just wanted to ask...' Then he caught sight of his mother, still frozen in an attitude of adoration more commonly seen in religious iconography. 'Oh! Mother, you're here too.'

'Clearly. You sound surprised, Hugo. This *is* my house.'

I watched Hugo take a deep breath. He'd obviously nearly blurted something out that couldn't be said in the vicinity of his mother, and was now realising that my knowing his clothing secret was going to mean a whole other level of checking before he spoke. Maybe it had just been less confusing when nobody knew and 'keep quiet' had been the order of the day.

'I, err... I just wanted to ask if you'd seen The Master.' Hugo switched mental gears and went on. 'I didn't want him to be still shut into your bedroom.'

As Hugo had watched the cat saunter from my room and follow us down the stairs earlier, this was quite an inspired lie. But then, I told myself, he'd probably had quite a lot of practice at lying about things.

'No, it's fine,' I said. 'He's here, under the table.'

'Oh. Good. I was worried about what he might do on your bed, if he was shut in there for most of the day.' Hugo's eyes were wary, fixed on me with a kind of wounded begging. Did he really think I'd gone straight to his mother to pour out his cross-dressing secrets? Was that how he saw me?

'The Master and I are going for tea now.' Lady Tanith clicked her fingers in the region of my knees. 'And possibly an early night. I am feeling a little overwrought just now.' She clicked her fingers again but the cat resolutely refused to appear. He was sitting in the darkness beneath the desk, his blue eyes narrowed in a cat smile, and the tip of his tail twitching.

Tanith made a 'tch' sound, as though she suspected me of having the cat strapped to my leg, and, with a last moue of affection directed towards Oswald's gigantic face, stalked out.

As soon as the door closed, Hugo let out a long breath. 'Did you tell her?'

'No, Hugo, of *course* I didn't tell her. I already said I wouldn't tell anyone.'

There was a look on his handsome, high-cheekboned face, which told me he wasn't entirely sure, and that he was beginning to realise that someone else knowing his secret wasn't quite as much fun as he'd first thought. It wasn't all whispered comparisons of fabric or my opinion of the hang of a particular gown. It was having to trust another person. And he wasn't completely sure that he could or ever would.

At that point, I knew I could never marry Hugo.

'I'm sorry, of course you wouldn't.' He said it smoothly, confidently, but just too late. I'd seen the doubt.

'Anyway. What did you want to ask me? Now that your mother has gone?'

Hugo shook his head. That moment of fear, that second of thinking that I'd gone straight to his mother with his secret, had clearly impacted harder than he'd realised it would. 'Nothing. Doesn't matter.'

'Oh. OK.' Trying to pretend that I hadn't seen or understood, I flipped open the first book on my pile and ran my finger down the title page to find the publication date.

Over near the portrait, Hugo sighed and draped himself over the back of a chair. 'I didn't realise,' he said wearily. 'You knowing. It means I've got to be more careful.'

I wanted to tell him not to worry, that his mother wouldn't always be around. That one day she'd be gone and he'd be free to live his life wearing *all* of the dresses. But she was still his mother, and it seemed a bit tactless to predict her demise.

'I'm beginning to understand Jasper a little better now,' Hugo went on, still in full drape situation. 'He saw freedom beckoning and he went. When I talked to you about... about the dresses and everything else, I felt a little less isolated, if you see what I mean. As though someone understood, and I've never had that before. I presume that my brother wanted the same understanding and he was never going to find it here.'

'You could go too,' I suggested.

Hugo unfurled like a weary umbrella. 'No. You don't get it, Andi. There isn't another life out there waiting for me. This, Templewood, it's the only life I know and I'm afraid I'm stuck with it. What is there for me out there in the world? I've no friends, no qualifications apart from rowing for my house at school, and I don't think there are many jobs out there for men with a lot of upper body strength but no A levels.'

I couldn't refute that, having taken the only job I'd been able to find for a woman without even upper body strength.

'Anyway.' Hugo's voice was a little stronger now and he seemed to have shaken off the doldrums. 'I wanted to ask you if you thought I should try the Elizabeth Taylor dress tonight. I mean, now you know, I don't have to stick to the Marie outfit in case you see me, and it might be a good chance to make sure that the hem doesn't hang too high. It's slightly too small, but I can do what I do with the other dresses that don't quite fit and leave the zip down. It's fine if I put a stole or a shrug over the top so you can't see it's not done all the way up. I thought I might team it with the blue sandals?'

I nodded. 'Why not? Although the heels on those might be a bit high? For the length?'

'Mmm. Maybe I should stick to the kitten heels.' Hugo lapsed into thought for a moment before dragging himself back to the matter in hand. 'But, Mother being here, I'm always going to have to check, aren't I? Before I say anything, just in case she overhears. I never had to worry before, when I *couldn't* say anything.'

'What did Jasper do?' I asked, resigning myself to absolutely *never* getting this library catalogued. As soon as I felt I was making any inroads, another drama crept its way out of the woodwork. 'To get away, I mean.'

'I don't... look. We don't talk about Jasper.'

I remembered that I'd thought Jasper might have been being held captive in the house. It had been less frightening to think of him as the cause of those mysterious noises, rather than ghosts but that whole train of thought now sounded ridiculously overwrought and dramatic. There were no ghosts, only sadness and Hugo's ephemeral longing for freedom. 'Your mother does. And she visits him. Where does he live, the estate village? So he's given up his birthright, but he still lives close by; it can't really be family rift territory, surely?'

My thoughts about the mysterious Jasper were beginning to form into something uncomfortable again.

'Oh, all right.' Hugo swung around now and perched himself on the desk beside me. 'Look, Jazz is gay. He's always known that he wasn't going to marry a nice girl and do the decent thing by the estate, produce the next generation and all that, so he had to come out and tell Mother that he didn't want to inherit. I think' – he bent forwards a little so that he could see my face – 'you can appreciate the amount of silent reprobation that went on in this house after *that* little explosion was detonated.'

'She clearly got over it.'

'She's had a while. Jazz dropped the bombshell when he was twenty-two. I'm nine years younger, so I was thirteen when it happened. Suddenly, all Mother's focus switched to me. There I am, adolescent, just starting to discover that actually I look damned good in velvet, and I'm being groomed to take over the estate while my brother buggers off to live a life of splendid isolation and take up a course in design.' A deep breath. 'So, yes, I fully understand you resenting your sister for being able to live a life that you feel you've been denied.'

The uncomfortable feeling was intensifying. It had become a niggle that I couldn't fully explore, like having an itch in that part of your back that you can't reach, and you can't wait for everyone to leave you alone so that you can press yourself up against a doorframe and have a good scratch.

'But you're going to sell the estate anyway.' I tried to ignore my thoughts and focus on Hugo's distress. 'So you get what you want, in the end.'

He jumped up. 'It could be *years* though. Jazz has had his own way since 2003! Twenty-two years of being able to live the life he wants, while I'm here with Mother! And if I so much as *mention* selling the estate, then she'll dash off to the solicitor and get everything changed to an entailment or some kind of trust that means I physically *can't* sell, and I'll be doomed to living here until I die.'

'At least you'll have a roof over your head,' I said, somewhat sarcastically. 'And it will be all yours. I can either share a bus with my parents – who can't or won't get something more comfortable, because the bus has become the star of the show, or move into my sister's guest suite and have the care of her hyperactive children thrust at me, to help cover my keep. I suppose there's a very slim chance that I might, somehow, be able to find a job that will take someone with no qualifications or experience and yet, miraculously, pays enough to rent somewhere to live and pay my bills, but that's pretty unlikely. You can swan around in your lovely house, wearing all the velvet you want, and I'll still be the dependent unmarried daughter with no life!'

Hugo blinked at me. 'We'd both be unhappy, then.'

'Well, yes.'

'Or, we could go along with my mother's intentions. Marry, do up the house, sell, travel.' He looked half-hopeful.

'Are you proposing to me, Hugo?'

I'd injected just the right amount of jocularity into my tone, I saw it in his eyes. They stopped looking worried and gained a little more twinkle. 'No. You don't need to say anything, Andi, it's fine. I know the whole' – he made 'flary dress' motions with his hands along his body – 'isn't for everyone, and that's OK. Being my friend is enough. Although, if you really need me to marry you and save you from whatever, we could do that too.'

I shook my head. 'No. That only works in stories, Hugo. It's a lovely thought, but we'd resent one another and it would stop you from finding someone who might absolutely adore having a man who looks better than they do in a frock.'

'Do they exist?'

'I'm sure they do. A little bit outside my area of expertise, but they must.'

'And you really won't say anything to Mother?' Hugo looked happier again now. He began to drift towards the door.

'Cross my heart and hope to die.' I grinned at him.

'And you won't let on that you know about Jazz? Mother has just about come round to him after some truly dreadful years, but she's not happy about it.'

I sighed. 'Hugo, I don't want to incur your mother's wrath in any way that I may not currently be incurring it. I'm going to keep my head down, find…' Oops, nearly. So many people were keeping so much from one another that I'd almost forgotten that I was one of them. 'Finish cataloguing these books, and then go. To whatever life might offer me.'

Hugo flittered his fingers at me in farewell and closed the door behind him. I collapsed across the desk and keyboard in a slump that brought the cat out from under my legs, with a chirrup of complaint.

Books had made life and love sound *simple*. Even *fun*. Some of my more up-to-date reading had been cute romantic comedies, where, despite misunderstandings and grim secrets, everything worked out happily and the end was telegraphed right from the beginning.

According to books, I *had* to marry Hugo. But absolutely none of my reading, classic or modern, had mentioned what to do when narrative causality meets the hero who just isn't attractive to the heroine, and vice versa. Or did my life story switch tracks – become a marriage of convenience? Hugo and I marrying to save him from discovery and me from the life I was currently contemplating? I somehow doubted that I was going to undergo an epiphany and discover that I really *could* find him sexually desirable in a dress and heels, and I really didn't think that it would be fair to ask him to renounce the silk and velvet, that entire collection he had hanging upstairs in the locked room. It was part of who he was and my lack of attraction to it was my problem, not his.

The Master chirruped again and came around to jump up onto my lap, four tiny paws supporting his bulky body so that all his weight was concentrated on my leg in those four points of contact. He stared into my face, his blue eyes very bright in the burnished brown of his face and his pale coat shedding noticeable hairs all down my front.

Without thinking I began to stroke him, incurring a deep, rumbling purr and a stomp that felt as though it was bruising every inch of my thighs. 'This is too complicated for me, puss,' I muttered. 'What I suppose would be the dark moment in the story of my life. I'm not getting anywhere with the diary-finding, I'm not going to marry Hugo. I guess I should just admit that I'm wasting my time here. Less of a denouement and more of an intercession.'

A tiny brown nose raised and shoved itself into my eye. The purr intensified as I blinked my way clear and reared my head away from the contact, and a spaghetti-slim tail, seemingly with a life independent of its wearer, coiled around my wrist.

'You can stop that,' I said. 'If it hadn't been for you in the first place, Lady Tanith would have sent me back home straight away.'

Purr purr. Stomp stomp. Then, as though annoyed by my lack of any follow-up actions, The Master sprang down off my lap and strolled off to sit underneath Oswald's portrait, where he bent himself into a shape any acrobat would be proud of and began licking his back end.

I shook my head at him and went back to stare at my spreadsheet, but that little itch in the back of my brain flared into life again when it had nothing to distract it.

Hugo's brother. Who lived on the estate. Jasper.
They call me Jay.
No. Surely not.
I only live over there, in the estate village.
Please God, no.
He's a designer.
Could that design be – *garden* design?
Gay.
A little harder to be exact about, but that tattoo on the inside of his wrist? That tiny bunch of flowers with the rainbow coiled around it that sprang from the cuff of his dreadful gardening clothes? His reticence, his maintaining that life wasn't like the books, that it was heartbreak and no happy ending?
Oh God.

I mentally audited all my conversations with Jay, just in case I'd said something horribly incriminating about Hugo or Lady Tanith but couldn't remember him recoiling in shock at anything. In fact, hadn't *he* been the one to be dismissive of them both as bonkers?

But then, if Lady Tanith had reacted badly to his renouncing the estate – and Lady Tanith's normal behaviour left me in no doubt that her 'reacting badly' wasn't going to mean that she simply took to her bed with a headache – then Jasper probably was under no illusions about her bonkersness.

I groaned, dropping my forehead to rest on the desk. Right. Of course. *Of course.*

Then I straightened up. It didn't matter. Jay had been nothing but pleasant and friendly to me; his being Hugo's brother shouldn't matter at all. It wasn't my fault that I hadn't picked up on it – there was no strong family resemblance although both were dark haired and eyed. Hugo had the fine build and slender frame of their mother whilst Jay was rangier and more muscly – I hit my head against the desk again. Of *course* he was! He dug flowerbeds and cut bits off trees all day! And single – well, he was hardly going to flaunt a partner who may well have to contend with Lady Tanith, was he? She was rude enough to me, and I wasn't stuck here for any reason other than financial; any poor bloke unfortunate enough to be here for love would probably be put through the metaphorical mincer on a weekly basis.

Damn it, I'd *liked* him!

OK, so the only sensible course of action was to catalogue the books. Make increasingly feeble and doomed attempts to find Oswald's seemingly non-existent diaries. Try to scrape together enough money and a decent-enough reference, and perhaps I could – what? Find myself a job that didn't ask for qualifications, in a town small and cheap enough to rent a room in a shared house? Well, it wasn't *totally* impossible. People did it. They survived.

I *had* to realise that life wasn't like the books, that there was no gorgeous man, heir to a ready-made way of life, willing to sweep me off my feet and take me away. There were no ghosts walking the corridors of a down-at-heel mansion, waiting for me to discover their secret, avenge their murder and banish their spirit.

That, as Jay had said, sometimes life was just heartbreak, getting up, going to work and going to bed. No narrative, no fabulous adventures. Just life.

At this rate, I wouldn't even get a go at the heartbreak bit.

13

THE SECRET GARDEN – THE SECRET GARDEN, FRANCES H BURNETT

A few days later I met Jay again.

I had wandered down to the village for something to do, yet again, with my day off. Templewood had begun to feel static and cut-off, as though anything could be happening in the world outside and we would still be here, bent double under the weight of good manners and expectation. Lady Tanith didn't seem to take a newspaper or read online news stories and I wondered if it was because she wanted to inhabit a world where Oswald was still alive. Cock-ups by the current government or scandals of the rich and famous didn't seem to mean anything to her, stuck as she seemed to be in her own grieving.

It was bloody claustrophobic. Even the only-marginally-less closed off scenery of the little estate village was better than the house, where hours felt endlessly recycled, I thought, resting on the little gate in the yew hedge to watch two birds of unknown species fighting over berries. The sun leaned its weight against the hedge which left me in shadow, trying to appreciate the great outdoors while really hoping to flag down a passer-by just to have someone to talk to. Even a dog would do, I thought moodily, picking flakes of paint off the gate, aware that the heroines of novels very rarely had to make do with staring into space and monologuing while watching birds squaring up to one another. Fiction didn't seem to have much to say on the subject of boredom. Ennui was more picturesque but conjured images of wan tubercular heroines in muslin and I had too large a chest and too much nylon to ever be mistaken for a consumptive Miss.

'Hello.' The voice made me jump and I turned around so quickly that I panicked the birds into a metallic chinking as they flew off.

'Oh, Jay! You startled me,' I said, aware as I said it that I sounded like the heroine of a badly written romance. I stopped myself short of clasping my hand to my bosom. 'I didn't hear you coming.'

'Welcome to my world.' He was wearing shorts again, his knees were muddy and covered in grass stains and his socks were rolled down to the tops of his work boots. It made him look like a slightly wicked schoolboy. 'What are you up to?'

I didn't want to blurt out that I knew who he was now. He'd not used his full name when he'd introduced himself to me, so he didn't want me to know, for reasons of his own. Well, that was fine, I didn't care. But I hugged the secret knowledge to me, as though it gave me a measure of power. *He's Jasper. He's renounced his birthright and his brother resents him.* But, of course, now I knew, I couldn't say anything about Lady Tanith and her demands and I'd already let slip Hugo's resentment about his situation. I went a bit clammy round the neck when I remembered how much I'd blurted to Jay when we'd last met, and hoped he'd forgotten most of it.

'I'm out for a walk,' I said quickly to distract myself from the flush of embarrassment, despite all evidence to the contrary.

'Fed up with the Great and Good back at the house?'

I didn't dare acknowledge that. Partly because I wasn't sure who was the great and who the good, and partly because I was terrified I might let some more information slip that Jasper wasn't supposed to know. 'Mmmm,' was all I said, and he could take that however he wanted.

'Would you like a tour of the gardens?'

'Why?'

'What an odd question.' Jay rubbed a hand through his hair. 'Because they are here and you are here and it's my job and I thought you might like to know what's growing? Besides, I'm fed up with weeding and you look as though you might like some company.'

I was a little bit dumbfounded. For a son of Lady Tanith, Jay was incredibly straightforward and ordinary and, dare I say it, thoughtful. Then it struck me that renouncing your heritage, having a mother who had trouble processing this fact and a brother who could hardly bring himself to mention you, might make him rather lonely too. I looked at him. His hair was, as usual, awry and there was something rather endearing about the bare knees and socks, like a grown up *Just William*, only lacking the gang and awful dog.

'All right,' I said. 'That would be nice.'

'Good.' His face was animated now by a broad grin. 'Come on. I'll show you the roses first, very romantic are the roses.'

I had to sit down hard on the urge to tell him that I knew he was gay and so he could stop the slightly arch allusion that he was wooing me. It might have been my imagination, but that tattoo on his wrist seemed very much more in evidence today, the little bouquet tied by the rainbow flicking into view as he pointed to various shrubs and reeled off Latin names.

'I'm impressed,' I said, when he'd shown me his *sorbus aucuparia* and a particularly lovely bed of *dianthus caryophyllus* on our way to the roses. 'How do you know all their names?'

Jay gave me a knowing smile. 'Years of study, hours spent memorising, working with them on a daily basis – and the names are written on little labels, look.' He pointed. Thrust deep among the leaves were indeed small white labels with the Latin names written on.

'Oh. I thought you were being clever.'

Jay's smile broadened. 'Andi, you are too easily impressed. Actually, I wrote the labels, so I have to know the names anyway, but gardening is ninety per cent basic grunt work and ten per cent being stylish. So I like to wheel out the knowledge when I can.'

'Ten per cent stylish,' I said, trying not to stare obviously at his outfit and messy hair.

'I scrub up well. Do you like plants? Have you ever done any gardening?' The smile had faded now and he was rubbing his wrist as though unaware that he seemed to be trying to erase his tattoo.

I shook my head. 'Never had a garden. Buses aren't known for their acres of...' I hunted around for something to use as an example; 'grass,' was what I settled on.

'I suppose not. You've never lived in a house at all?' He really did seem to want to know and it was refreshing change from Hugo's lack of curiosity about my upbringing.

'No. I was born on the bus – no, actually I was born in a hospital, my parents being prepared to compromise their society-smashing beliefs for childbirth. But I always lived on the bus, so no gardens unless you count hours spent playing in parks.' I looked out across the shining grass, where sunlight glimmered off the distant pond and chased through flickering leaves in fairy-wing shadows. 'It's lovely though,' I said, half to myself. 'I didn't know what I was missing.'

'Also a phenomenal amount of getting soaked to the skin, muddy to the elbows and stung, prickled, snagged and ripped by rampant vegetation,' Jay said. 'It's not all skipping through daffodils in the sunshine, whatever Wordsworth might lead you to believe.'

'Wordsworth, that well known market gardener?'

'He was the only author I had to hand.' Jay beamed at me again. 'I bet your sister has got a garden.'

So, he'd remembered my outburst about Jude. I felt that hot sweatiness pull close around me again. 'Well, yes,' I admitted. 'But she learned gardening at school, they all had little plots they were allowed to grow things on. It was a *very* posh school.' Then I remembered that he had probably gone to Eton or somewhere and wanted to bite my tongue off.

'Don't be bitter, Andi,' Jay said quietly, which I thought was a bit rich coming from someone who'd dumped an estate and a mother onto his brother. 'She's still your sister, and it's not her fault that you didn't get the life you wanted.'

I snorted, unbecomingly, at that.

'Anyway. I had better go and make myself look busy. Will you be all right?' His question surprised me, as did his tone. It was oddly gentle and concerned and it crossed my mind to wonder whether he thought Lady Tanith was planning my downfall, in league with Mrs Compton.

'Yes,' I said stiffly. 'Of course. Thank you very much for showing me the garden.' I didn't immediately move off, and neither did he. We stood for a few seconds as though reluctant to part.

'Oh, and I still need my jumper back,' he said eventually. 'So, you know, next time you're passing, because it's bloody freezing at 5 a.m. now.'

His levity was cheering. He wasn't holding anything over me. 'Don't tell me you've only got one jumper.' I looked him up and down. 'Actually no, I can believe that.'

'Oy! I'll have you know that I have a varied wardrobe; it just so happens that one is my favourite jumper and it keeps out the cold really well. So unless you want me to fade away to nothing but a small cough and a blood-stained hanky like one of your louche hero-types, get it back to me, please.'

I grinned as I turned to walk back to Templewood Hall. Jay might be Hugo's brother and as all kinds of messed up as the rest of the family, but he was kind and he made me smile.

He must take after his father's side of the family, because he surely didn't get that sense of the ridiculous and humour from his mother.

14

BAG END – THE HOBBIT, J R R TOLKIEN

Another week crawled its way past, like a horror-fiction zombie.

Summer was inching to a close now. The leaves on the beautiful trees all over the estate were lightly touched with burning colours, the flower displays flared and died back to architectural seed heads and vibrant foliage. The tinkle of the pond fountain began to sound less wonderfully cooling and more like a presage of bad weather.

Hugo and I had great fun with his clothing collection, though. Now I had stopped thinking of him as my future, it was a lot easier to take an interest in his 'hobby', and he sometimes let me try on some of the couture collection. For the first time in my life I found out what it felt like to wear evening gowns teamed with Manolo heels, and if the price was that the man beside me was similarly dressed – well, that was fine. We'd lock ourselves in the Yellow Room most evenings, once Lady Tanith was safely asleep, and dress up, chat and generally form a friendship which was much better for not having an enormous Dior-shaped shadow over it.

Hugo was fun. He was amusing, intelligent and attractive and I found myself having moments where I would wonder whether I really *could* make this my life. But then he'd step out from behind the changing screens in his blonde wig and a dress allegedly once worn by Marilyn Monroe and shoes that cost more than I would earn in a lifetime, and I would know that I couldn't. He looked better in the dresses than I did too, having the straight up-and-down figure that could be padded in appropriate places, whereas I already had the padding and it wasn't always in the right place for the dresses to hang properly.

We talked about our upbringing and experiences. I learned more than I needed to know about what boys got up to at prep school, and Hugo found out that life on the road wasn't a romantic gypsy-idyll of living off the land.

Hugo lived under a weight of expectation. 'Once it was obvious I'd inherit, my life was over,' he said sadly, pulling a zip down slightly to give him room to slump onto the floor.

'Couldn't you have refused? Told your mother to leave the place to a cats' home or something?'

Hugo turned big eyes up to me. 'Would *you* want to say no to my mother?'

I thought about this. 'I see your point.'

'Besides – I do have a sense of duty. Oh, not to Templewood, that's just a house, but to Mother. I know she seems to be sensible and stable...' He busied himself pleating fabric between his fingers, so couldn't see me rolling my eyes. 'But she's very fragile really. When he renounced the estate, Jazz took me to one side and asked me to look after her. It was an easy enough promise back then, she was hysterical and I was thirteen. Over the years I've come to realise just how much of myself I've had to give up to Templewood.'

Hugo said all this in a completely matter-of-fact way, without a trace of self-pity and I realised that he really did love Lady Tanith. I wanted to ask him what kind of love she had for him; how she could happily require him to live this solitary, undemonstrative existence, all good manners and keeping up appearances. It made me realise that money wasn't everything, and that I might have lived in a bus but at least my parents – distant and preoccupied though they might have been – had shown that they loved me, when I'd been a child. Once I'd become an adult they'd somewhat cast me adrift and become wrapped up in their own world, but really? Did that matter? I had my freedom, such as it was. Poor Hugo didn't even have that.

We did have points of contact in our parents though; my father, with his early retirement and large pension fund, sounded similar to Hugo's father Richard: family wealth, no need to work, cruising through life doing what he wanted. Although, in Richard's case, this seemed to consist of keeping the estate up to scratch and indulging in even more book buying – half the library stock was down to him, and his trips abroad to acquire more books had, apparently, given Lady Tanith the opportunity to learn how to manage the estate in his absence. Hence Richard's bequeathing it to her to run on behalf of their sons, rather than directly to his eldest son Jasper.

And when I wasn't pretending to be a Hollywood star at her first premiere, or listening to tales from Hugo's boyhood, I was sneezing my way through cataloguing.

There were no diaries. I'd come to terms with that. If Oswald really *had* kept any, then maybe he'd disposed of them before he set off for Switzerland. Maybe he'd destroyed them in grief when Caroline died. Maybe he'd buried them in the garden, under the arcane workings for the fountain, in the middle of that flowerbed. I didn't know. They certainly weren't anywhere that I could find them, in that dusty, still-too-dark room where I sat for most of every day, staring at a spreadsheet until my eyes bulged.

One morning I woke to my 'day off' and couldn't face my usual routine of going for a walk and hoping to meet Jay again, sitting in my room eating a sandwich that I had furtively made whilst avoiding Mrs Compton's infrequent kitchen activities, and then having an early night. This Sunday being bright and fine, I decided to do some laundry. Not exactly a pastime that was going to bring the men flocking, but then they had so far not hurled themselves through my door whatever my activity, and I needed clean jeans.

Hugo had shown me the washer-drier machine, hidden away at the back of the boot room behind a panelled cupboard door designed to keep the signs of domestic drudgery from the upper class, and I occasionally braved the wrath of Mrs Compton to wash my things.

Today she caught me. 'Slut,' she muttered, walking past me as I wandered back upstairs with my knickers on display in a plastic basket. I thought this was a bit over the top as none of my underwear had any slutty tendencies and all my knickers were quite substantial. I just smiled. Mrs Compton seemed to suffer from a form of class-orientated Tourettes and couldn't stop herself from bursting out in epithets when she saw me. She could, however, restrain herself nicely in the vicinity of Lady Tanith and

Hugo, so I didn't think it was a psychological problem, other than that occasioned by thinking I was beneath everyone.

I took the load of clean and dry laundry back to my room and began sorting through my remaining clothes for other things to wash. The dress needed cleaning. We were, I was aware, looming up to the next twenty-first. I was dreading having to dress up, but I was looking forward to the slap-up breakfast and three course dinner that resulted. I pulled the dress out and laid it on the bed, then went for a rummage in the cupboard I used to keep my clothing in.

There at the front was Jay's jumper. The one he'd draped around me when I'd been soaked, sitting in the icehouse entrance on the day of the storm. I hadn't seen him around much since my tour of the garden, except as a figure on the horizon in big boots and donkey jacket, wielding loppers or a digging tool that looked as though he may be off to a day of serial murdering, so I'd forgotten that I still had his jumper.

He'd asked for it back twice. Here it was, smelling slightly musty. I should take it back, just in case he came up to me during the memorial service to ask for it again, and then I'd have to answer questions from Lady Tanith and Hugo about how I knew Jasper. I really didn't want to give Lady Tanith any more excuses for pursing her lips at me and sighing.

I picked up the jumper, pushed it into the carrier bag that had been my repository for my worn and dirty clothes, and set out. It gave a purpose to my day off and, I reasoned, was merely an extension of my usual stroll around the grounds, although why I needed to justify my activities to myself I wasn't sure. Something of Lady Tanith and Mrs Compton's attitudes perhaps were getting to me more than I cared to admit.

The day had come in misty. Not cold, or warm, just a grey envelope that curtained the world from Templewood, and echoed the dust that I encountered every day. I set out along the path to the estate village, feeling as though I were fighting my way through a haunting. The gravel crunched into the silence, trees were bleak outlines, and drooping autumn flowers occasionally flopped from their restraining beds like sanatorium patients trying to escape.

It was further to the gate in the yew hedge than I had remembered. My jeans and trainers were damp by the time I got there, and the wrought-iron curlicues of the metal gate held beads of water, prism-copies of the grey surrounding me. It was all very atmospheric and portentous. Even the yew, sagging under the weight of its own history, had pleated and curved into horrific shapes that could, to the susceptible, look like agonised faces. I opened the gate, trod my careful way through the churchyard, and on out the other side into the little square of houses.

I knew Mrs Compton lived in one. She had an army of 'day girls' – most of them older than her – who came in to help with the never-ending task of trying to keep Templewood clean, or at least habitable, so some of those must live here too. And there must be other garden staff, although I'd only ever seen Jay, but he wasn't single-handedly keeping the flowerbeds in line and the further reaches of the estate grass cut. There were the carpenters and joiners and plumbers and others who worked locally and were entitled to an estate cottage and whom I occasionally saw wandering about at a distance.

They just weren't in evidence now.

Even though it was a Sunday afternoon, all the houses looked deserted, in their square surrounding a green which bore a maypole like the mast of a schooner which had sunk into the ground. No children played, no dogs barked. It looked like the opening titles of a horror film. I realised that I had no idea where Jay lived, in this Village of the Damned. I couldn't go around and knock on every door, could I? I was half afraid that doing so might awaken something that had been better left asleep, so I walked a small circle on the grass of the village green and tried to look for clues.

All the cottages were identical. Low eaves of thatch, which meant that the upper stories had windows that poked out through the reeds. Small lower casements, diamond-paned in black. Identical red doors, with a glass panel, letting light into, no doubt, identical hallways.

But only one had a climbing rose, past its best now but still spurting its way over the façade in a last show of petals. An immaculate flower border lay under the single downstairs window, bearing a late display of dahlias with their pom-pom heads decorated with fog-sequins like a button box overturned.

It was somewhere to start, anyway, so I crossed the green, leaving a trail of silver footprints behind me, and knocked on the door.

After a few moments of hush, there came a shuffling, and Jay opened the door. He was wearing a fleecy suit and enormous knitted socks.

'Whassamatter?' he asked, blearily, scratching a hand through his hair.

'I brought your jumper back.' I thrust the bag towards him. 'Thank you,' I added.

A gradual, blinking wakefulness arrived on his face. 'Oh! Oh, right. Yes. Right. Good.'

He took the bag, but I'd looped it over my wrist, so we were, for a moment, joined by a Sainsbury's cable, him trying to pull it off over my hand, while I tried to disentangle it so it would slide off. We wrangled for a second.

'Look, it's bloody freezing; come in a second while we get this bag off.' Jay scuffed a few steps back, his socks slithering on the patterned tiles of the hallway floor, and I, drawn by the orange plastic, followed him inside.

A closed door to our right was presumably the living room, fronting onto the green. At the end of the hallway I could see a kitchen, where a couch lined one wall and an Aga another. A cast-off blanket showed that Jay had been lying on the couch.

'Are you all right?' I asked him. 'You're not ill? I wouldn't have come if I'd thought you were ill, I just wanted to bring your jumper back and I found it in with my washing and remembered you wanted it.'

'Oh. A conversation. Hold on a minute.' He let go of the bag and turned, shuffling a floor-clearing way into the kitchen. I followed and caught up as he looped the second hearing aid into place. 'Right. Go.'

Cursing myself for forgetting his deafness, I repeated myself, although I mostly edited it down to asking if he was feeling all right and that I'd brought his jumper back.

I got a smile. 'No. Not ill. I'm good. Just – well, it's Sunday. It's my day off, and if I choose to spend it lying around in my PJs eating crisps and watching Netflix while scratching myself, well. What else are Sundays for?'

I looked around the kitchen. It was warm and bright and tidy and some mismatched blue and white crockery stood on a small dresser in the corner. There was no huge teetering pile of washing up waiting to be done, or damp just-out-of-the-washer clothes mouldering in a basket, and it struck me as unnaturally neat until I realised I was comparing Jay to the only other man I really knew, who was Jude's husband Ollie, whose opinion of housework could be summed up as 'ignore it until it goes away'. 'Too many late nights being dark and tortured?'

'Ah.' A hand scrubbed through his hair again. 'You remembered that.'

'Yes.' I wasn't quite sure *why* I had remembered it. The vaguely Heathcliffian surroundings, perhaps, in that muddy shelter.

'Well, I may have exaggerated a touch. I have terrible insomnia. Awful. So I sleep when I can, which was today…' Now he pointed at the couch. 'Until a literary-inspired presence from the Big House woke me up.'

'No, I didn't,' I said, confidently. 'You must have already been awake.'

Jay tilted his head. 'I… might not have been?'

'You didn't have your hearing aids in. If you'd been asleep you wouldn't have heard me knock.' I waved a hand at the hallway and the front door. 'You were awake and you saw me through the glass door.'

The head tilted further. 'Did your voracious reading happen to include *Sherlock Holmes*, by any chance?'

'It might have done,' I admitted, slightly ashamed. This was Jay's house. He was perfectly entitled to spend his time however he wanted, and it was none of my business whether he'd been awake or asleep. 'Anyway. I'd better go.'

Jay laughed. 'Oh stay and have a cup of coffee or something. You're here now and I've blown my cover as a brooding hero by answering the door wearing a onesie and slipper socks, haven't I?'

Feeling slightly more cheerful, I sat down on the sofa. 'I think you rather shot the brooding hero down when you mentioned watching Netflix, eating crisps and scratching yourself.' I stopped myself from going on to mention that, anyway, I knew he was gay.

'True. Can't, somehow, imagine Mr Darcy rattling about Pemberley dressed like an overgrown nine-year-old whilst filling his face with cheese and onion.' Jay put the kettle on the Aga and spooned coffee out of a labelled jar into two mugs. 'Anyway. How's life up at the House? Have you found those diaries yet?'

Oh God. I'd forgotten that I'd mentioned the diaries. Lady Tanith didn't want her sons to know about them until she'd had chance to 'vet' them first. 'Er. No. I'm beginning to think they're mythical.'

'So you're still cataloguing? How's that going?' He leaned back against the rail of the Aga and looked at me. I found that I was trying to pinpoint his resemblance to Hugo and failing. Jay certainly didn't *look* nine years older than his brother. Perhaps... perhaps Oswald had been *Jasper's* father? But Richard was Hugo's? I tried to remember everything I'd ever gleaned about precedence of inheritance, and whether the age gap between the brothers was sufficient to mean that Jasper had been born around the time that Oswald died. 'I'm sorry, was it a difficult question?'

'Oh, no, sorry. I was... thinking. Yes, still cataloguing. It's going to take me years at this rate, if Lady Tanith doesn't throw me out on my ear first, but I don't think she will because the cat seems to like me.'

'The Master? Yes, he likes me too.'

'Clearly he's an impeccable judge of character then,' I said, and it came out more sarcastically than I meant it to.

'Ah, I'm not so bad.' The coffee was made, and Jay and I sat side by side on the couch to drink it. 'Compared to most people round here, anyway. Have you met Mrs Compton?'

'Oh yes. And you're right. She makes Caligula look like a friendly and polite citizen.'

'She's my next-door neighbour. No wonder she adores Lady Tanith; they were clearly both cast from the same mould. I keep waiting for the evil to seep through the dividing wall, like damp.'

We sipped our coffee. I looked sideways at Jay, who, despite a fair amount of static resistance, had crossed one leg over the other. His upper sock was trailing, his sleeves were up around his elbows and his tattoo was bold along the inside of his wrist.

I had to say something.

'Does the tattoo – does it mean something?'

The mug stopped moving. The trailing sock went still. 'Yes.' Jay hardly lifted his mouth from the mug to speak, so the word was echoey. 'Yes, it does.'

Well, being gay wasn't something to be ashamed of, was it? I mean, unless you were Lady Tanith, of course.

'Is it, like, something to do with Pride?' It was the best way I could think of to let him know that I knew about him, and I was rather smug about the subtlety with which I introduced the subject.

Coffee slopped down his fleecy legs. 'What? No!'

'I'm sorry. I know I'm not supposed to know, and I haven't said anything, only Hugo got a bit – emotional, and he told me.'

Jay was staring at me, eyes huge. The coffee stain was spreading along his knee and the mug was still at an acute angle that meant more spillage wasn't out of the question. 'What the hell? I mean, what can Hugo possibly have to say about *me*?'

I stared back. 'I know there's an age gap, but he's still your brother.'

Jay stood up now. His socks meant he slid a small circle on the floor, like an agitated dog trying to escape a bee. 'No he isn't! I'm sure I would have noticed.'

Something in my chest fell, like a suitcase from a wardrobe. 'He's not? You aren't Jasper?'

'Of course I'm not bloody Jasper! Jasper lives three houses down, but he spends most of his time in London! Why would you think I was Jasper?'

I tried to remember how I'd rationalised it all to myself. 'You said they call you Jay?' was the best I could come up with.

Jay crouched down in front of me. The fleecy onesie bagged just about everywhere it was possible for an all-in-one to bag. 'My name is James,' he said carefully. 'James Williford. I am not, nor have I ever been, please God, related to anyone at Templewood.' His voice shook slightly, I wasn't sure whether with emotion or whether he was trying not to laugh. 'Do you think,' he said, still carefully, 'that you might have been trying to impose narrative structure onto the randomness of life again?'

'It seemed logical,' I muttered into my mug, trying not to look at his face, where amusement was definitely winning out. 'Jay – Jasper. Garden design. And I thought the tattoo might be some kind of gay symbol.'

Jay rubbed at his wrist and pulled his sleeve down to cover the image of those bursting flowers. 'Jasper's gay?' he asked. 'Well, that certainly explains a lot.'

'Only Lady Tanith doesn't want people to know.'

'I bet she doesn't.' Jay had his eyes screwed up, as though he was trying to reframe the way he saw me. 'So you've been going along all this time, thinking that I was part of that, quite frankly, lunatic set-up over at the house? Is that why you talked to me? Is that why you let me show you around the gardens?'

'What?'

'Well, you've been hanging around outside a lot. Then there was the night it rained and we met in the icehouse, and you were *very* chatty when we talked about gardening. Have you been lurking around trying to befriend me because you thought I was a son of the house?' Jay put his endangered coffee down on the pine worktop. 'Because somehow I slotted into your literarily inclined view of how life goes?'

'No!' I got to my feet too. It was unpleasant, being suspected of nefarious practices by a man wearing an all-in-one sleepsuit and huge grey socks. 'I just put two and two together…'

'…and made eleven…'

'Yes, maybe. But I only even suspected you might be Jasper the other day. I didn't want to mention it before because you didn't seem to want me to know.'

'I didn't *know*! If I'd thought you thought I was Hugo's brother I would have disabused you of *that* little notion straight away,' Jay said, heatedly. 'So you went round the gardens with me, thinking that I was Jasper? And not saying anything?'

'How could I? There wasn't much of an opportunity to bring it up, when you were quizzing me about the bus and Jude and things like that. And anyway, I thought I wasn't supposed to know and that you were keeping quiet about your family connections,' I finished, and put the coffee mug down next to his, only harder. 'And I resent your implication that I would only talk to you because I thought you were Hugo's brother.'

With that I swept my way out of the kitchen and, after a brief tussle with the front door, out onto the green. Jay made no attempt to follow me and I wasn't surprised. Mostly, because I didn't think he would want to be seen out in public wearing that terrifying outfit, and also because I could see his point of view.

By my own admission I'd shown that I had half-hearted designs on Hugo and then told Jay that I had found out something that had put me off him. If I *had* thought he was Jasper, particularly before I knew Jasper to be gay –

would I have rewritten the story? Would I have decided that my lot was to marry the elder son, not to inherit, but to enjoy the family wealth and background?

I could see how Jay might think so. *But it wasn't true!* The thought rankled. It wasn't fair either, to assume that I was – in the words of Mrs Compton – a 'gold digger'. All right, I may have come here in the first place with a lot of novel-inspired assumptions and conclusions but I'd put those aside, hadn't I? I'd found out for myself that life wasn't what books had led me to believe it would be, with its meet-cutes and its happy endings.

So, angry with myself, but even angrier with Jay, I stamped my way back across the green, still silent in the mist, and back to the house.

15

THE PRIORY – FOOTSTEPS IN THE DARK, GEORGETTE HEYER

Hugo had brought a few bottles of wine up to the Yellow Room and we were sitting on the floor getting slowly drunk.

'It's Oswald Day tomorrow.' Hugo stretched his legs out and stared admiringly at his feet, clad now in a pair of Dior heels. The rest of him was wearing Chanel, and I told him that it was tacky to mix-and-match designers, but he didn't care.

'Yep. I even washed my dress.' I poured myself another glass. I had never really had much chance to drink alcohol. My parents didn't drink, but Jude had introduced me to WKD on one of her visits home from school, and I quite liked the buzzy relaxation it gave me.

Hugo nodded in appreciation. 'You could always wear one of mine, you know. If you were careful.' He waved an expansive, and slightly drunken, hand at the wardrobes, which all stood open to display their jewel-coloured contents, like three boxes of Quality Street.

'Wasted on me.' I rolled my glass between my fingers. 'But why don't you wear one?'

He tipped his head back in surprise. 'But Mother would see!'

'She has to find out sometime, Hugo. You can't live like this forever. And don't you think you'd stop resenting Jasper so much if you could come out and say, "This is me, I like couture dresses and I look pretty bloody good in them as well"?'

Hugo pulled his legs up under his chin, digging the heels into the carpet. 'Andi. You know my mother. She'd disinherit me faster than you can say "Balenciaga".'

'But would that be so bad? You don't want the estate anyway. You could travel, go out, wear what you want and not have to be restricted to this one little room.' I held up my glass and mock-toasted him. 'Be your own person.'

'You don't know what it was like.' He wrapped silver-clad arms around his knees, sitting like a small, scolded child, only much better dressed. 'When Jazz came out, when he told her that he wouldn't take over the estate, she was *distraught*. Almost as bad as Mrs Compton described her when Oswald died. Mother has – expectations, you see. She likes life to go the way she has it planned out in her head and she doesn't deal well with deviations. That's why she reacted so badly to Oswald dying in Switzerland – not so much because he died, but because he was supposed to come back and marry her. She can be rather – rigid in her thinking. Her father was a duke, you know,' he finished, as though this explained everything about his mother.

'Yes, she said,' I muttered vaguely.

'Anyway, if she disinherits me, I will have to go out and get a job.' Hugo sounded rather more prosaic now. 'All I've ever done is help Mother manage the estate. Like I told you before, I'm not exactly overwhelmed with qualifications, and I think I've just spent too much time at Templewood.'

He sounded so hopeless that I put my head on his shoulder. 'There's a whole world out there, Hugo. Allegedly.'

'I've got nothing else.' He was staring out, past the colourful fashion collection, through the night-darkened window. 'Mother sort of gathered me in, if that doesn't sound too weird. When Jazz... once she knew that he didn't intend to inherit, it became her project to turn me into the Lord of Templewood.' Earnest eyes found mine. 'It's just not *me*, Andi.'

'I don't suppose it's Jasper either. I've never met him.'

Hugo sighed so deeply that my head bounced. 'He's around, somewhere,' he said vaguely. 'He works from home, but he's often down in London. I wish *I* could go to London.'

'Then go. Tell your mother you're away one weekend and go.' I patted the general direction of his arm.

He shrugged now and patted me in return. 'Not sure I've got the confidence for that, Andi. I've always been a bit – well, shy. I'm afraid prep school didn't toughen me up as much as my parents hoped. I wouldn't have the faintest idea how to get about in London or where to go or stay.'

Unworldly, I thought, that was Hugo. Unworldly and his mother wasn't doing him any favours trying to keep him close. She was just making him lonely and isolated and unfit for life beyond the estate. Poor Hugo, who wasn't so dissimilar to me, apart from looking a whole lot better in designer wear. Unfit for life. I nudged him with my shoulder. 'You and I are a right pair, aren't we?' I said.

'You could take me to London,' he said eagerly. 'Show me the sights. I'm fine if I've got someone with me.'

I thought of being Hugo's personal tour guide and minder. Steering him around the city like an eighteenth-century earl dropped into the twenty-first century. Fine for a time-slip rom-com but I had the feeling that in real life it would just be annoying. Hugo might be gorgeous, but he was foppish and ineffectual and I didn't want to have to become a bossy organiser like Jude just to get from place to place.

The sudden thought that perhaps my sister hadn't wanted to be bossy and controlling either, hit me. Perhaps Jude had had to become what she needed to be. If she hadn't channelled her inner Miss Trunchbull she'd be in the same position as me, so she'd done what she had to do, despite the upset it had caused. Just like Jasper.

'We really *do* have a lot in common,' I blurted out.

'I'm sorry?'

'I've never been to London either,' I improvised, not wanting to even try to explain my thought processes. 'So I'd be no good as a guide. I went where my parents decided.' All my life, dictated by my parents. No education, no job prospects, just bumbling through life with a vague hope that it would turn out all right in the end. Shit.

'Yes. I have a lot of sympathy for your position. Which is why I've always talked Mother into keeping you on, when she's been, well... having one of her moments.'

I froze. 'She's talked about firing me?'

'Sometimes. Oh, not often! Just – sometimes. She mutters about you not doing your job and how you haven't found what she wants you to find. I think she may be trying to get you to look for books that are valuable? That she can sell to raise money for the estate?' He looked at me quizzically. 'Mother is only really interested in Oswald's books, anything else is disposable. Besides, a lot of it is Father's collection and she and Father – well, it wasn't the most *affectionate* of marriages, from what I remember.'

'It's... something like that.' I hid my face in my wine glass now.

'Thought so. Sometimes she has a bit of a go about you but I always leap to your defence, Andi. I know how much you need to stay.' A pause. 'Are you *sure* you won't just marry me? It would solve such a lot of problems for both of us.'

I raised my head and looked properly at him. Bony, hairy legs, visible from the knee down under the layers of skirt and ending in a slightly-too-small pair of Dior narrow-toed pumps. His top half wore a bodice covered by a silver jacket, with a padded bra. ('Just to give the dress shape, I'm not into women's underwear.') His wig had moved slightly, due to alcohol. He looked like a debauched society beauty who just hadn't taken much care of her personal grooming lately.

And I knew, once again, that I couldn't marry him. Poor, desolate Hugo, heir to an estate that he didn't want, and a future he was going to hate.

'Sorry, Hugo.' I put my now-empty glass down. 'It wouldn't work. And even if we *were* married, you still couldn't dress up when your mother was about.'

'Suppose not.' He hiccupped. 'I'll just have to wait for Mother to drop off her perch, take over Templewood, get it in a fit state to sell and then' – he made a wild hand movement that nearly spilled his wine – 'head for the hills. Find myself an assistant to steer me through. Maybe I could learn to make friends. An all-boys boarding school wasn't my best preparation for life, but at least I'd have money behind me from the sale of the estate.'

'You can't *buy* friends, Hugo,' I said sternly.

'No.' His momentary animation was gone. 'I know that. If it was simple, like being rich got you companionship, then I'd be fine. I just don't have the right personality to be a playboy, do I?'

I shook my head. Then a thought struck me. 'Who *would* inherit, though? If Jasper doesn't want Templewood, and your mother disinherited you, who would she leave it to?'

'I don't bloody know.' Hugo poured himself more wine. 'Probably leave it to the gardener or something, knowing Mother. Or Mrs Compton. Someone who would "properly take care of the place".' He mimicked Lady Tanith's Dreadfully Upper Class accent.

Oh no, don't give me that thought. I excused myself and headed off to bed, weaving my way down the landing and past the hanging balcony to my room. *Don't start another story, where Jay will inherit if I can persuade Hugo to tell his mother about the frock-wearing. Jay and I...* I stopped, flopping down onto my mattress. *Jay already only thinks that I talked to him because I thought there was something in it for me. When actually... actually I rather like him anyway. Even if –* my eyes began to close *– his clothing choices are nowhere near as lovely as Hugo's.*

Thankfully, I had set an alarm, because I would have slept through Lady Tanith's treasured twenty-first of the month breakfast otherwise. Although that might have been rather better, because I felt decidedly fragile when I tiptoed my way down the stairs to the Breakfast Room and was confronted by the smell of kippers and kidneys, Mrs Compton having taken a leaf out of the *Pride and Prejudice* cookbook this morning.

'Good morning, Andi.' Hugo looked like I felt and we exchanged a glance of regret over the toast and kedgeree.

'Church at eleven thirty sharp, both of you.' Lady Tanith sipped a delicate cup of tea and nibbled a small piece of roll. 'And, after that, a chat in the library, Andromeda, if you would, please.'

My stomach jumped. 'Can we not have the chat in the library before church?' I asked, sticking firmly to only a cup of coffee, despite the goodies on display.

'No. I have work to do. After church.' She got to her feet. 'And appropriately dressed, please. Both of you.'

As she closed the door, Hugo gave me a wide-eyed stare of panic. 'Oh God. You don't think she knows, do you?'

'I think it's more of a dig at us both for wearing jeans on the morning of an Oswald Day. To be honest, I think she'd probably prefer you in a ball gown. Honouring his memory and all that.'

'Don't even joke about it.' Hugo subsided. 'Honestly, I never used to worry about... about Mother finding out. Now *you* know, I'm in a state of perpetual agony.'

'So *tell her.*'

He dropped his gaze. 'You know I can't. For her, for me, for the estate. It's all right, Andi, I've kept this up for the last twenty years, I can keep it up for a bit longer.'

Not for the century or so that your mother is going to live on, I thought, leaving the room to head upstairs. I needed a wash and to wake up properly before I lurched to the library for a morning's dedicated slumping and headache-losing before church. Lady Tanith was so nearly a vampire that it had crossed my mind, when I was still thinking that Marie was real and that I had psychic powers, that this might turn out to be some kind of paranormal horror story. I'd be drained of my blood and life force, to give new energy to Lady Tanith, and I'd continue searching through the library for eternity. Especially given all the mysterious thumpings and footsteps that went on around this place, and the fact that it was so large it could have housed an entire pack of Igors, plus laboratories.

But it wasn't. It was just life, 'boredom and shit', as Jay had described it.

I felt a bit of a pang when I remembered him and his accusations. He'd jumped to unfair conclusions about me, and that made him a judgemental idiot. Which was a shame, when I thought about how nice he'd been that night of the storm, then in the morning, giving me coffee and talking to me about my generally thwarted great expectations, and the tour of the gardens when he'd been wonderfully practical. Jay was genuinely straightforward and straightforwardness and practicality seemed to be in very short supply around the rest of Templewood.

Oh well. Onwards and... onwards. I went to my room to splash my face with cold water before I started in the library, to try to make myself feel awake and able to cope with a day of dusty tomes, a church service, and Lady Tanith. As I climbed the stairs, I wondered how my parents were doing out in Canada. Film crews, travelling and the general bustle of making a TV series didn't leave them much time for postcards and they would probably have phoned Jude with updates. I hadn't even given them the number for Templewood, although I had sent Jude an email to tell her where I was and what I was doing.

Somehow, life here seemed to exist in a bubble. Contact from my family would have been strange, like a message from another planet. They'd be busy, and they knew I could get in touch in an emergency. Jude was probably waiting for me to message and say I was at Truro railway station, could she come and pick me up and was it all right if I stayed in her annexe? Even though this whole venture had been her idea, I'd been able to tell at the time that she gave it about a week before I came running back, unable to cope with real life.

Ha! I sluiced my face. I was showing her! Then I remembered how I'd felt last night and my wondering whether Jude had had to adopt a personality to get away from our upbringing. Perhaps *she* was showing *me*. Being yourself wasn't enough, sometimes you had to find your inner dragon to get through life.

I wondered if Hugo had an inner dragon and if he did, how I could tempt it out so he could have a life.

From overhead, in the attic, came the creaking again. I'd learned to ignore the strange noises that the house made, wind whistling through gaps in the woodwork, rattles and bangs and drips, but I had never got used to the footsteps. If that was what they were. I was still clinging on to the hope that mice or squirrels in the attic could account for the regular, board-to-board groan, as though the woodwork was being subjected to pressure.

I raised my head. It could be rats? But only if they were extremely large – which I didn't want to think about. Birds? I knew they scuffled in and out somewhere above my window, I'd seen their shapes as newly fledged youngsters dropped into the air and launched out across the acres. Swifts had built nests like small, upturned pots under the guttering and frequently lined up along fences or overhead wires to prepare for leaving. Maybe they were responsible for the noises in the attic?

No ghosts, I told myself firmly. There were no ghosts. No madwomen in attics, no secret girlfriends. There was a perfectly reasonable excuse for that slow, soft tread. Hugo was downstairs in the Breakfast Room still, making a brave and spirited attempt to force down some scrambled egg – or at least, he had been when I left him. He had no reason for secrecy now, anyway.

So, was Lady Tanith in the attic? Why would she have any need, or desire, to go up there? She'd got the whole of the house to stalk around in, being haughty and officious, and unless she'd got ranks of minions in the attic to command, I couldn't see her putting in the effort to fiddle about in dusty, deserted rooms.

It must be Mrs Compton, I thought with a sudden relief, as I tracked the noises across the ceiling, from the bathroom, along the landing, to come to a sudden halt above the wing that contained the library below and Lady Tanith's rooms above. I wasn't normally upstairs at this time of day. I'd usually go directly from breakfast to the library, so Mrs Compton may well spend her mornings dusting and polishing whatever lay at the top of the house. She must, after all, do *something* with her time, because she certainly wasn't spending it on cleaning the rest of the house. Or maybe – I tilted my head to try to catch a sound, but there was nothing – it really *was* rats? Rats were, I hated to think it, more likely than Mrs Compton cleaning.

The library was cold. Despite the fact that there was an enormous fireplace in one wall, it was obvious that nobody had thought that heating the room was a priority, and I shivered my way through another shelf-worth of dusty tomes. Nothing of any note had come to light, apart from some rather nice early editions of Dickens with illustrations, which I'd whiled away a pleasant couple of hours with, catching up with favourite characters. Most of the rest were bound editions of court reports; histories of countries now absorbed into their neighbours and renamed and which, some cursory reading told me, were probably a lot better off no longer under the rule of whoever wrote the histories; or interminable numbers of the driest novels I'd ever opened.

I hadn't yet found any of Oswald's writings, let alone his diaries, although I could only too well imagine him in here, bent over the desk with his pen and sheaves of paper, composing away. I wondered if he had ever come dashing in from a day on the estate, in full shooting kit or riding gear, trailing mud and inspiration, to scribble down some lines of poetry that had come to him as he had... done whatever he did around the place.

Then I thought of the truly dreadful poetry that Lady Tanith had quoted at me, and hoped that, if he had, someone else had had the sense to burn it.

I looked up at the painted face which glared at me as though reading my thoughts, and wondered what had really gone on in this house. A man, in full middle-age with an ailing and frail wife, and a young and – although it pained me to admit it – beautiful woman. Perhaps it had been inevitable. Mid-life crisis meets doting admirer, well, there was only one outcome, wasn't there? Maybe Caroline had colluded in their relationship? Perhaps she had known all along that her husband was seducing her companion? Maybe – the thought crept into the back of my head, almost unwanted – maybe that was why Lady Tanith wanted so badly to find those diaries? Perhaps they would prove that Caroline had tacitly approved of her relationship with Oswald, her lusty and in-the-prime husband, while she was ill and incapable. Could the diaries relieve Lady Tanith of a guilt she'd carried all these years, about her relationship with Oswald?

Then the thought of Lady Tanith feeling guilt about anything, ever, met my daydreaming, and I shook my head. I was doing it again, trying to impose a narrative onto someone's random actions. Lady Tanith wanted the diaries because she wanted them, that was all. Nothing secret, just her desire to publish, probably with appropriate editing, his final works to complete the set.

No stories. No narrative. Just, as Jay had said, heartbreak and then the daily grind.

I changed into my dress at the appointed hour, and made my way to the church, with Hugo toddling alongside, full of excitement about an online auction for some dresses that had, apparently, once been owned by Princess Grace of Monaco.

'I'm not sure of their wearability,' he chuntered. 'But I could keep them to look at, couldn't I, Andi?'

I smiled at him, rather sadly. 'Hugo, you can't keep on living like this you know.'

He deflated instantly. 'I do know, Andi. I really do.' His lovely face retreated into lines of defeat and sadness. 'But I don't know how to stop.'

'Do you really not have any friends at *all*?'

Hugo held the gate for me and I brushed between the yew hedges ahead of him, feeling the prick and scratch of the needles like real life trying to intrude again. 'Not really. There's a few people I email sometimes, some dress suppliers, a few costume historians. But I've never met any of them, we're more like pen pals. After all, I can't leave Mother.'

We were early to the church and took our places in the pew at the front, where Lady Tanith was already seated, head bowed and veil in place. Behind us, I could hear the coughs and shuffles of the estate workers filing into their seats, but I didn't turn around to see if Jay was there. A hot wash of shame came over me every time I remembered our last encounter. He'd jumped to conclusions, but then, hadn't I been leaping to fairly large ones myself since I came here? I'd thought he was Jasper, on really flimsy evidence, when I could have asked Hugo whether his brother was a gardener instead of assuming he must be. So Jay's presumption that I'd only talked to him because I thought he was Hugo's brother could be seen as a fairly natural progression of ideas.

I got hot again with second-hand embarrassment, but it was just as well because the chill in the church rivalled that of the library. There weren't enough people in here to warm the place up, and there was clearly no heating, or none that anyone chose to turn on. I wished I'd worn a thicker top over the dress. I wished I *had* a thicker top. Maybe I could get away with borrowing one of the ancient furs ('rumoured to have been part of Marlene Dietrich's collection') that Hugo had tucked away in the third wardrobe. No. I'd never worn fur in my life, objected to it on principle, and my mother would have disowned me if I had.

I gave a tiny inner giggle, which Lady Tanith clearly picked up on because she side-eyed me during the sermon. My mother had nothing to disown me *from*. We'd always lived a fairly impecunious life, at least, until the YouTube channel had taken off and the TV companies had started sniffing around. My father's money had bought the bus, paid expenses and Jude's eye-watering school bills. I was hardly going to inherit a fortune, and given that my parents were in their late fifties and in excellent health, by the time I inherited anything, should there be anything *to* inherit, I'd probably be in my sixties and not know what to do with it. Plus, it would probably be a heap of rusted metal in a barn. I snorted again and Lady Tanith elbowed me.

'A sense of *propriety*, Andromeda, please!' she hissed.

I composed my features to look suitably attentive to the ongoing service and tried to keep them that way as the service finished. Lady Tanith led the way out of the church and I, not willing to risk another elbow, kept my distance, letting Hugo take his mother's arm.

'Andi.'

I turned around to see Jay, wearing the suit he always wore for church and an inexpertly knotted tie, behind me. He was sitting in one of the pews at the very back of the church as everyone filed out past him.

'Jay.' I had been going to acknowledge him and walk on, but he caught my arm as I reached the pew.

'Can I talk to you?' he asked. He looked tired and roughly shaven, his hair scooped away from his face.

'What about?' I stopped, and Mrs Compton pushed her way past me with a look of supreme malediction, as though I were consorting with Satan himself. But then, she looked at me like that when I was doing nothing more blameworthy than stroking the cat, so I took no notice.

'Oh, not "about" anything. Just, you know, generally.' Jay smiled. 'I'm really sorry if I was rude to you the other day.'

I waited for him to come up with a 'but', but he didn't. He let the apology lie, unexcused, so I slid into the pew next to him.

'And I'm sorry if I gave the impression that I only talked to you because I thought you were part of the family,' I said. 'I should have known that you're far too nice to be anything to do with Lady Tanith and her family.'

Jay snorted a laugh. 'I don't know. Jasper's all right. And I've met Hugo quite a few times, he seems OK.'

'Look, I've got to go,' I said, conscious of Hugo and Lady Tanith just outside the church door, mingling with the tenants. 'Lady Tanith wants a chat in the library.'

'With the lead piping?'

'I'm sorry?'

'Nothing. It's a game. Cluedo.' Jay shook his head. 'Please don't tell me you never played Cluedo on the long, dark nights in your bus.'

I remembered the long, dark nights in the bus. Jude away at school, my parents fussing about doing something. Dad checking the engine, Mum sorting out stuff for the next laundrette we passed or making a list of provisions we'd need when we got to the next town. Me, reading. Always reading, in a corner somewhere, with a little battery-powered light.

'Not really. But come up to the house after lunch. I'll be in the library. We can talk in there.'

Jay hesitated, lowering his voice as Mrs Compton came back past us again and strafed us both with her disgust. 'I'm not sure. Lady Tanith probably doesn't allow ground staff in the house. I wouldn't want you to get into trouble for fraternising, if she caught you.'

'It's fine. I'll let you in through the window. Once she's read me the riot act, I suspect she'll have to go for a lie down anyway. Lady Tanith seems to spend an inordinate amount of time lying down or resting, and I suspect that a conversation with me will enrage her into a couple of hours' shut-eye. Besides,' I grinned, 'the door locks.'

Jay gave a one-sided nod. 'All right then. I'll creep up to the house like a boot boy meeting the tweeny, shall I?'

'I have no idea what you just said, but yes.' I looked up to see Hugo making frantic beckoning motions to me, behind his mother's back. 'I'd better go.'

'Right. I'll come up later and peer through the window to make sure you're alone. Don't be alarmed if you see me squeezed up against the glass.' Jay looked happier now, less tired.

'As long as you haven't got your willy in your hand again...'

Of course, at that point Mrs Compton, who had apparently returned for a lost umbrella, walked back up the aisle again, bearing the forgotten brolly and an obvious desire to try to overhear us. My final words sent her eyebrows into her hairline and the rest of her scuttling outside as though the mention of willies offended every sensibility she had.

'Willy decently restrained. Trust me.' Jay grinned again. 'Go on. Hugo's having a small fit out there.' He nodded towards the doorway. Mrs Compton had reached Lady Tanith and was giving her a meaningful look, whilst Hugo was rotating with anxiety and making 'come on' motions that made it look as though he was groping the air.

Feeling a lot happier, suddenly, I squeezed my way out of the pew and went outside to join Lady Tanith, Hugo, and the combusting Mrs Compton.

16

THE BURROW – HARRY POTTER, J K ROWLING

'I can't help feeling' – Lady Tanith looked across the desk at me – 'that you haven't really been trying to find' – she lowered her voice although Hugo was in the kitchen, helping Mrs Compton load the dishwasher after lunch – '*Oswald's diaries.* Not putting in sufficient effort.'

Behind us the door squeaked open a few centimetres and The Master oozed in through the gap.

'I've looked everywhere I can think of,' I said. 'Honestly, Lady Tanith. Are you *sure* that they were definitely in here?'

'Why would I not be?' Lady Tanith patted her lap in invitation, but the cat strolled up to me and yowled his Siamese yell.

'Because, short of dismantling the walls, I can't think of anywhere else to look, and I haven't found them. I have managed to catalogue all those books, though.' I waved at the one wall of shelving that I'd cleared, entered onto the spreadsheet, dusted and returned.

'Hmm.' Lady Tanith blew through her nose and eyed me strangely. The Master jumped onto my lap and sat facing her across the desk with his back to me and the tip of his tail twitching. His solid weight forming a barrier between me and his mistress, was reassuring. 'I can't help feeling you could be doing more.'

'I'll keep looking. Why must they be in here, though? Couldn't Oswald have put them somewhere else in the house?' Without thinking I began stroking the cat's ears and the top of his chocolate head. He purred.

'Oswald did all his writing in here, his novels, his poetry and his diaries. The other things...' Tanith hesitated as the cat put his front paws onto the desk and eyeballed her, almost as though he were interviewing her. 'The other things I know the whereabouts of,' she went on. 'But not the diaries. They *must* be in here.'

'Have you thought about taking up the floor?' I asked, sarcastically.

'Well, yes. We removed the carpeting and checked for loose boards, hidden vaults, that sort of thing,' Lady Tanith replied as though taking up the floor was as reasonable as dusting the furniture. 'But there was nothing. Let me tell you, I am considering terminating your employment. Replacing you with someone who is a little more... diligent, shall we say.'

The cat yowled again. I carried on stroking, whilst I thought furiously. Being fired from what was, essentially, a data-entry job, wasn't going to look great on my CV, such as it was. Leaving Templewood would mean leaving Hugo friendless, and me, either in the bus mouldering away the winter, or child-wrangling for Jude.

'However.' Lady Tanith switched her attention from the cat back to me. 'Hugo seems to like you. We really must secure the next generation, so that Templewood remains in the Dawe family, if you understand me, and he has so few friends apart from the boys he was at school with, who rarely visit. You have no society connections, of course, and you are rather' – a curled lip and a contemptuous pass of the beady stare – 'less physically fortunate than I would have chosen for my son, but beggars really can't be choosers here, and he's not getting any younger.' Now she leaned forward until she was practically on my lap. 'So I would be *most grateful*,' she said, giving the words a spin that made them sound threatening, 'if you and Hugo were to form – an alliance. It must be legally sanctioned, of course, none of this "out of wedlock" nonsense. And a watertight pre-nuptial agreement would be required.'

Lady Tanith stood up now. 'And find those diaries,' she said. 'You're only here because Hugo and The Master like you.' She swept out of the library and closed the door with a genteel little click that rebounded from the panelled walls like a gunshot.

'Oh heck,' I said to the cat, who seemed, as far as a cat can, to agree.

About an hour or so later, I was alerted to Jay's presence outside the window by The Master who bit me lightly on the wrist and then leaped off my lap to stand by the wall. When I looked up, there was Jay's dark form outside, his face smeared against the glass like a cartoon villain.

'Knock it off.' I opened the window next to him, to avoid breaking his nose. 'And come in.'

Jay put both hands on the lower sill, hopped, and swung his legs inside. The rest of him followed, wearing his gardening clothes, and boots. He had a rolled-up newspaper under his arm.

'What's that? Ancient court reports that prove that the Templewood estate should belong to some distant relative with whom we were previously unacquainted?'

Jay gave me a straight stare. 'It's to put down so I don't get mud on the carpet.' He spread the paper on the floor and stepped onto it. 'Told you. Life's not like the books.'

By carefully spreading the papers, he crossed the room and sat down on one of the leather sofas that I was using to pile books on. He looked at the dust-ridden volumes as he moved them onto the floor.

'Wow. These look like riveting stuff.'

'Almost not at all.' I sat down on one of the more comfortable armchairs, and The Master plopped back up onto my lap again. 'So, how are you?'

'I'm...' Jay pushed his hair back with both hands. 'I'm fine. I've not seen you about lately?'

I waved at the window. 'Weather. Plus Lady Tanith is now giving me ultimatums about finding these diaries and/or marrying Hugo to secure the succession, preferably both.'

'Well, that's this weekend taken care of.' Jay leaned back on the sofa. 'What are you doing next week?'

'Stop it, she's serious.' I looked at him, casual and relaxed with one leg folded over the other, gobbets of wet mud dropping from his boot onto the paper. 'What about you?'

'What about me?'

'In all your tortured darkness.'

'Ah, yes, that.' Jay leaned forward and made a squeaking noise which made The Master prick up his ears. 'I may have exaggerated a wee bit.'

'You're dark,' I observed.

'Not tortured though.'

I remembered his face, that night in the storm, sitting in the icehouse. He had looked tortured then, face drawn and he'd been hunched around himself as though in pain. Plus, being out in the middle of the night in a storm was a bit of a giveaway. 'I think you might be,' I said softly.

Jay pushed his hair back again. His hearing aids were in, and I wondered if he did the hair thing subconsciously, to show them off. To let everyone know that he wasn't perfect. As he raised his arms, his sleeve fell back and the tattoo on his wrist became lines, telling a story I didn't yet know.

'OK, maybe a little bit. But nothing terrible,' he said. 'Being partially deaf is bad enough, but it's not really torture-worthy, just a pain. Great when I don't want to listen, though. I take my aids out and, bang, people can rant away to their heart's content and I'm practically oblivious.'

The Master jumped down from my lap and up onto the sofa beside Jay, looking into his face with those huge blue eyes. Jay smiled and began stroking the creamy back.

'It's the tattoo, isn't it?' I asked, still gentle. 'You want everyone to think that your hearing is the problem, but it's that drawing on your wrist, that's what it's all about.'

Jay stopped watching The Master and looked at me, a sudden, direct look that held – something, a depth and an assessment, as though he was trying to work me out. 'I take it back. Those books did teach you something worth knowing,' he said. His voice was level, but quiet.

'Not so much the books, more meeting different people every couple of weeks. I had to learn to sum people up fast, you see. Too many of them thought we were Travellers, so we got a lot of resentment and downright hatred, when people thought we were the vanguard of a load of others who were going to come and camp in the middle of their town or village. You needed to be able to spot those people and steer clear. Most people were fine, though. Friendly, up to a point.'

'Ah, I see.'

'Would you like a cup of tea?' I waved at the flask on the table.

'Not if Mrs Compton made it, no. I think that woman wants to be the last man standing as the world crashes and burns, and she's not above arsenic and petrol bombs to make sure it happens.'

'I made the tea.' I stood up and poured us two plastic cups of tea. 'Returning the favour from the other week. You made me coffee.'

'I did.'

The cup formed a barrier, as I had hoped it would. It had worked for me talking to Jay; somehow having something to do with your hands made opening up easier. I sat down on the chair opposite him.

'The tattoo is in memory of my sister.' Jay shook his cuff and held out his arm. Against the tanned skin the black lines blended, as though he'd been born with them like a birthmark. 'Her name was Flora, hence the flowers. She loved rainbows too, and she told me whenever I saw one, she'd be there, which is why I have that symbol too.'

'What happened?' I was sipping as I spoke, and he frowned.

'Sorry. I can half-hear you but I can't see your mouth. I do a combination of working out words and lipreading. These things help but they have their limitations.' He pointed at his ear. 'Makes for some *incredibly* amusing misunderstandings.'

I knew he was trying to distract me. Something bad had happened. I put the cup down and looked levelly at him. 'Tell me.'

A half smile, as though he knew what he was doing and he knew I knew. He began to stroke the cat again and his tattoo flickered in and out of sight, like a stop-frame cartoon.

'I think you can deduce from my use of the words "in memory", that she died.' He kept his eyes on the cat. 'A rare form of leukaemia. She was sixteen, three years younger than me. That's pretty much it.'

'And that night in the icehouse?'

'You don't let up, do you?' But it was said with a smile. 'As I said, I have dreadful insomnia. Sometimes, when it rains – I can't believe I'm saying this, it sounds like it's straight from some dreadful overwrought novel – when it rains, and I have my aids in, it's like I can hear her voice. Whispering, you know? That night I'd had an acute dose of self-pity, and I was sitting outside just listening. Pretending Flora was talking to me, giving me advice. She was great at telling me what to do, the job of little sisters everywhere, knowing better than their older siblings.'

The Master climbed onto Jay's lap, as though to console him, treadling his paws.

'And that's it. That's my torture. Not really a torture, just – a memory. A sad memory that's ten years gone.'

'Oh, Jay,' I said. I could hear his loss in his voice. 'I'm so sorry.'

A shrug. 'I was at uni when she died. I'd been studying biosciences, but I lost heart, quit and came home. Mum and Dad are gardeners, Mum has a landscaping business, so I went into that. Turns out I'm quite good at plants.'

'And fountains.' I needed to make him smile, to lift that terrible expression of lost lives, lost opportunities from his face.

I succeeded. 'Ah yes. That pond is a horror show all on its own. Whoever thought of putting the controls in the middle of a flowerbed wants shooting. To be honest, they probably were shot. The Holmdale family weren't noted for dying peacefully in their beds.'

He stopped talking and leaned his head back, looking around at the library. I saw him taking in the dark panelling, the racked shelving, ladders and random seating, then, finally, the enormous portrait. He pulled a face.

'That's Oswald,' I said. 'Hugo's grandfather, previous owner, dreadful poet and long-lost love of Lady Tanith. Although not her husband, before you ask; she married his son.'

'An American TV soap just called, they're missing their plot line.' Jay shivered. 'Blimey, it's freezing in here.'

'Yes. I've asked Hugo if I can have a portable heater. I didn't dare ask Lady Tanith; she'd probably just set me on fire, cut out the middle man.'

There was a moment of quiet. Jay really was easy to be quiet with, he sat lightly amid it, instead of forming a hole that needed filling. At last he said, 'It really all comes down to siblings, doesn't it?'

I'd been staring at a wall of books whose spines informed me that they were the collected minutes of the Yorkshire Fly Fishing Society. I was absolutely dreading getting around to those. 'Sorry? What does?'

Jay raised his eyebrows. 'If we're thinking narratively. You, with a sister you resent for having the life you want...'

'I do not! Not if it means having to be married to Ollie. He farts way too much and he's thinking of taking up golf.'

'You know what I mean. She got away. Went to school.'

I sighed. 'Oh, that. Yes. You're right, I do resent her a bit. She's so much the person I wish I could be.'

Jay shifted on the sofa and another glob of mud fell from his boots onto the newspaper. 'You're not so bad,' he said. 'And then there's Hugo, resenting his brother for having freedom and not being bound up with the estate.'

I had a fleeting memory of Hugo, tied to the Yellow Room by designer chains. 'True.'

'And there's me. I mean, I don't have sibling issues as such, but I miss Flora so much that it *feels* like issues. Issues with nobody to blame because she would far rather have been here than not. Nobody's fault. Just life. And you can't go on blaming life forever, can you?'

'I'm going to have a bloody good go.' I poured myself more tea.

It was Jay's turn to look around the walls again now. 'All these books. All these stories,' he said.

'To be fair, quite a lot of them are non-fiction.' I carefully held the tea mug down so he could see my face. I was learning.

'Maybe, but even the non-fiction has been ironed into a narrative, hasn't it? Otherwise it's just random events. *Life* is random events. Books have to have some kind of arc and if only life followed that pattern it would be so much easier, wouldn't it? If we all knew we had a purpose, or an end goal. A final chapter.'

I looked at him. There was a kind of amusement on his face, but it was a dark amusement of the sort you get from reading Poe under the bedclothes. 'You think about things way too much,' I said.

He sighed now. 'Yeah. Flora always said that about me too. But there's not much to do around here except think and read *Gardeners' World*. I could talk about buddleia propagation if you'd prefer.'

'Maybe talking about gardening would be more comfortable,' I said. 'I've got about forty thousand books still to get through, and your opinion of them is beginning to make me want to throw them all out of that window instead.'

So we drank our tea and talked about gardening for the next hour or so. I actually knew more about plants than I thought I did – thanks to my Wiccan period when I'd read everything on herbs I could find, and I'd remembered quite a lot from our previous tour of the gardens – and it was only when the windows started to darken that Jay stood up. 'Look, I'd better go. Things to get on with. Those trees won't prune themselves, you know.' He took half a careful step towards me. 'Come over to mine, next Sunday,' he said. 'We could have lunch.'

'Do you promise not to wear the onesie?'

He was already halfway over the window sill on his way out, collecting up the muddy newspapers behind him as he went, like a children's game. 'The onesie, along with my willy, will not be in evidence.'

'You aren't going to let me forget that, are you?' I stood with my arms on the ledge, watching him drop down onto the garden below.

'Nope. Neither, I suspect, will Mrs Compton. I don't think she wants you to marry Master Hugo, so watch out for botulism and poisonous frogs in your bed.'

'In this house,' I said, as he waved a hand in farewell, 'that's almost a permanent state of alert.'

In the twilight, I could almost believe even Oswald smiled at that.

17

PEQUOD – MOBY DICK, HERMAN MELVILLE

I redoubled my searching efforts, mostly visibly and mostly to reassure Lady Tanith that I wasn't just sitting in the library twiddling my thumbs and drinking tea. I cleared all the shelves I hadn't made my way through already, piling books randomly around the floor in teetering heaps, moved all the furniture, rolled up the carpet and generally made the place look as though I were leaving no stone unturned.

There *were* no stones to turn. I pressed, pulled and twisted every jutting moulding and shelf edging, to reveal an enormous lack of secret passages, priest holes or hiding places of any description. Oswald's giant expression now looked to be disappointment tinged with relief. Anything this well-hidden wasn't *meant* to be found, surely. I knew Lady Tanith wanted to publish the diaries, together with reprints of Oswald's novels and poems, 'for the students of the future, who will, no doubt, regard him as the genius he was.' But maybe the diaries were less of an insight into his working methods, and more of a record of his sexual exploits? Lady Tanith may have been his muse, but perhaps he had been less interested in listing the ways she inspired his creative juices and more in noting the various, and no doubt ambitious, ways she inspired all his other juices?

But my efforts reassured Lady Tanith to the extent that she allowed me to have a small gas-fired heater in the library. The room was so big that the heater didn't do much more than take the edge off the cold, but by sitting almost right up against it to fill in the spreadsheet, I could at least keep my fingers mobile.

When Sunday rolled around, I put on some clean jeans and set out for Jay's house on the green. The sun had cracked the clouds today, giving rise to a deceptively mild day as though summer were coming, rather than going. The grass was greener, the flowers were perky and scenting the air, and there were a few people moving about in the village. The carpenter whom I had come across around Templewood was painting a window frame and two ladies I recognised as part of Mrs Compton's coven of cleaning helpers were sitting on a bench chatting. A man walking a dog raised a hand in greeting, and two small children, poking the ground with sticks, stopped their prodding for a moment to stare at me as I walked up to Jay's front door and knocked. I didn't examine the idea that everything looked better because I was going to be seeing Jay; it seemed superfluous.

'He in't in, miss,' the larger of the children offered. 'He had to go down to trains, yesterday.'

Oh bugger.

'Aye. His mum were taken badly,' the smaller child said. 'But he left you a note.'

'Shurrup, stupid, note might not be for 'er.'

''Tis so! Cos, cos he told me, right. He told me a lady were coming and to make sure she saw the note. So it's you who's stupid, Marcus Dalby!'

The two of them set to what looked to be a pleasurable and often repeated scrap, while I fished out the note from where it had been jammed under the doorknocker.

Andi,

So sorry to have to call off our lunch, but my mum has broken her arm in the middle of preparations for a London landscaping event, so I'm heading home to give Dad a hand for a few days, to make sure all the basics are covered. Hopefully we can reschedule once I'm back.

Take care, don't work too hard and don't eat anything that looks like

paté, I haven't seen Mr Compton around in a while and Mrs C has got a really effective mincer and one hell of a temper. Catch you later.
Jay x

Despite my disappointment, I found I was laughing. Jay had thought of me to the extent of leaving a note, which was good. I pushed it into my pocket and headed back, past the still-fighting boys, through the churchyard, past Oswald's phallic memorial and into the gardens of Templewood Hall.

Hugo and his mother had gone out to lunch. I'd watched them drive away before I'd left, grateful that I didn't have to explain where I was going to either of them. Not that Hugo would have minded, he seemed to quite like Jay whenever he spoke about him, but Lady Tanith seemed to think that I should be sealed into the library and not released until I'd found those bloody diaries.

The house was empty when I got back. It even *felt* empty. Mrs Compton also had Sundays off, 'unless it's an Oswald Day,' Hugo had remarked, so there was no ghastly presence stalking the corridors with pithy, insulting one-liners to aim at my head. It was just me and The Master.

I made myself a sandwich, being careful to avoid anything that looked as though Mrs Compton had had a hand in its manufacture, and wondered how, when she could cook such wonderful meals on Oswald days, she managed to churn out such utter slop the rest of the month. Then I took my sandwich for a walk around the downstairs rooms for no other reason than I didn't know what to do with myself.

The sun continued to shine, and the rooms continued in their peeling paint and emptiness. The Master strolled along slightly behind me, like a small, round chaperone, cocking his head when I opened each door as though querying why I could *possibly* want to go into the Morning Room or the Drawing Room when there were no comfortable fires to sit in front of. I tweaked a few cupboards in case Oswald's diaries had migrated from the library, but found nothing more interesting than about forty thousand back copies of the *Radio Times* from the 1970s and loads of disused biros. Still eating, I trudged upstairs, with half a mind to get changed and go into the library to see if there was a Netflix account set up on the computer while nobody was around to see me watching it, but I only got as far as the top of the stairs when The Master took off. As though he'd been bitten by something, he leaped into the air and ran full pelt the length of the landing that ran away from my room and across the top of the house towards Lady Tanith's wing, with a yowl that sounded like pain.

'Master? Puss?' I called, walking in the direction he'd gone, but cautiously. I didn't know this part of the house, which was strictly Lady Tanith's territory and, as she was terrifying enough in the public rooms, I had never wanted to encounter her one-to-one in her private suite. I had a vague fear that it might be full of bodies, or, even worse, living people kept chained up.

'Puss? Are you all right?' I stopped, but everything was quiet. Great. It would just be my luck for the cat to have some kind of fit and drop dead on my watch. A distant yowl set me off again, walking an interminable corridor, where the few windows gave a view over the high, far hills where the bracken was turning to flame and the sky met the land so sharply that it was almost audible. This side of the house looked out towards the moorland rather than the domesticated garden view of the wing that Hugo and I occupied; the panelling was older and covered with the drill holes of woodworm, the curtains more sun bleached and tattered. Lady Tanith was clearly dedicated to keeping everything here exactly as Oswald would have known it, to the extent of not so much as replacing a light bulb.

Another corner, a closer yowl and I was standing surrounded by doors, while the cat writhed on the carpet.

'Are you all right? What's the matter?' I bent down towards The Master. He was trying to hook a paw under the nearest door, alternately pressing his nose to the gap and prodding a clawed foot into the space. 'Is it a rat? Or a mouse? Oh, please not a rat...' Hugo was terrified of rats. Not because of their essential rodenty nature, but because he was afraid one would get into his clothing collection and chew holes. It was one reason that he was happy to give The Master the run of the house – the other, of course, being that his mother wanted the cat to have the run of the house, and he was not going to stand up against her any time soon.

'Is there something in there?' I asked the cat.

In answer, he lay on his side and poked the paw further in.

I tried the door. It wasn't locked, to my surprise, and opened onto a small and narrow staircase of the kind that servants used to access the attic rooms without being visible to the household in general. The Master shot up the stairs as though he were being summoned by magic and I, aware of some vague duty of care to the cat, followed him.

The attics were huge. A big, rambling space, split into smaller rooms littered with boxes, broken vases, big hats, old board games, almost anything one could shove up into an attic. Huge beams arched above my head and occasionally demarcated the floor into sections as I padded after the cat, who had vanished except for an occasionally sighted twitch of dark tail and a spooky screeching.

Gosh, the space was big. I looked around, trying to get my bearings. Tiny windows in the eaves gave me glimpses of bits of sky or treetops, none of which was much good for ascertaining my position, and the boarded floor, which was remarkably free from dust, gave no clues either. I had to look for landmarks among the junk as I went, and when I turned left at the same broken hat stand twice, I gave up and resigned myself to being lost.

'Puss! Master, come *on*.' I hoped the cat knew where he was. Presumably, he'd also know how to get out of here, if I could only find him. 'Puss?'

A muffled miaow. I rounded another corner and saw a chocolate tail and paws squeezing their way through a narrow gap between two beams. Hoping for a shortcut, or at least, not a *nest* of rats, I followed him.

And stopped.

And stared.

And guessed what the noises in the ceiling had been.

In a secret corner, under a small window, stood a table. On that table, in a rather terrifying parody of a religious setting, there were some candles standing in front of some photographs, which were propped against the wall.

I went closer. One photograph was quite large, a black and white shot of what had evidently been a wedding, although the way the paper had been cut in half told me that the bride had been excised with a pair of scissors, leaving the groom alone and handsome in his morning suit, smiling at the camera. It was Oswald. Younger than his portrait and showing the immaculate bone structure that Hugo had inherited, he stood among similarly besuited guests, none of whom were visible as more than mannequins of elegance.

All the other pictures were of Oswald too: Oswald fishing, Oswald astride a large, bow-fronted horse, Oswald sitting on a fence with a small child. In pride of place, right in the centre of the table and resting on a pile of books which had Oswald's name printed on the front in gold embossing and various pretentious titles, was a colour photograph of Oswald, looking rather ill-at-ease, standing next to a radiant, and much younger, Lady Tanith.

The footsteps I'd been hearing and putting down to ghosts, or the even more unbelievable concept of Mrs Compton cleaning, must be Lady Tanith's visits to what I was trying not to think of as an altar to Oswald. Ghosts might have been preferable.

Oh boy. I turned sharply and began to tiptoe my way back, between the beams, down the attic and as far away from the shrine to Oswald Dawe as I could go. At some point in my retreat, The Master caught up with me, a deceased rodent of some variety in his jaws and a contented look on his little furry face, but I was too horrified even to be repulsed.

Lady Tanith was bonkers. Absolutely and totally quacking round the pond. I'd thought she'd limited herself to the enormous painting and some misty memories, but no, she'd gone full *Misery*. I'd half expected to find Oswald's corpse in there, desiccated and withered on the table, covered in flowers.

The cat and I found, by some miracle, the tiny staircase down to the main house and I ran down almost without touching the treads, slamming the door shut behind me, as though the resultant draught could take the memory of what I'd seen from my mind. *The pictures. The way she'd cut Caroline out of her own wedding photograph. The candles. The books.*

I flew along the landing to my room, hurled myself onto the bed and pulled the pillow over my head. *She'd set up a shrine to Oswald in the attic.* There wasn't enough urrrggghh in the world to cover how I felt about that. Lady Tanith must visit it regularly; there were no cobwebs anywhere on the table or pictures, and the noises above my head, although irregular, came pretty often.

From the other side of my room there was the sound of The Master eating his prey, with a disgusting amount of crunching. I groaned and pulled the pillow harder over my ears to try to block it out. To try to block out *everything*, the bone-chewing, the thought of that memorial table...

Then something odd happened. Which, given what had gone before, made it very odd indeed.

I began to feel sorry for Lady Tanith.

Oh, not hugely sorry, not yet. But the tiniest corner of pity crept into my heart when I thought of her, up there in the attic, alone at night, with Oswald's pictures. And I thought how dreadful it was that they had had such a deep involvement that it had impacted her so hard when he died. She'd been cheated of her promised happy ending, left with nothing but the booby prize of Oswald's son, when she'd been so desperately in love with his father, who had loved her, left her and never come back.

Obviously, she was still an absolute cow, and this kind of hero-worship was only one step from gibbering madness, but, even so. She must have suffered so much, waiting for her beloved to come back, and hearing of his death. No wonder she was desperate to find his diaries. She wanted to relive those happy times, when Oswald had been hers, even if only for short periods. Oswald himself must have suffered too, torn between his duty to his languishing wife and his love for the vibrant, energetic Lady Tanith. No wonder she had become his muse. No wonder he hadn't known which way to turn.

I *had* to find those diaries. Not for me, well, maybe a little bit for me, so I wouldn't get thrown out of Templewood with winter coming, but for Lady Tanith's peace of mind. To reunite her, in however small a way, with Oswald. To let her read through his notes, hopefully some of his wonderful memories of his time with her, then she could publish and show the public – however many of them were interested – that their love had been true and inspirational to his work.

Just because *I* thought Oswald couldn't write his way out of a deckchair, that didn't mean everyone thought the same. After all, I didn't think much of Tolstoy, but plenty of other people did. There were probably students of Oswald's work out in the world, poring over his every word, analysing every grim, obviously rhymed line. Those diaries could be valuable to the world of literary research. I could be a hero!

I took the pillow off my head and got up. The Master 'brrrrrpd' at me questioningly, and then followed as I set out towards the library again, with a new resolution in my steps.

I bloody well *would* find those diaries, if I had to take the room apart to do so.

18

221B, BAKER STREET – SHERLOCK HOLMES, A CONAN DOYLE

By Tuesday, my resolution was wavering.

Under the watchful eye of Oswald, I had stripped all the shelves again and piled the books on the floor. Then I had systematically examined each individual shelf, pulling, prodding, wiggling and yanking. After that, I'd taken the bookcases as a whole, dragging any unattached away from the panelling so that I could tap the walls, lifting to look for spaces underneath and checking for hidey-holes or suspiciously hollow sounding places.

After two days of this, with absolutely no result other than occasionally toppling book mountains, I was filthy, exhausted, and building a whole new set of muscles that I was absolutely never going to need again.

I stood, resting my back against the table, and surveyed the room. Or what I could see of it through the clouds of irritated dust, which swirled and coiled through the air as though I had disturbed a nest of tiny insects.

'Nope,' I said to Oswald and The Master, who were both staring at me as though they believed I had taken leave of my senses, and in this house I had quite a lot of competition for that stare. 'They really aren't in here, are they?'

The cat blinked and licked his front again, so that he could stretch his chin upward and better appreciate the warmth from the fire on his chest. Oswald just glared.

There was a tap at the window and I turned to see the form of Jay, nose flattened on the glass panels. I waved and went over.

'Hello, how are you?' Jay leaned against the ledge outside and peered through the gap. I'd opened the window a crack in a hopeful attempt to release some of the dust into the wild. It hadn't worked.

'Fed up. How's your mum? Thanks for leaving me the note.'

'She's fine, thanks. Mending nicely and the installation for the landscaping show is all done. And if I hadn't left the note, you'd probably be launching books at my head right now. Can I come in, or are you under observation?'

I opened the window wider. 'Come in. Hugo is doing an internet shop with Mrs Compton, mainly to prevent her from buying arsenic and cyanide, and Lady Tanith is upstairs somewhere, supposedly lying down, but that's a *whole* other story.'

Jay hopped in. He didn't need the paper. Today he wasn't wearing his work clothes and it was nice to see him in normal jeans and a T-shirt that actually fitted. 'I was gone *three days*,' he said, once he'd landed on the floor inside. 'You mean that there's yet more bonkers stuff gone on while I've been away?'

In hushed tones, although not too hushed because he had to watch my lips carefully and ask for me to repeat a few things, I told Jay about what I'd found in the attic. He stretched his eyes very wide.

'Good grief. That's halfway into sectioning territory. So she goes up there and...?'

'Well, I don't exactly know. She may just find it comforting to have all Oswald's things in one place where she can see them, and she only goes up to look through the photographs, read his books and remember good times,' I said, giving the benefit of the doubt so much leeway that it threatened to capsize. 'Perhaps she just lights a candle to his memory.'

'Or it could be blood sacrifices, chanting and trying to invoke Oswald's spirit,' Jay said, pulling a face. 'You need to tell Hugo.'

'What? No, I don't, do I? I mean, it's private, it's Lady Tanith's business. Like Hugo's...' I bit my tongue. 'Hugo has his own peccadillos that he doesn't want his mother to know about.'

'Are they teetering on the edge of being something that means the police should be informed?' Jay sat on the sofa, leaning forward over his knees.

'No! Of course not. But, to be fair, neither are Lady Tanith's.' I felt the pity again, making my heart lurch. 'Day to day she's fine. Well, no, not fine, obviously, but she's hardly running amok with a chainsaw. She keeps the estate ticking over, she's in charge of the finances...' I had an awful moment of wondering what would happen to the finances when Hugo had free rein with the money and the ability to attend all the vintage and historic clothing sales in the world. 'She's apparently sane, more or less. She just really, really loved Oswald.'

'But *fifty years*.' Jay dropped his head and fiddled with his hearing aids. 'Fifty years, Andi. That's not love. It's not even obsession. I think Lady Tanith has levelled up on the obsession thing and she's into – I dunno, whatever comes next.' He looked up at me now. 'And that might be something you want to think about, if you can't find these diaries.'

We both stared around the library, which looked like a room in a photoshoot for *Hoarders' Weekly*.

'She's going to go postal, isn't she?' I said, eventually.

'Well, if they aren't here, they aren't here,' Jay said, standing up and coming over. The Master oozed out from in front of the fire to rub against Jay's legs, purring. 'You can't make them be here. You're sure they definitely aren't among the sacred tomes up in the attic?'

I shook my head. 'Pretty sure. The books up there looked to be properly bound and titled from the extremely quick glance I had from between my fingers, whilst screaming.'

'Maybe Lady Tanith got it wrong, and Oswald got rid of the diaries.'

'Right. *You* tell her that,' I said, rubbing my arms. 'When I'm a very long way away. Like Montreal or something.'

Jay put a hand on my wrist. 'You've thought about going out to join your parents? When you hate everything about their lifestyle?'

I didn't know how to say it. These last couple of nights I'd run through my potential futures, lying in bed with my head itching from the dust and with desperation building. I couldn't live in the bus, it was uninhabitable, and I was saying this after having spent a couple of months at Templewood.

Jude would welcome me, of course, as would Ollie, but there, among all her carefully curated ornaments, working a cleaning job or in a shop or behind a bar I would always be aware of my Cinderella status. The girl who wouldn't speak up for herself. The second-best sister.

It had dawned on me that I could just swallow my pride, join my parents and take up my empire. Let them put me in front of the camera to talk about my experiences growing up as the daughter of a pair of late-to-the-party hippies, with no fixed abode. The freedom of the road before us and the lack of any roots behind. I could spin it and make it sound TV-worthy. I'd learned how to keep secrets, after all, at Templewood.

'Oh, I don't know,' I said. 'It was just an idea.'

Jay moved away and over to the nearest pile of books. He began picking them up, one at a time, staring at the spines and riffling the pages. This did not help the overloaded dusty atmosphere. 'I missed you, you know,' he said suddenly, eyes on a page of particularly dense print.

'Did you?' I stared at him. The idea was outlandish, ridiculous. Nobody had, as far as I was aware, ever missed me before.

'Mmmm. I'd had plans for our lunch.'

'Oh yes,' I said cautiously.

'Roast beef, Yorkshire puddings, the full works. Trifle, I thought, for pudding.' He was still keeping his eyes on the book. I wondered if he wanted to give all of them this close attention; if so, I could resign and hand my job over to him.

'That sounds nice.'

'And then I was going to make you a suggestion.' One eye looked up at me now, angled so I could see a glint in it. I thought, very briefly, about the warmth of his body when we'd sat in the icehouse.

'Er,' I said.

'I was going to ask you if you'd ever considered training as a gardener.' The book snapped shut, breaking the mood which had become weighted with something – a look, a touch, an imagining.

'*What?*' I started to laugh now. Jay really was the master of tension-breaking.

'I just thought, you seem to like the outdoors, you're not afraid of rain, you're determined and creative and good with people. And I'm not going to be here forever, charming though Templewood is. Even before Mum's accident I was thinking about going back and taking over the landscaping business, training up someone to work alongside me. What do you think?'

'Er,' I said again, probably wearing the same expression as a prisoner who has been incarcerated forever in a tiny cell suddenly seeing the door swing open and the whole of life going on outside and who has no idea how to function in society.

'I mean, I know you, and you know about the' – he pointed at his ears – 'and the...' He flashed his wrist. 'It saves time explaining, and you know that you can't just shout to me across a site and have me respond. It doesn't have to be... you and me, I think we've got a... but that's incidental, I don't mind if you don't want... it could just be as business partners, but I know I'd like... if you felt the same... I'm going to stop talking now, because you look like a fish.'

I closed my mouth. 'But... but you hardly know me!'

'I wouldn't know anyone else I interviewed to come and work with me either,' Jay pointed out, reasonably. 'And I know quite a bit about you. Plus, you've seen me with my willy in my hand; that tends to bond people quite fast.'

I laughed now. 'And you've seen me in transparent wet pyjamas.'

'That did feed into my decision somewhat, I will admit.'

I flopped down onto the sofa, as though all my bones had been removed. The Master, sensing a lap opportunity, left Jay's legs alone to plonk himself up next to me and prod me with a paw. 'Can I think about it?' I asked weakly. 'It's come as a bit of a shock.'

'Of course.' Jay came and sat next to me. 'You'd be mad not to.'

'In this house, "mad" is a sliding scale,' I said, stroking the cat almost without thinking, as though those blue eyes were hypnotic.

'It's not sliding,' Jay reached across me to assist in the cat-stroking, bumping against my shoulder in a touch that was – promising, was the only way I could describe it. 'You are at one end, perpendicular and hanging on grimly, and absolutely all the other inhabitants are falling off the far side.'

'You're all right,' I said, robustly.

'I don't live here. Jasper's OK, but he got away. The others – how's Hugo, on a general basis? He's always seemed all right.'

'Yes. Hugo's, er, hobbies aren't mad. Just a bit "special interest". It's really only Lady Tanith who's hanging over the abyss. Oh, and Mrs Compton.'

We sat for a moment. The heater, powered by the cylinder of gas which I had been instructed by Lady Tanith 'needs to last the whole month', popped and the cat purred. Jay was solid beside me, adjusting one side of his hearing aid, dark and maybe just a little bit tortured, but not so badly that he was beyond redemption. He'd lost a sister. I'd lost mine that day she'd demanded a normal life. His hadn't wanted to leave him, mine couldn't get away fast enough.

Everyone had their demons.

I tipped my head back against the leather cushions and looked up at Oswald; his huge face seemed somewhat sympathetic today, or maybe that was because I was seeing it through dust. I wondered what demons he had carried. Apart, obviously, from Lady Tanith.

As I looked up at the portrait, The Master jumped down off my lap, leaving our stroking hands forced to entwine fingers in a clasp of understanding. We sat for a few moments longer in a feeling of dawning peace and acceptance and potential for happiness, and the cat perched himself on a pile of books that sprawled open-paged, like dancers at the finale of the Can-Can. He 'wowed' loudly.

'What's the matter with him?' Jay asked, without moving.

'Dunno. He really likes sitting under that picture.' I didn't move either. This was nice. No, it was more than nice, it was lovely.

'Do you think he really is the reincarnation of Oswald?'

'I hope not. He's in bed with me most nights.' I watched the cat, stretching himself full length against the firmly-fixed-and-not-containing-secret-cupboards panelling beneath the portrait, claws extended, as though he were trying to reach high enough to pull at the picture, the lower edge of the frame of which was around a metre and a half off the ground. 'What are you doing? Puss?'

The cat looked at me over his shoulder, blue eyes blazing, then went back to clawing the wall.

'Rats, do you think?' Jay went to stand up, realised he was still holding my hand, and sat back down again.

A sudden realisation struck me. 'Oh my God!'

Now Jay let go of my fingers and leaped to his feet. 'What? What's wrong? Are you all right?'

I stood up too. 'I've never moved the picture!'

He stared at me. 'You've never what? Moved the picture? Why the hell would you?'

'Because it's the only bloody place in this room that I haven't practically taken to bits and rebuilt. It was put here when Oswald was still alive! I've been treating it as though it's part of the wall, but it's not, it's attached to the panelling. Come on.'

The Master shot out of the way as, between us, we heaved the big table across the room to the spot underneath the portrait. Then, with a hand from Jay, I climbed up onto it, which unfortunately put me level with Oswald's groin, and stretched my arms full length to grasp both sides of the frame. This pushed my face into the painted crotch, but I still couldn't stretch far enough. Jay had to hop up next to me, and with him holding one side and me holding the other, we managed to slide the picture upwards enough to disengage it from whatever fixture was holding it in place.

In a choreographed movement worthy of any ballet, we spun around and let Oswald slip gently to the ground behind us, where he flopped forwards to rest his face against the nearest bookcase, like a drunk passing out at a bus stop. Now revealed was a stretch of panelling, slightly paler than the rest, having been protected from whatever had gone on in here for the best part of seventy years. It bore some vicious fixing arrangements, which had been keeping the portrait not only up, but so close to the wall that I hadn't realised it *could* be removed. I wouldn't have put it past Lady Tanith to have glued it up there.

The panelling also had a crack in it.

At first it looked like a crack in the wood, where the weight of years had pulled two planks apart, just an ordinary result of ageing and drying out. But a closer look revealed it to be some kind of hinge.

My heart began to beat faster. I'd bitten my lip in my eagerness to remove the portrait and the blood had the metallic taste of anticipation. *This could be it.*

'How does it open?' I stuck my nails in the gap and tried to prise the two halves apart.

'I don't know. But, look, look at the portrait fixing on the wall there.' Jay stretched up, and by standing on tiptoe he could just reach the lower attachment that had fixed the picture in place. 'It moves. Bit rusty now, of course, but it's a pivot. In Oswald's day you could have moved the picture to one side with a fingertip.'

I stared at him. 'Ten minutes ago that would have been brilliant information. You mean we struggled to get that thing down when we could have just moved it?'

'I don't know it if it still works. It's pretty old and it might have seized. But it does mean that *Oswald* could move the picture without taking it down.'

Jay and I looked again at the crack in the panelling. 'Right,' I said. 'That's coming off if I have to take to it with an axe.'

'If there is a hiding place here and Oswald used it by moving the picture, it shouldn't be *that* hard to open, we just have to find out how.' Jay stood back and looked at the panel with his head on one side.

'OK, Jonathon Creek, *you* work it out,' I panted, trying to pull at the wood again.

Jay slithered down off the table and began to walk around, staring at the wall. 'He must have used one hand to hold the picture back,' he said, 'so it must only take one hand to open. And it should be doable from here, assuming that that portrait isn't life sized and Oswald wasn't twenty feet tall.'

I got down next to him. The Master came and sat with us, all three of us now gazing at the oak panelling. 'So it must be something really simple that we're missing,' I said. 'Like just pressing it, or something.'

To demonstrate, I pressed the panel, and to our collective astonishment it popped out, sliding smoothly open to reveal a small space behind. And in that space...

'Well, bugger me,' Jay breathed.

A stack of six books. Slim, hardbacked notebooks, edges ruffled and worn. Almost reverently I leaned in and took them out. When I opened the first one, I could see the ink was still as bright blue as the day it was written –

these had been put away and never looked at; the pages had the virginal flatness of new paper. Even, it seemed, Oswald hadn't reread them.

> September the fourth 1968
> Caroline complained more of pains today. The doctor called and we have an appointment at the hospital for next week, but I suspect there will be little they can do. Whether it is rheumatism or some other form of degeneration I do not know, but she is largely confined to bed and unable to do for herself. I do what I can, but brushing her hair is beyond me.
> Started another novel tonight. I feel this one may sum up the small joys to be obtained from a life mired in unhappiness.
> Wilkins reports the dairy returns to be lower, instructed him to move the herd to the Upper Pasture.
> Richard has a cold.

Jay read the entry over my shoulder. 'He was quite a boring bloke, wasn't he?' he observed.

'It's a diary, not a column for *Penthouse*,' I said tartly. 'What were you expecting? What sort of things do you put in your diary?'

Jay pulled a face. 'Fair point,' he said. 'Mine is all about next year's planting and which seeds I should be starting off. Anyway, objective achieved. You've found the missing diaries, well done. Lady Tanith will be ecstatic. Actually, we might want to have some Valium on standby.'

I held the diaries to my chest for a moment. Yes, Lady Tanith would be delighted. But, also, would she now terminate my employment? After all, the whole 'catalogue my library' had been a ruse in the first place. She could well decide that I'd done my job and I could go.

Jay was offering me a chance at a life. Gardening didn't need loads of qualifications, plants didn't care if you didn't have GCSEs, as long as you knew where to put them and made sure they had water and things like that. I knew, somehow I just *knew* that I could be good at it. That I would enjoy working with Jay, in whatever context we found ourselves.

But I needed more time. More time to get to know him properly. Maybe a few dinners, more flasks of coffee drunk at strange hours, more casual encounters that could lead to more... *something*. If I left Templewood now, I only had two places to go and both of them were a long way from this bubble in time; from Jay and also from Hugo, who needed a friend.

'I think I might hang on to them for a little while,' I said, still clutching the bundle of notebooks. 'Lady Tanith doesn't need to know we've found them yet.'

Jay was looking at me, one eyebrow quirked as though he knew how my mind was working. 'All right,' he said at last. 'We'd better put Oswald back then, hadn't we?'

We hauled the portrait back into place, with a lot of swearing, broken nails, and the occasional yowl as we trod on the cat. Then we had to drag the table back and make everything look as it had. Eventually, the portrait was rehung, the furniture dragged back where it belonged, and now the library was, once again, just a whole load of books in random piles on the floor.

'I did all that for nothing,' I panted, looking at the heaps. 'Got them all off the shelves and generated enough dust to test-drive a thousand hoovers.'

'On the plus side,' Jay observed, 'at least it looks as though you are serious about finding those diaries. Ought to keep Lady Tanith quiet for at least a week. Can you let me out of the window again, please. I should go home and sort myself out for tomorrow. I have to mow obscene slogans into the lawns for the final time this year.'

With one eye on the diaries, in case they evaporated, I opened the window and Jay climbed up onto the sill. 'Goodbye then,' I said, suddenly awkward. 'And thanks for helping.'

'No problem. Well, no very big problem, anyway. I'll probably see you tomorrow.'

Our faces were very close. Jay was sitting on the ledge facing into the room, bending forward over his knees to look into my eyes.

'Yes,' I said. 'And no pissing in the bushes.'

He raised a hand and cupped my cheek. 'No pissing about of any kind.' His voice was very quiet. 'Just plain, direct action.' He leaned in a little further and I moved closer. His hand was warm, the callouses rough against my skin. I closed my eyes; his breath was on my face, his mouth so very close to my lips that it felt as though we were already kissing. 'All right?'

'Oh yes,' I murmured.

There was the briefest of contact, just a feather-touch of his mouth against mine, and then he lost his balance and toppled backwards out of the window to vanish into the drop onto the lawn.

'Oh, bugger,' floated up to me.

'Are you all right?'

No answer. Then his head popped up, reattaching both hearing aids. 'Sorry. They fell out.' A breathless kind of pause, a wiggle of eyebrow, and then he was gone, moving away with both hands in his jeans pockets so his elbows stuck out like wings, and he was whistling.

19

GARDENCOURT – PORTRAIT OF A LADY, HENRY JAMES

'Do you fancy a bottle of wine tonight?' Hugo asked that evening over dinner. 'I've had a delivery that I'd like your opinion on.'

This had become our shorthand for a fashion show, when he'd had a new arrival. Hugo would try it on first, then I'd have a go, and we'd check the label for authenticity, browse the internet to see if anyone famous had worn it recently, and then finish a bottle of wine whilst Hugo slipped into something more comfortable and I quietly despaired of my life choices.

But things were different now. I actually *had* some life choices, courtesy of Jay, which I needed to think about, and I wanted to take Oswald's diaries to my bed and spend an evening combing through the more salacious entries. I wasn't actually going to *use* any knowledge I obtained, but if I produced the diaries later with a knowing smile and a wink, Lady Tanith would know that I knew and she may let me hang around the house a bit longer.

Just a couple of days with the diaries, that was all I wanted. Time to skim read. It would probably be all that my nerves and imagination could take but it would mean I was in a position of – no, not power, because that would imply an evil twist that just wasn't me. I wasn't going to use the diaries for blackmail or anything like that. After all, who was there to blackmail? Oswald and Caroline were already dead, Hugo and Jasper knew their mother had been... important to Oswald. Any revelations about that relationship that the diaries contained would surely be worth no more than a nod and a shrug? So reading the diaries would be for me. For personal satisfaction, so I would know what all this hunting around the library had been all about. Perhaps I could get to know Oswald a little better too; his enormous visage had been quite a confidante during these weeks amid the dusty tedium; it would be nice to get behind the austere stare a little.

'Can we do it tomorrow?' I rolled my eyes at Lady Tanith, who was sitting at the dining table with us, unusually for her. She'd clearly finished whatever she had to do earlier and was choosing to cramp our style instead. 'I'd rather like an early night tonight, Hugo.'

'I believe my son is requesting your company,' Lady Tanith said stiffly. 'And you are a guest in this house.'

'I know what Hugo is requesting, Lady Tanith,' I said, my voice heavy with double-meaning.

'It doesn't matter,' Hugo added, very quickly. I hoped he hadn't thought I was about to dob him in. 'Tomorrow is fine, honestly, Mother.' He began collecting plates, noisily, trying to end the conversation.

Lady Tanith raised her eyebrows at me. She was still trying to force Hugo and me together and seemed increasingly annoyed at our lack of evident intentions for one another. Although, even if we *had* had any intentions, I liked to think we'd have been classy enough to keep them from his mother.

'It's a date,' I said, which made him smile and Lady Tanith settle back into her chair with a disgruntled air.

'Hmph,' she snorted. Just for one second I was tempted to tell her that it was only a date in the calendar sense but I didn't, and Hugo, sensing the worst was over, stopped clattering crockery.

'In fact.' I stood up. 'I think I'll go to bed now. Goodnight.'

Hugo returned my goodnight, with a slightly crestfallen expression on his face. He was obviously looking forward to unveiling his new purchase and my postponing the event was leaving him at a loose end, but it just reiterated my decision. I could *not* marry Hugo. And I *particularly* couldn't marry him knowing that Lady Tanith would only endure me as the mother of the future heirs to Templewood. The position of power she would have over me would be unbearable, and the thought of raising children as supercilious towards me as she was, made me shudder. Although I did grin at the idea of popping babies out in very quick succession and then insisting that Lady Tanith babysit them all. *That* would sort out her attitude.

Then I sighed. As if I'd leave any child of mine in the care of House Grim. Besides, Lady Tanith would hire nannies to 'help out', and then Hugo would fall in love with one of them; I'd read those books too.

As I went up to my room, preceded by The Master, who was now forcing his way into my bed most nights, where he was a great stand in for a hot water bottle so I'd stopped scooping him back out and closing the door on his whiskery face, I thought again about Jay's offer and my alternatives.

Should I swallow anything that was left of my pride and ask Mum and Dad for the airfare to Canada and join them? They would be only too delighted if I took back everything I'd ever said about hashtag NomadicExistence, hashtag Vanlife, hashtag TooOldForThisShit. They would hand over the travelling empire to me in a few years, I could get my bus driving licence and I could carry on making TV shows about resentful locals, lack of amenities and the trials and tribulations of parking a single-decker bus in public car parks. I'd have money, as long as the TV companies stayed interested, and the whole freedom of the road movement seemed to be growing in popularity again, as early-retirers sold the bungalow and bought a camper van. Yes. I could be a cult figure, and a rich one at that.

Or, I could try to make a go of landscape gardening. I had the feeling that Jay would make an incredible teacher – a frisson crept down my spine at the thought of his fingers and that near kiss – and that I would actually enjoy learning about plants and planting conditions and how to design a garden.

Was sticking to my principles really worth starting again?

Another thought of Jay, with his direct gaze, his messy hair and those long brown legs in shorts. Of *course* my principles were worth it.

I got into my pyjamas, then I propped my pillows up, sorted the volumes into date order, and began reading. I started with the earliest, 1968, and read all about Caroline's gradual slide into frailty, which seemed to be linked to arthritis and maybe some other conditions that Oswald was too delicate to mention. He also tried out some phrases he was thinking of using in his next novel – I could have told him not to bother, he seemed to be the king of the mixed metaphor and obvious description – and talked about the management of the estate in general. It was, in short, not exactly riveting stuff. There wasn't as much of 'Oswald' as I'd hoped for. I wanted emotions, dreams for the future. I wanted high drama, character development and, in short, *story*. I hadn't considered that the diaries of a real person, as opposed to, say, *Bridget Jones*, might just be a catalogue of daily events and a record of milk yields.

I read about the decisions Oswald made: redesigning the gardens, letting out more farmland, finding someone to provide help for Caroline, but nothing of the guilt he must have felt about having to do so.

The first mention of Tanith came halfway through the year. Some old friends had a ward, which I had thought a thing that only existed in fiction – they were guardians for the daughter of a cousin. She had lost both parents; her mother had died very suddenly when the girl was five, and then her father had remarried and moved to South America with his new wife. The girl, Tanith, had been left in the care of Oswald's friend and he was now looking for a position for her.

I put the book down for a moment, my eyes burning. So Tanith had lost her mother when she was little more than a toddler? Then her father hadn't wanted to take her with him when he moved continents? She was the product of such cold-heartedness that it made a tear plop onto the diary page. How *could* her father have left his little girl behind? Her mother had only just died, she must have been bereft and scared and lonely. I had a sudden urge to seek out Lady Tanith and hug her, but I managed to suppress it without too much difficulty. Tanith had had a lifetime of ignoring emotion and I doubted that she'd welcome any outbursts from me.

Was *this* why she really wanted the diaries? Because she knew that Oswald would have laid her past bare and revealed her to be, at heart, just a terrified abandoned child, and didn't want her own children to see what she'd been through? I guessed that being shown to have had a less-than-perfectly upper-class upbringing might let people into secrets that Tanith would rather keep buried. It was why she kept her sons close. Fear of loss must have ruled her life – no wonder losing Oswald had hit her so badly.

Oh God. Poor, poor Tanith. She daren't have her past exposed, because she would worry that her boys might not understand. That little girl, alone and friendless and brought up by distant cousins... I wiped the back of my wrist over my eyes. Of course. It all made sense now. Those cousins had contacted Oswald, asking if he had anything for the now adult girl. Nothing too menial, a light role which would help her learn to run a household. Oswald considered her to be suitable. But he never ruminated on the possibility of giving up the estate, taking Caroline away somewhere they could be together more. He didn't consider spending more time with his wife, or agonise on paper as to what would happen to the estate when his son Richard – who sounded a bit ineffectual and more concerned with his city friends than learning how to manage Templewood – inherited.

I wanted emotion from Oswald, outpourings of grief and anxiety! There was no narrative arc, other than that provided by the passing of the year, no character growth that I could see either. Literature had, once again, misled me. He never mused about the background of the companion he was thinking of taking on for his wife. Not one word was written about how fragile she must be, how friendless and lonely, or how much good she might bring to the household. Oswald, in short, had all the empathy of a house brick. It did not bode well for his novels.

But as I read on, the story of Templewood, Caroline and Oswald and their son still managed to absorb me, even without the personal touches I wanted. I got to the end of 1968 and laid the book down with the feeling of anticipation that I'd got used to from reading books which ended on a cliffhanger, preparing me for the excitement to come in the next-in-series. 1969. That was when Lady Tanith had come to Templewood Hall. Perhaps this was where dear Oswald switched up a gear and discovered he had Hidden Passions?

I wriggled myself more comfortably on the pillows and opened the next volume.

***

The birds were starting their feeble twittering complaints at the first glimmers of dawn when I put the last volume down. My eyes itched, but I hadn't been able to stop reading. And now I needed to talk to someone.

Not Hugo, obviously. I couldn't talk to Lady Tanith, because… because I just couldn't, and anyway…

So I got out of bed, put on the thickest clothes I had and, leaving the cat to resettle in the warm bit of bed I'd left, I went out into the first early brightness. The sky was grey, the night gradually dragging the day over the sky as it retreated, and everything wore long shadows of the retiring darkness, and drizzle. I padded my way out of the back door, around the house and down the path.

Jay would be up. He was a gardener. Whatever time of day – and night, too, come to that – I went outside, there he would be, snipping and mowing and generally gardening. Dawn was probably his natural time, he'd be skipping about somewhere, snipping roses or tying back some trailing growth in a top beaded with condensation, and shorts.

I kept an eye open, but couldn't see him anywhere, so decided to start at Ground Zero and went to his cottage. Jay, it turned out, wasn't skipping anywhere and was, in fact, irritable and newly awoken when I banged at his door, rang the bell and pressed the buzzer that he'd had installed to bypass his need to wear his hearing aids at night.

'What? Andi? What...? It's about ten past midnight, isn't it? Why aren't you asleep? Never mind, I've not got my aids in, hold on, I'll come down.'

The upstairs window banged shut and I jiggled on the step for a few moments until Jay, in a T-shirt with Homer Simpson looking very past his best on, and boxer shorts, opened the door.

'I thought you'd be up,' I said, apologetically, sliding into the hall.

Jay didn't answer. He led the way through to the kitchen, which was warm and brighter than the rest of the house, fumbled on the table, and found his hearing aids. 'All right,' he said, as though he were trying to lose the last dregs of dreams. 'All right. I'm here. What's the panic?'

'I'm sorry,' I said as soon as he turned round. 'I thought – gardening, up at dawn, digging and... and... everything...' I trailed off, at his grin.

'In spring, maybe. In summer, yep, up early to get the watering done. But it's autumn. Most things are shutting down. I'm keeping the autumn colour beds going but now I don't need to cut the grass every five minutes or weed absolutely everywhere, I get a lie-in. Until a very strange woman turns up on my doorstep while the sparrows are still in bed.'

'I'm sorry,' I said again, still hopping from foot to foot, powered by the rocket fuel of discovery. 'But I needed to talk to someone.'

'And you thought of me? I'm flattered.' Jay ran a hand through his hair, which didn't help the middle-of-the-night look. 'Right. Let me put the kettle on.'

While he did so, I took out the diaries that I'd carried over, clamped once more to my bosom and laid them on the table. Jay turned around from filling the kettle and plonking it onto the Aga plate, saw them and raised his eyebrows.

'*That* exciting, eh?' He looked at the diaries and then at me. 'I do hope that you aren't so filled with lust as a result of those that you've come over to have your wicked way with me. It's early, I might need a bit of a run up.'

'Sorry, no,' I said, and then wondered why I'd apologised. 'I read them all last night and I have to offload.'

Jay whistled. 'All right. All right. Sit down, stop dancing. Would you like some toast?'

'*Toast*?' Obediently I pulled out a chair and sat down.

'For you this is clearly earth-shattering. For me, it's dawn, I was asleep, I need toast. I'm making some anyway and need to know whether to make extra.'

His pragmatism in the face of my evident incredulity was both calming and incredibly annoying. 'Yes. No! Look, this is important!'

'Better make it wholemeal then. Right, you talk, I'll toast. Go.'

I took a deep breath. Where to start?

'You know that Lady Tanith came to be a companion to Caroline, Oswald's wife?'

'I'd gathered that, yes.'

'And Lady Tanith became his muse, they fell in love but Oswald was too honourable to leave Caroline, so they had an affair under her nose. When she died, he took some time out, went to Switzerland and died there. That's the story, right?'

The kettle whistled and Jay poured water into mugs. I waited until he turned back around to see my face. He'd got his hearing aids in, but I didn't want to have to repeat any of this.

'Right.' He raised his eyebrows. 'Are you saying that's not what happened?'

I took a deep breath. 'Not according to Oswald.'

'Maybe he edited things? Didn't want to be seen in a bad light? Seducing the young companion while his wife was quietly dying upstairs?'

I shook my head impatiently. 'He didn't need to worry. These diaries were hidden, weren't they? If he'd wanted them to be squeaky clean, maybe for publication, he would have either written a fake set, put them somewhere easy to find, or he'd have self-edited and not hidden them at all. These were his own, private recollections and records – trust me, there is a *lot* about the running of the estate in here. Maybe he'd been going to edit them or destroy them when he got back from Switzerland, only he didn't *come* back.'

I took the mug of tea. Over in the corner, two slices of toast popped, and I had to wait for those to be buttered before I carried on.

'I'm imagining all kinds of nefarious dealings.' Jay handed me a slice, warm and dripping with melted butter. 'Carry on.'

'That's just it. There *weren't* any nefarious dealings. Oswald really did not like Lady Tanith at all. He took her in as a favour to a friend because her mother was dead and her father had left her and this friend had brought her up and needed somewhere for her to go. To be honest, he really ought to have wondered a little bit more about what a background like that might do to a person.'

'Oh dear,' Jay said, biting his toast.

'He calls her things like "that annoying child" and "my bleating shadow". Apparently Lady Tanith inserted herself into his life; she was *everywhere*. Oswald was trying to write – she'd be there, in the library, talking, trying to give him ideas or lines he could use.'

Jay pulled a face. 'That sounds... irritating.'

'According to Oswald it was more than irritating. I actually started to feel really sorry for him. He even took to hiding in the icehouse to try to get away from her, but she followed him there too. By 1972 the poor man was desperate.'

'Wow.'

'Yes. She was obviously damaged. I mean, everyone she'd ever loved had dumped her, she was desperate for something to love and she fixated on poor Oswald. Round about May he got absolutely scathing about her. He was clearly being fairly polite to her face but letting it all out in his diary.

There are *pages* of stuff about how she wouldn't leave him alone, how she trailed behind him, how he was going to have to leave Caroline – to whom he was, incidentally, absolutely devoted – and go down to London just to get a break from Lady Tanith.'

Jay licked his fingers and got up to put more bread in the toaster. 'Why didn't he just tell her to push off? Explain that he needed space to write? Lock the library door?'

'Apparently the door didn't lock, not until late 1972, when he got one put on. But Lady Tanith would take a chair and sit outside, talking through the door. And Caroline liked her; Lady Tanith made her life easier and gave her someone to talk to – when she wasn't pestering Oswald, obviously. To be honest, I'm not sure Lady Tanith would have gone, even if he'd given her her marching orders. She was too much in love with Oswald. It just wasn't returned. At all,' I added, in case there was any doubt.

'So – so all that stuff about her being his muse? About them being devoted to each other? That's all in Tanith's *head*?' Jay leaned against the Aga as though he needed its support in his shock. 'She made it all up?'

'Fifty years, Jay. I'm not sure she even knows what was true and what she just invented. She didn't do it deliberately I don't think. She just didn't know what love was meant to look like.'

'Bugger me.' He scraped his hair back with both hands. 'Fifty years. Fifty years of that bloody memorial service every month. For a man who didn't even like her.'

I made a 'there you go' face.

'So, she's got a shrine in the attic, she lays flowers at that stone, she's been staring at that portrait, for *fifty years*! It was pretty weird when we thought they'd been lovers, now it's not just weird it's – well, treatment territory, I'd have said.'

'I think it's grief,' I said, taking another slice of toast.

'Grief? No. I *know* about grief, Andi.' Jay rubbed, probably unconsciously, at the tattoo on his wrist. 'Grief is carrying someone with you, in your soul. It's wanting to live your life for them too, because they didn't get the chance. It's hearing their voice in the rain, wishing they could have met... Look, what Lady Tanith has, that's not grief. That's self-indulgence.'

I looked at him over my crust. 'You don't have a monopoly,' I said softly.

'Sorry? You're eating and...' Jay waved a hand at my face. 'That bit wasn't clear.'

'You can't speak for everyone's grief. The way you feel about your sister, that's *your* grief. Lady Tanith has her own grief. OK, yes, it's over the top and utterly bonkers from our perspective, especially knowing now that she's grieving for someone who really disliked her, but she's still entitled to it, Jay.'

This was as close as I could come to explaining what I felt about Lady Tanith. The pity I had come to feel, more and more, as I'd read those diaries. Oswald, who had been too – I wanted to say soft, but he'd been kind, really – too *kind* to sit Lady Tanith down and tell her that she could never be anything to him. Or perhaps – the thought had come at about two in the morning – perhaps he had been afraid to say anything? Perhaps he'd half thought that Lady Tanith might lose any reason she had and do something awful to Caroline just to have him free for her? And he'd needed Lady Tanith, whatever he thought of her. He'd loved his wife, but he couldn't care for her, couldn't be with her all the time. He'd had his writing.

And he'd been bloody stupid.

But Lady Tanith had rewritten history. Perhaps she'd always believed it. Maybe she'd taken Oswald's attempts to shake her off as being his artistic temperament. His inability to declare love for her, as loyalty to his wife.

After all, she hadn't had the best start in life. But pity only took you so far, before you wanted to shake her really hard and tell her how much she had interfered with Oswald's life. He may even have written twice as many dreadful novels and even more execrable poetry, if she hadn't been over his shoulder all the time, 'helping'. So maybe it wasn't medicating she needed, so much as a medal.

Jay took a deep breath which sounded more like a gasp. 'Yes,' he said. 'Of course. You're right. Everyone loses someone in their own way and everyone deals with it in their own way. I can't speak for the entire world of loss.' He came over and flopped beside me on a chair at the table. 'Thank you,' he said, softly.

'What for? Telling you you aren't the only person ever to lose a loved one?'

'For stopping me from being so self-absorbed. Grief starts out dark and tortured and it ends up – well, like Lady Tanith.' He shook his head. 'Poor woman. All those years telling herself that he loved her.'

'But it does rather beg the question,' I said, pointing at the diaries on the table. 'What do I do with those? Lady Tanith isn't going to be happy until she gets them, but I can't let her see them... or can I?'

He pulled a ferocious face. 'Argh. That's a tough one.'

'It might be good for her. To see life as it really was, not as she's constructed it to be. I mean, she *must* have known, surely, men don't run away and hide when they see you coming if you're their muse and the love of their life. Even Lady Tanith must know that, deep down.'

'Or' – Jay pushed my cup of tea towards me – 'or it might send her over the edge and she kills everyone who might know and then takes to the woods, gibbering and bloodstained.'

I gave him a hard stare. 'Or she might just be really upset.'

'As I said, gibbering and bloodstained. Anyway. Ethical dilemma; this is much more your territory than mine.'

'Is it?'

'Well, you've got all that "go and live with my sister, or please my parents by taking on their world" stuff, haven't you?' He dropped his face into his mug. 'Or coming in with me.'

He wasn't looking at me. Carefully not looking at me. As though he were afraid of what I might say next.

'That's not ethics. That's just practicality,' I said, trying for cheery upbeatness. 'But I'm assuming that learning how to landscape gardens won't involve *Peppa Pig* or passing an HGV driving test.'

A quick, hopeful sidelong glance came from the direction of his mug. 'Nope. Or at least, not that I've noticed so far, as long as you can come to terms with a ride-on mower. Gardening can also be somewhat pig-adjacent.'

'Well then.'

Jay smiled, a slow thoughtful smile. 'Great. But what about these diaries? What are you going to do? Could you redact them? Tear out the pages where Oswald is at his most vicious about her? Pretend, I dunno, that there's a particularly selective breed of worm that only eats some paper?'

I gave a deep sigh that let out a lot of the tension I'd been holding. 'I really don't know. I should just give them to her, of course. She's an adult, responsible for managing her own expectations and responses. I should just hand them over, not say that I've read them, and let her discover what Oswald really thought, in her own time.'

'But?' Jay crossed his legs and his shoulder made contact with mine. It was nice.

'Well, bloodstains, gibbering and all that. And, I feel sorry for her. I don't know if I could bear being the person who blew her world apart. She wants to read them, to edit them for publication, even though no reader is ever going to comb through that lot to find Oswald's motivations for his novels. She's not going to publish them without going through them first, so I can't even tell myself that she won't ever see what he said.'

'So, pretend you never found them.'

I focused on the hairy brown knee beside me. 'She knows they're there in the library somewhere. I can pretend to keep looking, of course, but I've got no idea how long I can keep it up before she fires me and brings in someone else.' I pulled a face. 'Someone a lot quicker on the uptake than me, who finds the hiding place. If it's empty, Lady Tanith will draw a whole lot of conclusions that I'd rather she didn't – like I found them and ran off with them, and if I put them back, then I'm just kicking this further down the road to make it not my responsibility.' I sighed again. 'I'm buggered, whatever I decide.'

Jay whistled again. 'And now it's my problem too, thanks for that.'

I stiffened. 'I'm sorry, I didn't think...'

'Don't be daft. It's good, in a very weird and protracted kind of way. Shows you trust me.'

'Does it?'

'Well, you obviously realise that I'm not going to run straight to Lady Tanith or Hugo and tell them that you found the diaries, am I? That's trust.' Jay looked at me sideways again. 'You really haven't trusted many people in life, have you?'

'There's never been a need,' I said briskly. 'So, advice. What do I *do*?'

'We could run away?' Jay suggested, half-hopefully.

'Lady Tanith would have a case against us for breaking the terms of our employment, and don't tell me she wouldn't use it. Besides – besides, I don't want to leave Hugo in the lurch. He's all right.' Then I thought of Hugo, in full-length satin and velvet, swinging an evening bag with no one to turn to. 'He's got his demons too, but he's been nothing but kind to me. I can't dump him and go and hide.'

'So tell him what you've found. Lady Tanith is his mother, maybe this is more his responsibility than it is ours?'

I stood up, noisily pushing the chair back. 'I've thought of that as well. But the boys were brought up on the story of their mother's doomed love for Oswald. Is it fair to expose them to the fact that she has never really known what love is? With all the implications that might have for the way she's treated them?'

'It might explain an awful lot about life for them, though,' Jay put in. He stood up too. 'What's not fair, is that this has fallen on you.'

Jay reached out. I felt my skin cool at the thought of his approaching touch, and then prickle with heat, but he reached past me and picked up his plate of toast.

'I'm going to give it a couple of days,' I said, not sure whether I felt disappointed or not that he hadn't touched me. 'Nobody knows that we found anything in there. I've got a bit of leeway to weigh up the pros and cons and maybe introduce the topic to Hugo.'

'You and Hugo...' Jay put the plate down again. He didn't seem to know what to do with his hands.

'No. I thought, right at the beginning... but no, Jay.'

'What about me? Was I in the frame at the beginning?' He was quite close to me now, Homer Simpson's bug eyes giving me something to focus on.

'I thought you were going to attack me with a pair of shears,' I admitted. 'But I do admit to a momentary *Lady Chatterley* consideration.'

Jay's expression brightened. 'Well, that's hopeful, at least. I did get a look in at being a lusty young stud.' Another small step, so close that I could see the light of the increasing dawn reflecting in his hair. 'But I promise to take things very, very slowly. All right?'

'I think that would be good, yes.' My voice came out very small, very quiet. He smelled of clean linen, of rumpled sheets and sleep, with a musky top note that was probably just shower gel or shampoo but to me smelled alluringly male. When I looked above Homer, Jay's head was on one side, and his eyes were asking me a question that I wanted to answer with my entire body. 'All right?' he whispered, a hand tangling into my hair to draw my face closer.

'Mmmm.' I stood on tiptoe to reach his mouth and we kissed, a toast-crumb and tea-flavoured kiss that somehow managed to conjure images of potential nights of tangled sheets and heat rather than burned bread and stewed leaves.

After a while, which could have been moments or could have been decades, Jay stepped back, although his fingers still grazed the skin of my cheek. 'Er,' he said. 'Well.'

'Mmmm?' I said again, lost now in a potential fantasy which leaned a lot more towards the raunchier side of my reading habits than Jane Austen would have cared for.

'I'd better get dressed and walk you back to the house.'

'Oh.' Disappointment and thwarted lust crashed together into my heart. I'd hoped – had I? – for more. But Jay wasn't a 'take advantage of the moment' sort of guy, I realised.

'You don't want to be caught sneaking in with that lot, do you?'

'No.' He was quite right, damn him. Whilst my literary-powered brain had been imagining moments of passion on the kitchen table, practicality had to win out. Jay had been right all along, life really couldn't be like the books. Us having wild sex here and now would mean getting back to the house to the likelihood of being met by either Lady Tanith, Hugo or Mrs Compton, and any one of them would query why I was carrying a load of books. And I couldn't leave them with Jay, in case I decided that telling Hugo was the only thing to do. I would need to show him absolute evidence of his mother's self-deception.

Jay gave me a wicked smile. He clearly knew what I'd been thinking. 'Right. Give me five minutes.' He set off for the hallway. 'Actually, better give me ten. Not sure I can get my trousers on yet.'

I laughed and let him go. Now that someone else knew about Lady Tanith and Oswald, I felt better. Lighter. I understood how Hugo felt, telling me about the dresses after keeping the secret to himself for years – sometimes you just needed someone else to know.

I walked around Jay's kitchen, tidying our plates and mugs into the deep butler's sink and wiping the table free of crumbs. Living in a small space in the bus for so long had taught me that if everything wasn't put away immediately, after twenty minutes you were wading through knee-level mess and trying to find somewhere to sit that didn't have cutlery on it. Then I looked at the walls, where botanical prints decorated the plain plaster, and stacks of gardening books and magazines were piled roughly but tidily in a corner.

There was one photograph. Unframed, tucked under a magnet on the fridge and slightly curled at the edges. A much younger Jay, hair tied back, and wearing a University of Durham sweatshirt, arm around a smiling girl whose head was pushed right up against his so they could both fit into the photograph. She looked frail but happy, short curls bouncing around her thin face and a look of mischief in her eyes.

I took the photo off the fridge and looked at it properly. Yes, I could see the sibling resemblance. Jay and Flora both had the same dark hair and eyes, the same high cheekbones and similar smiles. If he was at university when this was taken, it must have been fairly close to her death.

'That's the last picture.' Jay had come into the kitchen behind me, unheard. 'Flora wanted us to do a selfie. She'd come up to Durham to visit me.' Gently he took the picture from my hands and then stared down at it. 'We were both pretty rubbish at taking selfies,' he said quietly. 'This was the only one that had both our faces in.'

I thought of that photograph on the table in the attic. Oswald looking uncomfortable, with Lady Tanith squeezed in next to him, smiling happily. Who had taken it, Caroline? Richard? How had Oswald been persuaded to stand still next to Lady Tanith for long enough? Not that it mattered. She clearly treasured that picture, her and her beloved. The denial that Lady Tanith must live under was almost a solid weight. How could I ever blow her world apart with the evidence? But somehow, somehow she was going to *have* to find out, and then she'd know that I knew and... But love took so many forms. Did I have a right to impose my belief in the way it looked onto Tanith, who had presumably loved Oswald in her own way, even though that love hadn't been returned? Her feelings had still been valid.

I tried to imagine Tanith faced by utter reality and failed. Nothing was like books. This was people's *lives*.

'She'd have liked you.' Jay gently hooked the photograph back under the magnet. 'Flora. You would have made her laugh.'

'Why don't you frame it? Put it on the wall?' I watched the picture's edges curl back into place, shadowing Flora's happy smile under a twist of paper.

'It seems – too final, somehow, you know?' With one last glance at those happy faces, Jay turned away. 'Yes, right, I don't have the only way to grieve, I know that. But ten years... it's still not long enough.'

'So you can understand Lady Tanith? A bit?' I waited for him to swirl his waxed coat over his shoulders.

'Understand? Nope, not if I live to be two hundred. But sympathise with? I guess I can maybe do that.' Jay opened the front door. 'But only because it's probably my best idea for keeping safe if she finally loses it and ties us all up in the basement.' He ushered me through into the chill of the early morning. 'If she utters one "mwahahahahaha", I'm heading for the hills as fast as my sturdy gardener's legs can carry me.'

20

THE TALLIS HOUSE – ATONEMENT, IAN MCEWAN

Jay left me at the back door of the house. 'I've got some beds to reshape,' he said, although I had no idea what this involved, 'so I'll be around somewhere if you need me.'

'I'll be fine. As long as Lady Tanith doesn't suspect our big secret, she's not going to be any worse today than she is on any other day.'

'Well, you know. Need me, just scream.' Jay shoved his hands into the pockets of his coat. 'I'd like to kiss you goodbye, but Lady Tanith is probably glued to the front window, keeping an eye out for hanky-panky among the staff.'

'Yes, better not.' I felt the heat of the earlier kiss ripple through me again, an overcoat against the cold morning. 'I'll see you later.'

'You will.' Jay melted off again into the bushes, as though he were part foliage himself, while I squared my shoulders and opened the kitchen door, preparing myself for a day of outright lying.

I spent most of the day cataloguing, although in an even more desultory fashion than normal now that I knew I probably wasn't going to get to finish the whole library. I occasionally glanced up at Oswald, whose painted face had lost the slightly lascivious expression I'd imagined on it, and taken on a hunted look.

'You soft old bugger,' I said to it. 'You should have just sent her packing.'

Oswald's fixed glare told me that this would have left Caroline without anyone to assist her; that Lady Tanith probably would have taken being fired as Oswald's admission that he could no longer contain his feelings for her, and that she probably would have camped out in the woods rather than go home, simply to be close to her love. After all, what had been her alternative? The cousin who'd brought her up had presumably handed over responsibility for the young woman with a measure of relief and made it impossible for her to return there. She had nowhere else to go.

Tanith and I had more in common than I would ever have wanted to admit.

Pity fought with incredulity somewhere behind my heart. *How* could Lady Tanith have been so blithely unaware? But then I remembered some of the less fortunate people that we'd met out on the road. Travellers who didn't have my parents' advantages, those who moved around not because they wanted the freedom, but because they had nowhere to go. Those whose mental health was so fractured that they entertained some strange beliefs and imaginings. Lady Tanith was broken, yes, but she had the financial backing, the education, the wherewithal to maintain a normal life. Other than her firm and abiding belief in a relationship that had never existed, and an unpleasantness to anyone she considered lesser, she functioned perfectly well in society. She was managing the estate, she'd brought up her sons, she kept everything ticking over, ready for Hugo to inherit. The fact that she was still having monthly memorials for a man who had actively hidden from her, that she kept his house exactly as it had been when he'd lived in it and had a shrine to him in the attic – well, did that make her mad? Or very, very single-minded? Or just brave?

Around mid-morning, clearly in search of someone to upset, Lady Tanith wandered into the library. I felt the immediate leap of guilt fire into my cheeks, and kept my eyes fixed firmly on the computer screen as she walked around, looking at the piles of books that teetered against the walls.

'You *still* haven't found those diaries?' she asked, giving me a horrible moment of uncertainty when I wondered whether she could have overheard Jay and me yesterday, moving the furniture.

'Nope.' I kept my burning face down, pretending to drop a book so that I could hide as much of myself as possible under the table.

'I *know* they are here.' She picked up a book, looked at its spine, and flung it down again, where it let out of a puff of dust. 'Oswald wanted me to have them, so he put them away in here to keep them safe from prying eyes.'

I so, *so* wanted to say, 'Did he, did he *really*?' but knew it would be cruel. I wanted to ask why, if Oswald had wanted her to have the diaries, he hadn't just given them to her in the first place. I knew, though, that confronting delusional people with reality never worked. I'd tried often enough on my parents, asking why we couldn't just buy a house and live somewhere, and then we wouldn't have to worry about the bus breaking down or bad receptions from locals or not being able to find anywhere to empty the toilet and have a shower. They would just stare at me, as though it were I who was obsessed with travelling, never settling, showing off a new, viable way of life.

Presumably Oswald had known what reading those diaries might do to Tanith. He'd kept them for himself, memorabilia perhaps, or maybe he meant to publish them himself one day, with anything personal removed. But he'd hidden them away, somewhere she wouldn't find them, to save her from the knowledge they contained.

'I'm still looking,' I said, when I came back up off the floor, hoping my face had gone back to normal. 'In between cataloguing.' I fought my eyes, which wanted to stare beadily at Oswald's portrait in a treacherous betrayal.

'Hmm,' Tanith snorted. 'Clearly, you aren't looking hard enough. I think, a week more, and if you haven't found them by then, I will let you go and recruit someone else. Someone with a touch more *impetus*. More drive. That will be good for Hugo, too.' Then, to my horror, she stepped back and looked up at Oswald, but without her usual doting expression which always made her look as though her face was melting. She tipped her head to one side. 'Does Oswald look a little askew?' she asked.

'What! No!' I took a deep breath. 'No, he looks all right to me.'

From beneath the desk, The Master's head protruded and he let out a soft, multi-vowelled vocalisation. Lady Tanith's attention immediately switched.

'Ah, there you are,' she said, as though she'd come in purely to look for the cat. 'The Master seems very attached to you, Andromeda.'

'He's good company,' I said, and didn't mention the ever-attendant smell that came with him.

Lady Tanith 'hmmed' again and withdrew. I stroked the cat's head. 'Thanks,' I said, fondling the dark ears. 'I owe you. Again.'

The cat blinked at me, hopefully telling me that it was all right, he was being well paid back for all these favours by being allowed to snuggle up with me in the increasing chill of the nights. Our gas canister had sputtered its last gasp earlier, and I was trying to screw up enough courage to ask Hugo to ask Lady Tanith for a refill. I suspected The Master was sitting under the desk because it was the warmest place, cuddled up to my legs.

What was I going to do?

I couldn't let Lady Tanith see those diaries. Unless... just *maybe* she would read them and decide that they must never see the light of day. But she'd always suspect that *I* had read them. Would that make me Enemy Number One? And what would she *do*? What might *they* do *to her*, with her insubstantial memories of what she thought love was?

No. I'd have to destroy them. I could probably get Jay to put them through the leaf shredder, remove any trace of their existence. Could I convince her that I hadn't found the diaries or their hiding place and that Oswald must have destroyed them himself? I shook my head. Lady Tanith was so entrenched in her fantasy, and I was dreadful at lying, that I'd give myself away and she would know. I imagined that landscape gardening meant having a fairly high profile and being easily found – maybe I could persuade Jay to change his name? And move to Tierra del Fuego? After all, how long *could* Lady Tanith hate me for? Ignoring the fact that she'd managed to love and grieve for fifty years, how long would it be before she sighed and decided I wasn't worth the effort and investment in lawyers to hunt down?

What if she passed the hatred on to Hugo? Sweet, kind, Hugo, whom I'd have to leave to his solo fashion shows. Would he resent me too?

Oh God. There really wasn't an easy way out of this.

The cat meowed at me softly as I banged my forehead against the desk in desperation. *Why* had I ever found those bloody diaries? Why couldn't I have remained in blissful ignorance?

I looked up at Oswald. His stern rigidity in the portrait, painted before he ever let Lady Tanith into the house, must have been severely eroded by the presence of a woman besottedly in love. I knew from his diaries that he had kept the extent of her fixation from Caroline so as not to worry her, and that must have meant a good deal of tiptoeing around the staff who must surely have seen. He'd been the victim in all this. Lady Tanith had, in effect, been his stalker; living under his roof didn't make her behaviour any more acceptable than anyone else's. The realisation that, from fifty years' distance, I was seeing it as a slightly amusing tale of an appalling writer being followed about by an infatuated young girl, when in reality it must have been dreadful for him, hit me hard.

Lady Tanith had made Oswald's life hell. I owed her nothing. I should make the diaries public and blow her lies open.

But then I remembered those little posies of hand-picked flowers that she left on his memorial stone every twenty-first. Diaries could be very subjective, Oswald making himself the tragic hero of his own story. Maybe he *had* encouraged Lady Tanith's devotion, at least at first. Perhaps he'd liked someone's close interest in his work and by the time he realised that she was taking it all too seriously, it was too late. After all, even by his own admission he hadn't really done much to stop it – he'd just tried to avoid her. He *could* have sent her elsewhere, but he hadn't.

Did that painted face show a hint or two of malice? Of enjoying control?

Oh, this was ridiculous! I banged my forehead again. I had to stop feeling sorry for absolutely *everyone* here and come up with a plan before Lady Tanith forced me out of the house. It was far too soon for me to consider moving in with Jay, even as a housemate, and I needed a job anyway. I couldn't see Lady Tanith taking me on as an under-gardener – the phrase gave me a tiny tingle of anticipation – and she might even fire Jay too if she discovered we were in cahoots.

'Arggh!' I vocalised my utter frustration into the musty air of the library, making the cat leap from beneath the desk and flee to hide behind the sofa. Then I took a deep breath, feeling slightly better for having shaken paint flakes from the ceiling and made the one loose panel bounce on the wall. 'All right. I've got a week. Think rationally and think properly.'

A few seconds later, the library door was cautiously opened. 'Andi? Are you all right? I thought I heard – I mean, the library is a long way from our wing, but there was a noise?'

Hugo came in looking worried, presumably in case I'd fallen from the top of the library steps and was currently crumpled in a bloody heap on the floor.

'Sorry, Hugo. I...' I thought fast. 'I caught my finger. It hurt and I *may* have sworn a bit loudly.'

'Oh.' His face cleared with relief. 'You haven't forgotten tonight? We've got a date with the Yellow Room and a bottle of wine?'

'Mmmm,' I said, in vague agreement. I hadn't forgotten but I'd been hoping he had. Every time I looked at Hugo I found myself thinking *should I tell him? I should tell him, shouldn't I? Give him the diaries.* Then I'd worry about not only Lady Tanith's reaction, but Hugo's reaction to Lady Tanith's reaction, Hugo's thoughts about being lied to all these years, his worries about how to deal with his mother – I suppressed the urge to bang my head again. If he knew about her upbringing and her background he'd never, ever leave. I knew Hugo now and his sense of duty and affection would mean he would be stapled to her side until she died, all thoughts of an independent life of any kind gone.

'Only I haven't opened the new one yet. I thought I'd wait until you were there and we could look at it together?' There was such suppressed excitement in his voice, an anticipation of a treat, that I knew I couldn't say anything.

'Is that the Doris Day one?'

My remembering encouraged him. 'Yes! I wasn't sure you remembered. Yes, I won that one at auction, much cheaper than I thought so I'm not sure it's genuine now. But I want to look it over, I mean, if it's beautiful anyway does the history matter so much?'

'Not if you love it.' I smiled at him. His sheer joy was infectious. I hoped his mother's madness wasn't similarly catching. 'I'll be there. What time?'

'About nine? I've got some work to do before then. And once it's dark it will be more spectacular. If we put that little lamp in the middle of the floor, all the sequins show up so much better!'

'That sounds great.'

There was a pause. Hugo was walking around, pretending to look at the titles on the books at the top of the stacks piled around the walls. I felt my stomach leap. Did he know? Had he seen or heard something?

'You and Jay...' he started, carefully not looking at me. 'I saw you come back with him this morning?'

'Yes.' It was all I could say.

'I'm sorry. I didn't mean to pry. I was up at the balcony window. I'd been to the bathroom and I happened to glance out and you...'

'Yes,' I said again.

Hugo's face turned to me, wearing a resigned kind of frown. 'Ah. I had hoped, you and I... I know it's not perfect and you struggle with the dresses and everything, but I thought maybe I could... only at weekends, or something?'

Poor Hugo. Oswald and Lady Tanith shuffled over in my heart to make room for a moment's pity for Hugo too.

'I'm going to learn landscape gardening. When Jay leaves here I'll go with him,' I said.

'Ah.'

'He and I are...' I tailed off. It was far too soon to put words to what Jay and I were to one another.

'I see. I had hoped...'

'No, Hugo. We've had this conversation. I'm sorry. I can't marry you, lovely as you are.' I smiled. Hopefully my tone conveyed everything I thought and felt more gently than words could ever do. 'There will be someone out there for you.'

'I never meet anyone though.' He came and perched on the edge of my desk, half an eye on the screen. 'I'm stuck here. Nobody comes, and there's not much time to travel. Plus, you know, Mother. No sign of me being able to get away until I can sell up.'

I shook my head and patted his hand. 'I know. I can't really help you there. Maybe, when I leave, the person who comes to do the rest of this job might be more suitable?'

Hugo brightened unflatteringly fast and I realised that he didn't want *me*, he just wanted *someone*. 'True, true,' he said. 'By the way, what on *earth* did you have shoved down your front when you and Jay came back? You looked as though you were carrying half the contents of the library!'

Shock made my throat feel as though it bounced down into my stomach for a second and my brain froze in utter horror. Then I remembered Jay's kitchen. 'Just some gardening books that Jay has lent me,' I said, proud of the smoothness of my voice. 'I didn't want them to get wet, so I tucked them inside my top. Some of them are quite valuable, you know.'

'Oh, right.' Hugo stood up again. 'Right. So, tonight, nine o'clock? I don't want to mention it over dinner, if Mother is there, just in case. She already knows we're meeting, from last night, and I don't want her to get her hopes up any further.'

'See you later.' I turned back to the computer screen and pretended to type diligently, until I heard him leave, closing the door quietly behind him. Then I stopped, swivelled around in my chair, and saw The Master, eyeballing me silently from the depths of the gloom under the velvet couch. 'Don't you bloody start.'

The Master blinked, eyes sapphire in the darkness. He looked reproachful and for a second I wondered if he was reproving me for not being upfront with Hugo so I turned my back on him. *If this were a book,* I thought, *what would I do?* I typed in another entry, but I was working on automatic pilot. If this had been one of my novels, greedily consumed by lamplight whilst sitting on the floor in a corner of the bus, what would the heroine do?

Narratively speaking, she'd face up to Lady Tanith, wouldn't she? Sit her down, have a conversation. Lay out the diaries and tell her that she knew about the stalking of Oswald, and let Lady Tanith have her character arc, whereby she came to realise she had been at fault. Lady Tanith would come to her senses, agree to therapy for her childhood trauma, apologise to Hugo for keeping him a prisoner here, all in the name of Oswald's memory, they'd embrace and... fade to The End.

I ran the scene through in my head but couldn't find a part that didn't end in someone screaming. No. Life wasn't like the books. Books assumed that people would be rational, that they would behave in accordance with the narrative. Books didn't allow for the messiness of human nature and life had an inbuilt hatred for narrative causality.

I was buggered.

21

THORNFIELD HALL – JANE EYRE, CHARLOTTE BRONTË

Mrs Compton limped into the dining room, scraped up our empty plates with an immense amount of noise, and eyeballed Hugo and me.

'Her Ladyship has gone up,' she said. 'And I'm going home. My legs is awful.'

'Of course, Mrs Compton,' Hugo said evenly. 'Good night.'

'She said to tell you, "no hanky-panky".' Mrs Compton's focus switched to me and her stare could have drilled through granite. I smiled, as blandly as I could, although half of me wanted to swing at her with the soup ladle.

'I promise you there will be no hanky of the panky kind, or otherwise.' Hugo smiled too, more warmly than I thought the statement deserved, but then he'd grown up with Mrs Compton and probably didn't notice her rudeness any more.

'Well, then.'

A bit more ostentatious limping and then she and the crockery rattled their way out of the dining room and Hugo burst out laughing. 'I think she and Mother assume we're locking ourselves away in the Yellow Room to, err...'

I remembered some of Mrs Compton's more prejudicial side-remarks to me. 'I'm pretty sure that's what they think we're up to. Is that better, or worse than what we're really doing?'

'Infinitely preferable.' Hugo pushed his chair back. 'So, I'll meet you in there in, what, twenty minutes?'

I finished my coffee. 'Yep. I just need to shower. All the dust from the library gets in my hair.'

Hugo grinned and left the room. He was probably going up for a solo prowl around his collection before I arrived, but I really did need a shower. The Master, ever attendant at my side, blew into his fur, one leg cocked into the air.

'And you can't come,' I told him sternly.

One eye solemnly regarded me over his own hip.

'You're not allowed in the Yellow Room. Fur on velvet is a dreadful thing, look at the sofa in the library.'

The athletic stare continued.

'I'm going to shut you in here, so you don't sit outside the door and shout to come in.' I put down my cup. 'I'll let you out to come up with me when I go to bed, all right?'

The Master straightened, looked at me down his aristocratic dark nose, and twitched an ear.

'I'm taking that as acquiescence then.' I stood up. 'You really can be a dreadful nuisance sometimes. But it's warm in here and you can sit on the window seat. I'll see you later.'

Before the cat could jump up and try to squeeze out of the door with me, I fled through the gap and closed it firmly. Mrs Compton wouldn't be back in, she'd be taking her leg home, firm in her belief that we didn't know that tonight was Bingo night down in the town, so she'd clear the cups tomorrow morning. Somehow, I didn't think that even a full house would sweeten her general demeanour.

I showered, checked that the diaries were safe, tucked inside their Sainsbury's bag amid my clothing, and went to the Yellow Room to meet Hugo.

It was dark outside and the gentle light from the lamp he had set up on the floor glowed appealingly. I felt another momentary pang that this couldn't be my life. Would it really have been so dreadful? Then the moon, full and netted among the branches of the trees, shone over the grounds and I remembered Jay kissing me and knew that I would rather have him, the mud, learning to prune and plant and a gardener's cottage than this whole estate and a lifetime's worth of costume design.

'Right.' Hugo was oscillating with anticipation, the newly arrived package in his hand. 'Shall we open this?'

'You open it,' I said. 'I'm going to pour some wine.'

I leaned back on the floor pillows that stood in for furniture in here and waited for Hugo to appear from behind the screen in the corner.

'I'm teaming it with the diamanté Jimmy Choos,' he said. 'For the length.'

'Mmm,' I said, not really listening. Hugo didn't need my input, he just liked to drop designer names. Not his fault, of course, he couldn't talk about his interests anywhere else, so he had a lot of pent-up chat to get through when we found ourselves alone and outside his mother's influence.

There was a strange smell in the Yellow Room this evening. It came and went, faintly, as though blown in on a breeze. 'Ta da!' Hugo swirled out from behind the changing screen. 'What do you think?'

'Does it smell weird to you? Is it the dress?' I sniffed once or twice.

'Can't smell anything,' Hugo said briskly. 'Anyway. What about this?'

He did a twirl. I didn't know anything about fashion history, although Hugo was doing his best to enlighten me, but I wasn't completely sure about the provenance of this particular gown. 'It's very pretty, but I'm not sure about the Doris Day-ness of it.'

'They did only say that it was *rumoured* to have been worn by her.' Hugo stopped rotating and stroked the skirt. His joy and enthusiasm were infectious.

'It's lovely, whoever wore it, and does it really matter after all?'

'I do like the gowns to have history. It's part of the fun, imagining who wore ˙' ˙n and to which event. If I can find pictures it's even better. Holly-
˙   and all that.'

˙illow of vague, mysterious smell. It was faint, and had that
˙tion nudge, as though I ought to know what it was.

˙ugo, nearly seven feet tall in his enormous heels. The look
o   ˙re on his face made him extremely handsome, particularly
as   ˙n't got his wig on, his fair hair standing up at angles and his cheeks partially shaded by stubble. I made a sudden decision.

He *should* know. Maybe he could use the knowledge as leverage with

Lady Tanith? 'Let me live my own life and I won't mention what I know?' Could I do it? Could I destroy his innocent happiness and belief in his mother and her stories of her past?

But was it fair to keep it from him? If he understood, if he could see what had made her so desperate to keep first Jasper and then himself close – her lack of experience of how parental love should look or how *any* form of real love should look – it might make it easier for him to finally break away and have an independent life. 'I just need to pop to my room to fetch something,' I said. 'Be back in a minute.'

Hugo was stroking the fabric down over his hips, admiring the fall of the skirt. 'All right,' he said cheerily. 'I'll let you out. Usual knock to come back in though.'

'Of course.'

We'd had to develop a 'secret knock', to ensure he didn't throw the door blithely open to Lady Tanith or Mrs Compton, whilst fully encased in a Vera Wang sheath dress or similar. It gave everything a *Secret Seven* vibe, a childish fun pastime air which I hadn't objected to, because it matched Hugo's childlike glee.

Cautiously, and with much giggly staring up and down the landing, because we were pretty certain that Lady Tanith had gone to bed, and *I* was pretty certain that she'd been up in the loft at her home-made altar for most of the afternoon so would have taken to her room, Hugo unbolted the door and let me out.

'I'm going to put something else on while you're gone,' he said, as though promising me a treat. 'This one is a wee bit tight and I don't want the seams to give.'

I nodded, my mind far away in a time where he already knew. *Was showing him the diaries the right thing to do?*

I went next door to my room and fished the plastic bag out from where it sat in my bag under my neatly stored clothes. The smell was out here too, still faint and almost imperceptible, a chemical, swirling smell. Maybe Mrs Compton hadn't gone home as promised, but was cleaning with some industrial bug spray. Fumigation was probably what Templewood Hall needed.

Back to the Yellow Room, secret knock given, Hugo let me back in with a half-curious glance at the bag swinging from my hand, the weight of years of lies making it hang heavily. He was wearing his favourite dress, the full-length blue velvet with the spaghetti straps, still teamed with the Choos, and he'd put his blonde wig on. It gave him a certain Cate Blanchett look.

'Can you smell something weird?' I asked.

'Not really. What have you got there?' Hugo pointed at the plastic bag looped over my wrist. He looked so innocently happy; did I really have the right to blow his life out of the water? My heart felt swollen and just under my throat with the potential of what I was about to do.

'It...' I started, but that was as far as I got.

A tremendous clanging started, distant at first but closing in on us, a dreadful, mechanical wailing sound, seemingly issuing from the far wing of the house but advancing, and, at the same time, something heavy hit the window of the Yellow Room.

Hugo and I looked at one another.

'That's the smoke alarm,' he said.

'Then what the hell is *that*?' Another soft weight against the glass.

I went to the window and threw it open. Jay stood outside on the lawn below, with a couple of other people from the estate. 'Thank God you're in there!' he shouted up. 'I've been trying all the lit windows. The house is on fire, you need to get out, now!'

The words were in English, they were logical and spoken in a tone loud enough for me to hear, but somehow they made no sense.

'No it isn't,' I said.

Hugo clutched my arm. 'The house is on fire?' He was keeping himself hidden behind the curtains, from the group outside.

'I've called the fire brigade, but I don't know how long it will take them!' Jay called up again. 'Someone's gone for a ladder, I'm not sure you can get out any other way now! The fire's moving through the roof space by the look of it, but we don't know how far it's got, just get down here!'

In the background the wailing clamour had reached the landing. The smoke had clearly got far enough through the house to set off the alarms in this wing.

'Mother!' Hugo shouted, ran to the door, ran back, looked at me and then looked at his discarded clothing, jeans and shirt on the floor.

'Let's just get out,' I said. 'Lady Tanith will have heard the alarms, she'll get out from her side.'

'But if she's taken her tablets she might not wake up!' Hugo was staring at me again, his wig disarranged, holding his skirt bunched in both hands.

I chanced another glance out of the door. 'The fire is above us, at the front of the house.'

'Come *on*!' Jay yelled from outside. From somewhere deep in the house I heard a cracking sound, like a beam giving way.

'You can't go, Hugo.' I grabbed his arm. 'We have to get ourselves out.'

'But *Mother*,' he wailed.

I'd thought that whether or not to show the diaries to Hugo or Lady Tanith had been the epitome of my moral dilemmas, but now it seemed that was subsumed under 'do I let this man run back into a possible inferno to rescue a woman who has stunted and stifled his entire life?' Rescue human life, yes. Save Hugo from a future of furtive dressing-up and marriage to please his mother? Also, yes.

'See how far you can get.' I gave him a tiny push. 'If her wing is already on fire, leave it, she may already be out.'

Hugo opened the door and fled down the landing in the direction of the back of the house. I went to the top of the stairs, but it was obvious that the fire was above the library wing. From that side of the house the smoke was billowing into the hallway, filling it with grey clouds that smelled not smoky but of a far more solid kind of smell. There was a creaking sound from the disused bedrooms in that wing and ghostly shapes wound their way along the landing as smoke issued from under the doors. I couldn't feel any heat, but I knew enough to know that the smoke would reach and kill us faster than any flames.

'Hugo!' I shouted.

He came back, tottering in his shoes. 'What?'

'We can't go out this way. The fire must be in the library wing and spreading from there. We can't use the main stairs.'

From behind, I could hear Jay yelling at me from outside the window above the racket of the alarms, but then a voice cut through all the noise.

'What on *earth* is going on?' Lady Tanith, wearing a beautiful chiffon negligee, wafted like her own spirit, along the landing from the back of the house. 'Who is making that dreadful noise?'

She gave me a grim, hard stare, as though I may be solely responsible for the siren-like shrieking that was now reverberating through the entire house. Smoke puffed, coming up the staircase towards where we were standing, then cleared, revealing Hugo, full-length velvet and all.

'We need to get out,' he said calmly. 'The house is on fire.'

There was a tremendous bang from somewhere behind us. It sounded as though the library ceiling had fallen in, or was about to, and I could see a red glow now, just a sinister red line beneath the doors across the landing.

'We need to go now,' I said, my voice commendably level.

Lady Tanith stared at us both. 'You will have left the gas on in the library,' she said, haughty and gathering her swathes of chiffon around her, then she turned to her son. 'And what on *earth* are you wearing?'

'Ah. Um. Mother...' Hugo began. I was beginning to feel two genres clashing – my mild rom-com coming up hard against thriller, as the two of them stood at the top of the stairs amid the drifting smoke.

'We need to get *out*!' I shouted. From beyond the Yellow Room window Jay was still yelling. I could hear his voice cracking with his increasing volume and desperation. 'We may have to go out of the window.'

Lady Tanith took Hugo's arm. 'We can use the back stairs,' she said, ignoring the fact that her son was wobbling on his enormous heels.

'I'm not sure we can.' I pulled at Hugo's other arm, tugging the pair of them with me back into the Yellow Room, and closed the door so that we could block out the smoke and hear ourselves think. 'It sounds like ceilings are coming down. If we go down the back stairs we might find ourselves trapped in the kitchen.'

'We've got the ladder!' Jay was practically screaming now. 'Come *on*! Get *out*!'

Lady Tanith, showing remarkably little fear considering that Hugo and I were almost dragging her towards the window, stopped again. The smell of smoke was increasing and there were random banging and crashing sounds that were getting closer. There was also an ominous, and growing, background heat.

'What *have* you been doing? Is this yours?' She waved a hand at Hugo's dress, then glanced around the Yellow Room, where the wardrobe doors stood open and one or two garments were hanging outside the cupboards. 'And *this*?'

Hugo swallowed. I became aware that I still had the diaries swinging from my hand in their bag. I wondered if I could use them as a cudgel. 'We need to go,' I said urgently, trying to distract her.

Over at the window, the twin metal arms of a ladder made a clonk as they came to rest against the frame.

'Er,' Hugo said. 'Um. Yes. But we do need to get out, Mother.'

Lady Tanith raked him with another stare. 'Velvet.' She shook her head. 'What *possessed* you, Hugo? You clearly don't have the hips for velvet. And blue is *not* your colour at all. You could get away with a mulberry silk, satin at the very worst.'

Hugo's mouth dropped open. I tried to drive them both towards the window, where the ladder was tapping with impatience.

'And these are yours too?'

Hugo clearly couldn't speak, so I intervened. 'Yes, yes, these are all Hugo's. Now can we get down that ladder before the fire comes along the landing?'

From far away came the sound of something dropping, big, heavy and ominous, right through the house. The room was filling with smoke, and we'd all started to cough.

Without another word, Lady Tanith moved to the nearest wardrobe, reached in an arm and scooped the contents out onto the floor. Then she began throwing the dresses out of the window, to the evident and loud consternation of those waiting on the ground below, and the possible disruption of someone halfway up the ladder.

'Mother! What are you doing?' Hugo made a motion to stop her.

'These are *couture*!' She had to speak up over the general sounds of fire, smoke, coughing, and random yells from outside.

I made a face at him, and the three of us emptied the wardrobes out of the window in record time. By now, there were audible crackling noises, the heat had risen and there were sounds coming from the ceiling as though the rafters above us were giving up. Thumps and bangs, and a small hole had appeared in the plaster rose in the centre.

'Look, just go!'

At last Lady Tanith, with extreme dignity, slung a leg over the windowsill and climbed barefoot down the ladder in her negligee. I followed her and Hugo, wrenching off his diamanté shoes, which twinkled in the firelight, came after me. Being followed down a twenty-foot ladder by a man in velvet carrying six-inch heels was almost more of an experience than being in a burning building.

Jay wrapped his arms around me as we arrived on the grass. It was only from down here that I could see the full extent of the fire – the opposite wing was blazing from roof to floor level and the roof was almost fully alight. We all ran into the gardens, away from the inferno, to join the small crowd of watching villagers, several of whom were filming the conflagration with every sign of enjoyment. Jay kept an arm wrapped around me.

'My house!' Lady Tanith gave a little cry. 'My house! All my wonderful things!'

I had the uncharitable thought that most of her things could only be improved by an enormous blaze, and then I remembered the cat, shut away to prevent him from following Hugo and me. 'Oh my God! The Master! He's in the dining room!' I pointed at the windows, flaming with reflected light beneath my bedroom. The glass was as yet unbroken, but there was smoke filling the space and pressing itself against the window.

Lady Tanith screamed. Jay let me go and gave me a resigned look. 'It might be too late,' he said.

'We have to get him out.'

'But we can't. Look, the whole place is going up.'

'The fire is worst in the roof above the library. The dining room is ground floor in the other wing, it will be the last place the fire gets to.'

We all stared again at the windows of the dining room. Apart from the smoke which puffed and billowed against the glass, there was no sign of life.

'I'm sorry,' Jay said, and Lady Tanith screamed again. She turned and began to run back towards the flaming house. Hugo, showing a surprising turn of speed for a bloke in a frock, belted after her and tackled her to the ground, where she lay, sobbing.

'We have to get him out,' I whispered. 'I owe that cat. Plus, it might be the only thing that Tanith has a healthy relationship with.'

Jay gave me a resigned look. 'You're as batshit as the rest of them, aren't you?' he said, but there was a fondness to his tone which took the sting from his words.

I clutched Jay's arm. 'We can't leave him. We just *can't*.'

'All right,' he said tiredly. 'I'll do the heroics.'

Cautiously, with an arm up in front of his face to protect him from the heat and smoke, Jay approached the building. Massive rafters were coming down now, as though the roof was tired of the weight and slumping down through the house. Our wing was still intact but the tiles were cracking in the roof as the fire made its way through the space.

Jay drew his other arm back. He was wearing his gardening clothes, jumper and mud-encrusted trousers, and he flickered like an elemental in the ominous light from the fire. A siren wailed now, just audible above the sound of the alarms, and a blue light strobed its way along the drive. Its noise was almost drowned out by the sound of Jay swearing as his elbow rebounded off the glass of the dining room window without making so much as a crack.

From inside, a blue eye blinked amid the smoke.

'He's in there, he's alive!' Lady Tanith shrieked from her position on the ground.

Jay swore a bit more and clutched his elbow.

'Oh, for heaven's sake,' Hugo said. He climbed off Lady Tanith and ran to join Jay, recoiling once at the sheer heat, but pressing on until both the men were wreathed in the smoke which now encompassed the whole building. Hugo went back, collected one of the dropped Jimmy Choos and scampered towards the window. 'Stand back,' he shouted.

Jay stood back. The shoe hit the window, heel first. Hugo battered the steel tipped point against the glass, once, twice, and finally the window shattered, the flying glass being accompanied by a flying Siamese, who hurtled through the broken frame as soon as the gap was wide enough, and flew out onto the lawn as though rocket launched.

'Master!' Lady Tanith cried, getting elegantly to her feet and ignoring the fact that her silk nightwear was mud stained and tattered. Her voice was creaky with emotion and smoke.

The cat ran a few steps, stopped, stared at us, sneezed once and then sat down to begin licking its paws. Hugo and Jay followed, until we were all hunched together against the wall of the pond. At least, the men and I were hunched, Lady Tanith was bolt upright and quivering like an arrow that had just been fired into an oak door. The villagers, I noted, had backed even further off, although they were still filming with notable glee.

'We'll need to get further back,' Jay said, his voice a little tight, although I wasn't sure whether it was from emotion, confusion or pain. 'The fire brigade are here and they'll use the fountain connection for water.'

We stood up again and retreated further. I looked at our little smoke-stained group, Hugo in his now slightly ragged dress and carrying one shoe, his arm around his mother as they limped out into the broad reach of the gardens where the air was fresh and clean and not glowing. Lady Tanith, her back ramrod straight despite the gravel under her bare feet, wasn't leaning on him in the slightest. The estate workers who'd helped Jay with the ladder were, without a word, gathering up the collection of dresses that we'd flung from the windows and moving them away from the slowly collapsing walls.

I looked at Jay. 'What the hell is happening?' I asked.

He was also watching Hugo and Lady Tanith's limping and smoke-stained progress into the darkness. 'Right now, I haven't got the vaguest idea.' He put an arm around my shoulders. 'But you're out. You're safe. That'll do.'

The part of the house where the library was currently blazing, slumped further inwards. Ash flew out, little sprinkles of pale grey floating up on the breeze and encircling the building, blurring into the smoke and the flame and the additional spray from the water hoses, where the fire brigade were beginning to try to extinguish some of the fire.

'I need to go over there,' I said.

'But the place is falling down!' Jay clearly felt me tugging against his embrace. 'You can't! Anyway, the firefighters won't let you.'

'They won't see.' I ducked out from under his arm and ran around to the front of the house. There, the fire engine, still flashing intermittent blue lights, stood while people in uniform dashed around unspooling more hoses to attach to the pond supply. Firelight flickered out into the dark, echoing the blue strobe. Two people in helmets and masks moved me gently aside and then passed on. I waited until they were out of the way and then I got as close as I could to the flaming library.

The windows were all broken; flame was belching out through the gaps. The house was almost down to rubble here, the roof and the upper floors had collapsed to lie among the burning books, stone and wood and paper all glowing orange and red and giving off an immense heat. I had to shield my eyes and hold my elbow up to my face. It was like walking up to the biggest bonfire in the world.

'What are you *doing*?' Jay made a grab for me but missed, probably because his eyes were screwed up against the heat.

'Just... this.'

I loosened my burden so that it was held by the two handles, then, with a degree of effort, I swung it until momentum took over and then let go.

The bag, with its incriminating contents, flew higher and wider than I thought it would, through the long-gone window and deep into the conflagration beyond. I almost thought I could see it ignite as it went, but that was probably my imagination. I also thought I saw, as the final wall collapsed, the face of Sir Oswald, eyes aflame, dropping onto my hurled bundle but that was almost *certainly* imagination inspired by years of narrative structure and carefully rounded endings.

'You are crazy.' Jay pulled my arm again, now with more success, and I backed away with my eyebrows beginning to singe, until we were behind the fire engine and the bulk of the local fire brigade, who were running hoses everywhere amid lots of organised shouting. 'And you've got a lot of competition.'

Away, over past the bushes, I could see Hugo, his arm still around his mother. She was standing absolutely straight and immobile, watching her house go up in flames. She didn't even seem to be crying now. The only movement from them both was the passing breeze tugging at his velvet and her chiffon.

Two of the estate workers approached them, gentle hands held out and, in shock, the pair were helped away towards the village. Everyone was carrying dresses draped over arms and shoulders, looking like a costume department on the move.

'Let's go back to mine,' Jay said. 'We need to wait until the fire is out, and it might be morning before the place is secure.'

'But...' I gestured hopelessly towards Templewood, flaming and flaring out of every window space, walls gradually tumbling, like a hotel in hell. 'All the things...'

'The fire brigade will rescue what can be rescued.' Jay gave me a look. 'But the diaries will have gone up with the rest of the books.'

'That's all I could think of to do,' I said, taking his hand as he held it out to me. 'Destroy them with everything else. I came this close to telling Hugo, you know.'

Jay looked back at the house where plumes of water were being sprayed onto the burning remains. 'For the best, I think,' he said carefully. 'It all being gone, I mean.'

I stared back too. Most of the roof was gone now, fallen into the attic space. That table covered in photos, gone. The portrait, gone. *And,* I whispered to myself, *the diaries, gone, along with any evidence that they ever existed...* 'Definitely for the best,' I said, and then sagged against his supporting arm. 'I think I might be in shock.'

'My house then, for strong sweet tea and a shower. You smell charred.'

So I let him lead me away over the soft grass, following Hugo and Lady Tanith and the dress-carrying locals.

22

MANDERLEY (AGAIN) – REBECCA, DAPHNE DU MAURIER

The house burned all night. I sat at Jay's table, fingers wrapped around non-stop mugs of tea and wearing his baggy hoodie and some jogging bottoms that I had to tie up with an old dressing gown cord. Parts of my face stung, despite an evil smelling cream that Jay had found in the back of a cupboard and had liberally smeared onto my skin. But I was clean, I was warm and the worst of the shock was beginning to wear off, particularly now that my lap was being kept extra warm by the presence of The Master. He smelled horribly of smoke and the tip of his tail had a sore patch where it looked as though it could have been scorched, but he blinked up at me happily enough and his weighty presence stopped me from going to the window every few minutes to look out at the glowing sky.

Lady Tanith and Hugo had gone to Jasper's house. He wasn't there, but it turned out that the entire village knew where he kept the spare key and had left them to it. I was pretty sure they'd all gone home to mutter about Hugo's unconventional wear and Lady Tanith's uncharacteristic silence, but we were all safe. That was what mattered. How much sanity may remain intact was a question for the morning.

Jay occasionally muttered, 'Hugo and the dresses, eh?' or shook his head as though trying to rid himself of the sight of his employers in blue velvet and wafty chiffon, but he mostly kept an arm around me as we sat together on the sofa in his kitchen, stroking the cat's head.

Around dawn I fell into a light sleep, my head on Jay's shoulder but half-dreams telling me that I was still in a burning building jerked me awake every five minutes. The smell of smoke which lingered around us all, mostly from the cat's fur, didn't help. Vigorous cleaning activities gradually replaced the smoke smell with the smell of old fish, and we all stopped coughing quickly enough to realise that smoke inhalation wasn't going to be a problem.

Then it was morning proper and things couldn't be put off any longer. Jay and I bundled up in his gardening coats and set out for what remained of Templewood Hall.

The entire library wing was gone, nothing but a pile of rubble with split rafters protruding, like a mouth full of broken teeth. Next to it, the façade of the rest of the front stood, looking wobbly and unsupported. We walked around to the back, which revealed an empty shell, burned away to leave nothing but a few walls, and the remnants of the wing that Hugo and I slept in, still two storeys high but without a roof or any floors. Some tattered panelling jutted into what was left of the hall; cracked and stained black and white tiles still marked the floor. A stone figure lay toppled and headless amid the ruins and outside on the grass stood a few pieces of furniture which the firemen had pulled from the blaze or rescued from the water.

It stank. The whole site smelled of that half-chemical, half-smoke that I'd noticed up in the Yellow Room what felt like a century ago, and the grass surrounding the walls was trodden into mud and ruts where the fire brigade had done their best to save what could be saved.

Hugo and Lady Tanith were there too, standing shell-shocked and wearing borrowed clothing. Hugo had clearly raided his brother's wardrobe, because he was enveloped in a duster coat and had trainers on his feet. Lady Tanith must have been lent something by one of the villagers, because she was clad in a blue tweed skirt and a pink jumper with an elephant knitted into it.

Jay and I, hand in hand and accompanied by the delicate tread of The Master, went over to where they stood and we all stared.

'It's all gone,' Lady Tanith said faintly, her only acknowledgement of our presence. 'All of it.'

'Yes.' Hugo's eyes were shadowed with tiredness.

Around us, the fire brigade were rolling up hoses and packing away equipment. Someone had turned off the blue light, at least. They paid us no attention, for which I was grateful.

Lady Tanith turned to me. She looked almost skeletal in this early light, her skin drawn tight over her bones with weariness. The pink jumper did her colouring no favours either. 'You left the gas fire lit in the library, didn't you?'

'No.' My voice sounded raspy from the smoke and the shouting. 'The canister was empty, so it wasn't even on.'

'Well, it *must* have been you,' she snapped. One of the firemen walked past, arms full of something that dripped, and she grabbed them. 'Where did it start?' Lady Tanith asked, with no preamble such as 'thank you for your help'.

The firefighter, who looked about seventeen and had soot smudges on both cheeks, sighed. 'You're the owner, right? You need to talk to the boss,' she said. 'I'll send him on over.'

'Well, of course it was you,' Lady Tanith said in my direction, releasing the arm to let the exhausted firefighter carry on her journey across the Somme of lawn. 'Who else would be stupid and careless enough? I shall be suing, of course.'

I didn't react. I was too busy trying to stare into what remained of the library to make sure that there was no trace of the diaries left. It didn't look as though I needed to worry. Anything that was left of any of the books was reduced to single pages or charred covers, everything so water-soaked from the hoses that it was unrecognisable. There was nothing left of Oswald bar a small piece of standing wall from which an iron fixing drooped from one hinge. Lady Tanith was right. It was all gone.

'At least we rescued the dresses,' Lady Tanith went on. 'Hugo, how could you be so *ridiculous!*'

Hugo gave me a quick glance of agony, and then turned to his mother. 'I...' he began but she steamrollered on.

'Those dresses are *priceless*. They should have been in fireproof cupboards and protected! When I think of what could have happened... You have Moschino there, you know! And Dior!'

'Yes,' he said faintly. 'I know.'

'And vintage too! Some of those dresses are irreplaceable! Unique!'

'Yes, I know,' he said again. I got another 'help me' look over Lady Tanith's head, but I couldn't think of anything to say.

'Even your father had the sense to put his dresses away in storage!' Lady Tanith went on. 'Incidentally, he had some very good diamonds which would look wonderful with that velvet.'

Hugo's eyes became enormous and I saw his mouth flail for words. 'Dad?' was all he could come out with, and the word was almost lost in the arrival of a brusque, burly man, who'd taken off his fire helmet and looked tired, but In Charge.

'You the householder?' He addressed Hugo, who still couldn't manage more than a squeak.

'Templewood Hall is mine,' Lady Tanith said, with dignity.

The firefighter scratched a stubbled chin. 'Right, love,' he said, and the fact that this unwarranted mateyness went unchallenged only went to show me how shocked Lady Tanith really was. 'You're going to want to talk to your insurance company.'

'How and where did it start?' Lady Tanith turned the basilisk stare on me again. '*That* is the matter of most concern at present.'

'Best guess right now, in the roof. Looks like candles left alight.' Scratch, scratch. 'Course, we won't know until we do a proper examination, but that's what we think. Someone left a naked flame up in the attic, rafters caught and it went through the roof space. Good job you had the alarms fitted, but you should really have had a sprinkler system, place that size.'

He wandered off to berate his inferiors, and I looked at Lady Tanith. Something in my eyes must have told her that I knew, because she suddenly went very white.

'Come on.' Jay drew me gently aside to let another firefighter pass. 'Let's go and sit on the icehouse for a moment. Everyone has a lot to process just now.'

As we walked away, I heard Hugo say, 'Dad?' again, still faintly.

Lady Tanith didn't seem to be able to reply just yet.

Jay and I sat on the humped grass of the icehouse roof, looking out at the activity surrounding Templewood Hall. Tyre marks scored his carefully mown lawns, the bushes and flowers in the bed that concealed the fountain workings had been trodden down where the hoses had attached to the water supply. All the undergrowth that surrounded the house had either been burned to stubs or broken and battered by the weight of water poured into the building, and pools and puddles of it still stood on the earth.

'What a mess,' I said.

Jay squeezed me around the shoulders. 'It'll be fine,' he said. 'By next summer you'll never know there was a fire. All the perennials will come back, the grass will recover and the annuals would have died off anyway, come the first frost.'

'I actually meant the house.'

'Oh. Yes. Of course you did. Yes. That's – that's a bit of a mess too. Sorry. I was just being a gardener there for a minute.'

I smiled. 'Is that your default then? All about the plants?'

I got another squeeze and a sideways smile. 'Not always. I can diversify.' He fiddled with one of his hearing aids. 'Into surprising areas too. You wait and see.'

The warm flush came up again, welcome in this early morning chill. 'I shall look forward to it,' I said.

We stared on. A lump of stone that had been jutting precariously from the side of the west wing fell into the scorched ruins with a sound like resignation.

'Hugo likes dresses,' I said, eventually, when we had wrung all the visual potential out of the scene.

'I gathered,' Jay said, dryly. 'And you're not quite as keen, I take it.'

'It wasn't just that.' I kept my eyes on the rubble-strewn lawn in front of us. 'Not really.'

'No. Plus, here's me swanning in with my charisma and charm.'

'And that.' A pause. 'Do you think I'll make a good gardener?'

'I think you will make an excellent gardener.' Another momentary pressure around my shoulders. 'You will be fine.'

'All those hours I spent cataloguing the library.' I sighed. 'What a waste of time.'

We sat for a while longer, and then we were joined by Hugo and The Master. Lady Tanith we could see in the distance, berating the fire brigade and directing those of the locals foolish enough to come for a look at what was left of the house. She'd got them humping any saved furniture and goods off towards the village. Poor Jasper was going to come back from wherever he was to find his house full of smoke-scented Regency tables, and his mother.

'Well,' Hugo said, carefully spreading his brother's coat out underneath him and sitting down beside us. 'Today is turning out to be most surprising.'

He looked at me, sitting with Jay's arm around me, resting myself comfortably in the crook of his arm, and smiled.

'What are you going to do, though?' I asked.

'Well,' Hugo said again, 'it turns out that the house burning to the ground may be the best thing that's ever happened to me.'

'OK,' Jay said slowly. 'We might need a bit more detail on that one.'

'I take it you know about the...' Hugo hesitated, rearranging the folds of coat under his leg so as not to have to meet our eyes. 'The, um, the clothes. Thing.'

'I gathered.' Jay didn't look at Hugo as hard as Hugo wasn't looking at him. There seemed to be some kind of bloke-communication going on that I was outside of, and it consisted of absolutely not talking about anything, ever.

'So.' Hugo cleared his throat, obviously searching for the right words. 'According to Mother, Dad was... well he had... it was... and apparently he had quite a collection. They're in storage, somewhere in York. Some are on loan to the V&A.'

I found I was cupping my hands over my face. 'Oh,' I said faintly.

'And Mother is talking about using the insurance money from Templewood to build something, somewhere we could open ourselves, as a kind of clothing museum. Here, on the site so we wouldn't have to leave the estate.'

I heard Jay swallow.

'Which would be perfect, of course,' Hugo went on. 'We've got the core of a collection already, and I could go on buying trips and bring in more vintage couture, and Mother could stay and run the museum.'

'That sounds like quite a result,' Jay said.

'And she's not... I mean, she's lost all her Oswald things,' I said carefully. 'How is she taking that?'

Hugo looked quite perky. 'It's astonishing really,' he said. 'She doesn't seem to be all that worried, considering. She keeps talking about "acts of God" and it all being a dreadful accident.' He lapsed into what was clearly a frock-related dream.

Jay and I made eye contact. He was obviously thinking what I was thinking. Lady Tanith's candles on her home-made shrine had started the fire; she must have forgotten to extinguish them after this evening's Oswald-worshipping session. Perhaps the guilt of burning down the house and destroying all her own collection of artefacts had made her see sense. Or perhaps she was actually *glad*. Perhaps the fire had removed that obligation that she'd felt, to keep him alive in her memory. She had, after all, had a lot of experience of life-changing events and having to start again in different places. Maybe her background might actually have made her more resilient to new beginnings; perhaps knowing that things could change and improve would stand her in good stead here. I'd never really thought of Tanith as adaptable and flexible, but she couldn't have had the life she'd had without a certain degree of overcoming of stress. I gave a tiny smile. The fire might turn out to be the only way this could ever have ended.

Plus, it had destroyed Oswald's books, and, Lady Tanith would believe, any chance of finding those diaries. Well, she was right there.

'We probably won't need any gardening done for a while,' Hugo said eventually. I didn't know whether he was aware of it, but he was stroking his knee now, almost as though he could already feel that velvet or satin or silk beneath his fingers. A museum of historic costume would be Hugo's idea of heaven, plus he'd be allowed to travel, to actually look at new potential artefacts before he bought them, rather than having to rely on online photos. He would get to meet real people, make new friends. Maybe even meet people with similar interests to himself, eventually, and stop being that lonely little boy unhealthily co-dependent with his mother.

'That's fine.' Jay gave me a small wink. 'We're thinking of moving on soon anyway.'

'Good, good.' Then Hugo suddenly reached out and caught my hand. 'You will stay in contact, won't you?' I was surprised to see tears in his eyes as he looked at me. 'I don't have that many friends, and now you know about… the dresses, I couldn't bear us to lose sight of one another.'

'Of course we will.' I was touched. 'This has all been…' I groped for the right words. 'An experience,' I finished.

Jay just said, 'Mate,' and slapped Hugo's shoulder. I assumed this was some sort of guy acknowledgement.

'Plus, we have to keep an eye on you, to make sure that Lady Tanith hasn't suddenly decided to run amok, because of losing all her things,' I said, prosaically.

'She's not that bad.' Hugo smiled.

'She bloody is,' Jay murmured into my ear.

The cat wandered over from his exploration of some small mouse holes in the turf and his forensic examination of the sore end of his tail, and stuck his nose in my eye. Then the four of us sat back in the dew-damp grass to stare over the ruins of Templewood Hall and contemplate new futures. I leaned against Jay, feeling his reassuring arm around my shoulders, and contentment crept up through my body. I *had* a future, gardening with Jay. Hugo's museum would mean freedom for him and even Tanith was free now too. No more Oswald to obsess over. Maybe there *could* be a winsome retired professor for her to marry somewhere out there?

It didn't matter. We were all safe, it was a beautiful morning and things were looking up.

* * *

MORE FROM JANE LOVERING

Another book from Jane Lovering, *The Start of the Story*, is available to order now here:

https://mybook.to/StartOfStoryBackAd

ALSO BY JANE LOVERING

The Country Escape

Home on a Yorkshire Farm

A Midwinter Match

A Cottage Full of Secrets

The Forgotten House on the Moor

There's No Place Like Home

The Recipe for Happiness

The Island Cottage

One of a Kind

The Start of the Story

Happily Ever After

ABOUT THE AUTHOR

Jane Lovering is the bestselling and award-winning romantic comedy writer who won the RNA Contemporary Romantic Novel Award in 2023 with *A Cottage Full of Secrets*. She lives in Yorkshire and has a cat and a bonkers terrier, as well as five children who have now left home.

Sign up to Jane Lovering's mailing list here for news, competitions and updates on future books.

Visit Jane's website: www.janelovering.co.uk

Follow Jane on social media:

- facebook.com/Jane-Lovering-Author-106404969412833
- x.com/janelovering
- bookbub.com/authors/jane-lovering

BECOME A MEMBER OF THE SHELF CARE CLUB

The home of Boldwood's book club reads.

Find uplifting reads, sunny escapes, cosy romances, family dramas and more!

Sign up to the newsletter
https://bit.ly/theshelfcareclub

Boldwood

Boldwood Books is an award-winning fiction publishing company seeking out the best stories from around the world.

Find out more at www.boldwoodbooks.com

Join our reader community for brilliant books, competitions and offers!

Follow us
@BoldwoodBooks
@TheBoldBookClub

Sign up to our weekly deals newsletter

https://bit.ly/BoldwoodBNewsletter

www.ingramcontent.com/pod-product-compliance
Ingram Content Group UK Ltd.
Pitfield, Milton Keynes, MK11 3LW, UK
UKHW020322040225
454637UK00001B/9